Absinthe Makes the Heart Grow Fonder

Twenty Major was born some years ago in Dublin, Ireland. He lives on, or around, the South Circular Road with a dog called Bastardface and a cat called Throatripper.

He was nominated for the Nobel Peace Prize in 1984 but was beaten to the gong by Bishop Desmond Tutu who ran a vigorous dirty tricks campaign against him. His other mortal enemies include Daryl Hall, LL Cool J (who stole his rap) and any kind of clown.

Twenty Major writes a blog at www.twentymajor.net

Also by Twenty Major
The Order of the Phoenix Park

Absinthe Makes the Heart Grow Fonder

TWENTY MAJOR

HACHETTE
BOOKS
IRELAND

First published in Ireland in 2009 by Hachette Books Ireland
An Hachette UK company

1

A CIP catalogue record for this title is available from the British Library.

ISBN 978 0 340 95288 7

Typeset in Sabon MT and Gill Sans MT by Hachette Books Ireland
Cover design by Anu Design
Cover illustration by Fintan Taite

Printed and bound in the UK by
CPI Mackays, Chatham ME5 8TD

Hachette Books Ireland policy is to use papers that are
natural, renewable and recyclable products and made from wood grown in
sustainable forests. The logging and manufacturing processes are expected
to conform to the environmental regulations of the country of origin.

Hachette Books Ireland
8 Castlecourt Centre, Castleknock, Dublin 15, Ireland
A division of Hachette Livre UK
338 Euston Road, London NW1 3BH, England

For Yefiw

Prologue

The man came scurrying down the dark street clutching his side. He knew he'd broken a rib or two in the fall, but he couldn't worry about that now. He had to keep distance between him and the men chasing him; otherwise he was dead. They wouldn't stop and ask questions. They knew he'd taken the disc and that if it got into the wrong hands, such as the police or any journalist with their wits about them, it would mean big trouble for their organisation. Every stride sent shockwaves of pain through his body, and he tried to think as he kept moving. He didn't know how to hot-wire a car or to pick locks like people in films. Breaking a window would be as good as erecting a sign outside a building saying 'I'm in here!!' and the late hour meant passing traffic in this part of town was non-existent. There was no passing motorist to flag down, no last-minute taxi driver to help him get away.

It was at times like this he wished he'd kept fitter. Joining a gym and going six times in a year wasn't really good enough. If he got out of this, he promised himself he'd actually carry through some of his New Year's resolutions. He even promised to go to church every week although he'd long stopped believing in God.

He figured he needed all the help he could get.

Suddenly he found himself caught in the powerful headlights of a car skidding around the corner behind him. He looked back and tried to run faster but there was nowhere for him to go. He couldn't outrun a car – even if he had gone to the gym he figured that would have been difficult – but his instincts kicked in and he tried to stay as far ahead of them for as long as possible. He knew they were going to kill him whether he had the disc or not so he thought he might as well at least try to get the information out there. Reaching inside his pocket, he felt for the CD case, and, as he kept running, he thrust it through the shutters of a shop. He hoped somebody would find it. He hoped they'd look at the information and see that it had to go to the police. He hoped that by some stroke of luck his actions hadn't been in vain and his death would at least bring about the demise of the people now about to kill him.

Most of all though, he hoped that the fact his prologue was in completely the wrong book wouldn't matter too much.

Tuesday

I

Waking up is a terrible thing

The last thing I could remember before hearing the phone ring was having a discussion in Ron's with Dirty Dave about why some people, namely me, should be perfectly entitled to kill other people – I had a whole system worked out based on intelligence, education and how annoying a person's face was. But after that, it was all a blank. After some moments, I realised I was lying face down on my bed. The realisation you've made it home but have no recollection of getting there is always the most pleasant part about waking up the next morning. The phone was ringing, and it seemed to be coming from underneath the bed.

Those extra three or four pints in Ron's had my head pounding like a new prisoner's arse in Mountjoy after his first night behind bars. Then, glory of glories, the phone stopped. The silence was indescribably beautiful. One of those rare moments in life where you can appreciate the beauty of something despite being in terrible pain. Sadly the beauty was fleeting as the phone started to ring again. I pulled myself forwards and hung over the side of the bed, looking underneath. The blood rushing to my head enhanced the pain in the same way that the discovery that your teenage daughter has lost her virginity is made more painful by the fact that it was your best friend who did her. In your bed. And filmed it. And put it on YouTube.

Underneath the bed I saw my pants, a roll of tinfoil, an old slipper and, just within reach, the cordless house phone.

'Yes,' I said, rolling onto my back and closing my eyes.

'Where the fuck are you?' said Jimmy the Bollix, my best friend. Luckily I don't have a teenage daughter.

'I am in a coma,' I said.

'Only to be expected given how much you drank. The thing is though, we have a meeting in town in an hour, and you were supposed to be around here half an hour ago to discuss what we were going to do and say at said meeting.'

'Oh fuck. Fucking fucking fuck.'

'See you in twenty, Twenty. Hurry up.'

'Right, right. See you then.'

Fucking fuck. Why were there always meetings on the mornings you had the worst hangovers? Normally I would have been quite content to stay in bed till the afternoon but this wasn't the sort of meeting we could be late for, let alone not turn up to. I suppose I'd been living it up a bit since the Folkapalooza adventure when we'd managed to prevent the entire population of Dublin and, less importantly, the rest of Ireland, being turned into permanent cabbages who loved the music of Damien Rice and his ilk. It had been quite harrowing at times and, given how close we'd come to not managing to save the day, I had a bit of the old Lorenzo de Medici about me. I was eating, drinking and being merry – for who knows what some cunt might try and do tomorrow.

I reached out for the bottle of water I always keep to the side of my bed. I unscrewed the top and took a big mouthful of dry air. Mmmm, empty. Fuck. I got up, threw on a big dressing gown, took four painkillers from my bedside drawer and made my way into the kitchen. I swallowed the tablets with a swig from a carton of orange juice in the fridge, put the kettle on, then opened up the back door. My dog Bastardface emerged from his kennel to greet me.

'Hello, big fella,' I said before reaching into the pocket of my gown to take out my cigarettes. We stood there smoking in silence, the dog and I, before I went inside and drank a cup of coffee. There was no sign of the cat, Throatripper, just yet but that wasn't unusual. Sometimes he liked to stalk his prey for miles before pouncing.

I took a quick shower, trimmed my beard, buzzed my nose hair with this little contraption that was so ticklish it was all I could do not to titter out loud in a high-pitched voice, and got dressed. The dog was buzzing around expectantly, as if he wanted to go to the park, but the clean-up from the Folkapalooza concert was still ongoing and I couldn't go back to the scene of a crime. Not so soon anyway. The Phoenix Park is the only one big

Absinthe Makes the Heart Grow Fonder

enough for Bastardface. People just think it's a particularly ferocious-looking deer they're seeing race across the gallops. Anyway, I didn't have time. I had to be round in Jimmy's in ten minutes. I promised him I'd take him out later on, and he looked at me as if I'd just said Ryan Tubridy was going to sit and keep him company for five minutes but there was nothing I could do. I put him out the back with his breakfast (a suckling pig with the apple in its mouth and everything) and locked up the house.

I live on, or close to, the South Circular Road in Dublin. I have an old Victorian cottage quite near the city centre, and I love where I live. Jimmy lives about two minutes around the corner in a house which is surrounded on both sides by houses converted into flats. For most people this could cause problems as they have to deal with noisy tenants, but nobody would disturb Jimmy. The landlords tell the people who occupy the flats that border his walls that if they make too much noise then Jimmy'll come round, and any blood they spill on the carpet or that gets sprayed onto the walls will make their deposit non-refundable. I think it's the idea of losing their deposit more than the fact the next-door neighbour might make them bleed that keeps them quiet.

I strolled around, nodding at some of the locals. Asad and Habib, the two Muslim lads from up the road. Mad for the pints and bacon sandwiches they were. Old Paddy who drinks in Ron's and who you don't want to get into conversation with because there's no way out of it. Words, edgeways and all that. Bald Susan who runs the graphic design company. I call her Bald Susan because all her hair fell out and her name is Susan. Big Jim who works down the road in the local shop. You can always tell what he's had for breakfast because there are generally bits of it stuck in his enormous moustache. He's the kind of man you want to stay upwind of at all times. Trampy the tramp, with his bushy grey beard. He's all right, and I give him a few bob now and then even though he once threw a Cadbury's Creme Egg at my head. He spends it all on cheap hooch so at least he's not wasting it. All the colour of the local community.

I put out my cigarette underfoot before walking up the path to Jimmy's and ringing the doorbell.

'Ah, there you are!' he said with the smugness of one without a desperate hangover.

'Stop talking so loudly,' I said. I dry-swallowed another couple of painkillers.

'No time to come in,' he said, grabbing his coat and closing the door behind him, 'we've got half an hour to walk into town.'

'Walk? Are you mad? We'll get a taxi.'

'No fucking chance. You need the walk to clear your head. You're not going into this meeting without at least some of your wits about you.'

'I have to warn you that I may need to stop and vomit along the way.'

'You'll have your pick of the gardens then.'

We walked down through the Blackpitts, up past that old school that has been turned into a bar, onto Clanbrassil Street, up the road and down the side of the old Meath Hospital, across onto Camden Street and onwards to town. I smoked as I went. Jimmy didn't smoke because he doesn't smoke. I did feel slightly nauseous at one stage but managed not to vomit. I think that's because I didn't actually have any food in my stomach to chuck up. I'd eaten a sandwich at lunchtime the previous day but nothing since. I thought I should probably get a piece of fruit or something because my stomach makes very weird noises when it's empty but I didn't trust myself not to regurgitate it during the meeting. And that would be bad.

'Right,' said Jimmy, 'what's our plan?'

'I'm not sure we have a plan. We don't even know what he wants.'

'Hm, good point. He's going to ask us to do something for him though, isn't he?'

'Yes, I believe that's the whole point of calling in your marker on someone.'

'Har har. Look, you know me. I don't mind the old ultra-violence or action but I do not like risk. I don't want to be set up for a fall.'

'Well, me neither, but I don't think it's going to be anything like that. How would that benefit him?'

'Another good point. You should do more of your thinking when you're hungover, not drunk.'

'I'm not doing it on purpose. . . . Oh, I think I need a shit.'

'Save it till afterwards. It'll keep you on edge.'

'It's times like this I'm slightly jealous of Colostomy Chris.'

'Ah, old Bumtum himself. Anyway, leaving aside men who crap into bags, let's agree on one thing before we go in.'

'What's that?'

'That Phil Collins is a cunt.'

'Agreed.'

'Right then,' said Jimmy, stopping outside the door on South William Street, 'let's do it.'

He rang the buzzer, and a couple of moments later we were on our way upstairs.

2

At Tony's

We walked up two flights of stairs and came to a door on the top left of the landing. Outside was a brass plaque, which was blank. Before we could knock, the door opened. A burly man beckoned us inside to a kind of reception area, with potted plants and a leather couch but no receptionist. He gave us both the eye but said nothing. There was another door open to our left and from inside another guy, who looked like he could have been a professional gladiator, was dragging, by the collar, an unconscious man whose face appeared to have made repeated contact with a very hard surface. Just then a voice rang out. 'Twenty. Jimmy. Come on in.'

I don't even know how he knew it was us. I looked at Jimmy. He looked at me. I gulped slightly, and in we went.

'Ah, there yiz are,' said Tony Furriskey from behind a solid mahogany desk. He was rubbing a towel over his hands, and it was immediately obvious that the hard surface the unconscious man's face had made contact with was Tony's fists. 'It's been a while.'

'It has that,' I said, thinking in my head, not long enough though.

Tony Furriskey is in his mid-forties and one of the most vicious and powerful criminals in Dublin. His 'family'-run business makes millions each year from drugs, smuggling, protection rackets and armed robberies. His manor takes in Crumlin, Dolphin's Barn, Kilmainham, Rialto and Drimnagh on the south side of Dublin, and, while there are newcomers to the gangland scene in recent years, Tony is undoubtedly still the kingpin. When you read about pipe bombs and gang wars between Crumlin and Drimnagh, these are the smaller players because nobody in their right mind would trample on Tony's turf. His reputation goes before him, and he is a genuinely scary man capable of acts of incredible violence. While other bosses like to send their lieutenants out to do the kicking, punching and strangling, Tony still enjoys the 'dirty work', so to speak. Physically he's not the tallest, standing about five foot nine, but he is stocky and powerful with the kind of forearms that would make Popeye jealous. He has enormous hands, battle-scarred from so many fights and punch-ups, his knuckles are grossly misshapen, and, when clenched, his fists could punch holes in a steel door. His hair is cropped short, his eyes just slightly too close together, and his face adorned with a scar that runs from between his eyes, across his nose and down his left cheek. He got jumped in a bar when he was younger, slashed by a rival in a surprise attack. The old joke 'Yeah, but you should see the other guy' was Tony's favourite because nobody ever saw the other guy again. Well, not in person anyway. The legend goes that he was taken to the mountains and tortured for hours, with the whole thing recorded on video. Tony then called a meeting of the other gangsters, sat them down and showed them the film just so they'd know what they could expect if anybody tried that kind of move again.

Nobody ever did.

The true measure of his fearsome reputation came when a feckless, self-important tabloid journalist, famed for making up Batman-style nicknames for Dublin's criminals, rather unoriginally labelled the barrel-chested Tony as 'Fat Tony' in his column one Sunday. Despite the fact the journalist had twenty-four-hour garda protection, it was made very clear to him that should he ever repeat that slur he would live, for a short time, to bitterly regret it.

He never did.

That was the kind of guy Tony was. If you were told to do something and you did what you were told then you wouldn't have any problems with him. If you challenged his authority, then you could expect his full wrath to wreak down upon you, and that was never a good thing.

'So,' he said, 'did yiz get caught up in that painful shite the other week? All that acoustic bollox? I was out of the country but I do read the papers online and that.'

'Yeah,' I said, 'we got caught up in a bit all right.

Poxy thing. Can you imagine a world where Damien Rice was the nation's favourite?'

'Doesn't bear thinkin' about. Still, he's dead now, and the men that did it should be honoured like soldiers. Fuckin' heroes they are. How's the dog?'

'Vicious.'

'I've always liked that dog. Reminds me a bit of meself. Powerful, aggressive, relentless and a massive fuckin' tail! Wha'?! Hahaha.'

We laughed. When Tony makes a joke, however terrible, you laugh, unless you're feeling brave. And that was a two-out-of-ten joke.

'Story with yeh, Jimmy? Heard your brother died.'

'Yeah,' said Jimmy.

'Congratulations.'

'Cheers, Tony. It's been a long time coming.'

'Was he in a lot of pain?'

'The doctor told me afterwards that it would have been worse than having a large thistle inserted down your mickey then pulled out really slowly while having to read the *Sunday Times* and listen to David McSavage's attempts at comedy.'

'Ouch. What goes around comes around, right?'

'It sure does.'

'Speakin' of which . . .,' he began. I looked at Jimmy, Jimmy looked at me. 'Yiz won't have forgotten that little favour I did yiz a while back.'

'How could we forget, Tony?'

'Too much booze, a stroke, hypnotherapy, wha'?! Hahaha.' We laughed again, a one-out-of-ten this time, but

Tony wasn't renowned for his joke-telling as much as for his pain-inflicting, torturing, killing and general meanness.

Some time back, Jimmy and I had found ourselves caught up in a situation outside our normal scope, and the people we were dealing with had become quite, shall I say, agitated at our presence. That there were many of them and only two of us put the odds very much against us. It was over pints in Ron's one afternoon that we figured we had to ask for help, and Tony was the only one we could think of. Tony and Jimmy and I go back some years. Not that we were exactly buddies, but our paths had crossed enough times for us to be on reasonable terms. Sometimes Tony might outsource a bit of work to us – some collections, some driving, some merchandise that needed to be shifted – and we always, true professionals that we are, did a good job of it. I think he always appreciated the fact there was no nonsense with us, no problems, so we asked him if he might be able to get these people off our backs. In typical fashion, he gave his help on the proviso that we now 'owed him one'. So there was no question of us turning him down, whatever it was. In fact, even if you didn't owe him a favour and Tony asked you to do something for him you'd be best off agreeing to it if you didn't want to wake up dead.

'Right, well, here's the story. Yeh know me youngest, Cynthia?'

'Of course. How old is she now?'

'Twenty-two and beautiful as her mother was at that age.'

'Stunning so,' said Jimmy. 'How is the lovely Imelda this weather?'

'Ah grand. Got her a membership up at one of them Ben Dunne gyms. Old Ben owed me from that time I stopped that thing with that other thing getting in the papers. She goes every day, but the lady just likes to eat cakes. She's a diamond, a great, enormous diamond of a woman. Wouldn't change her for the world. Anyway, Cynthia hasn't developed the same addiction to cake as her mother, but she's involved with a fella that's no good as far as I'm concerned.'

'That can be a tricky situation, Tony.'

'Don't I know it? Can't say anythin' directly because she's smitten as she is and she'll just side with him if I give out, and the one place I want happiness is in me own house.'

'So what's his problem then? Drugs? Robbings? Gangs? Chelsea fan?'

'Ah, if only it was somethin' like that, I could bring him under me wing. I never had a son, Twenty. Three girls but no lad to take over the business when the time comes. I've got me nephew Portobello Jack, but it's not the same. I always dreamed of a son. I could teach him the old ways, how to do business, mark the territory, gouge someone's eye out without gettin' bits under the fingernails, all that shite. I thought maybe one of the girls would marry someone with a bit of street to them, but it didn't happen.'

'What about the other two?'

'Well, Laura married a fella who works for Eircom. As dry as an Arab's arsehole, and he doesn't like football.'

'Oh?'

'Yeah. Proper fuckin' weirdo. And Bernadette ended up hitched to an American called Randy.'

'Does he like football?'

'He pretends to, at least, but he's as honest as the day is long. He knows what I'm about, doesn't have a problem with it, but doesn't want to be involved. Says he wants to make his own way in the world. I've got to respect that.'

'What does he do?'

'He's an expert in artificial insemination.'

'That's noble work—'

'For cows, Twenty. He examines bull spunk all day long and matches potential mothers, then sends off vials of jism to be lashed up cow's gees.'

'Erm . . . well, someone has to do it, I suppose,' said Jimmy.

'Yeah, someone. Had to be me fuckin' son-in-law though, eh?'

'So, this new lad on the scene. If he's not a drug pusher or general miscreant, what's the problem?'

'He's just not right for me Cynthia, Twenty. Yiz know me, yiz know me family. Salt of the fuckin' earth, so we are, but this fella's miles removed from all that. Doesn't know the first thing about the real world, talks like a cunt, looks like a cunt too. And then when I found out what he does . . . well, that was fuckin' that as far as I was concerned.'

'Fucking hell,' I said, 'it must be rough. You'd best spill it then.'

'It's a bit embarrassin' actually, that someone like that is so close to being part of me family . . .'

'Look Tony,' said Jimmy, 'you know us. You know

what we've been through, what we've seen, the people we've dealt with. It can't be that shocking.'

'OK, then . . . he . . .' Tony sighed, 'he plays rugby for Blackrock College.'

3

The quest revealed

I thanked my lucky stars that my stomach was empty because if I had eaten anything, Tony Furriskey would have been covered in my sweet, sweet puke that very moment. Silence filled the room. 'Oh man, Tony. I'm so sorry,' I said eventually, still reeling from the shock. It must be one of the worst things a parent can go through, to have their child involved with somebody so very unsuitable. I suppose it's slightly easier if it's a son, but the idea of your daughter having sex – slippery, sweaty, smelly sex, rutting like a pair of young dogs on sheets covered with genital juice – with an insufferable arsehole like that must be almost impossible to bear.

'Tony . . . I . . . I don't know what to say,' said Jimmy, genuinely downcast.

'I know. Yeh can't imagine the hell I've been goin'

through. Every time that fucker is in the house with his "loike, ya know" this and "shore, oi'm lowded" that, I feel like snappin' his fuckin' neck. But the young one, she's head over fuckin' heels. And she's the apple of me eye, Jimmy. I have to pretend to like him and sit there listenin' to his witless shite about his life workin' for a bank and playin' that stupid game against teams like Terenure and St Mary's and all those other private-school motherfuckers.'

'Ouch,' I winced. 'Well, maybe it'll run its course. You know how flighty the young people are these days. You can't go anywhere without some guy or girl offering their hole to you, so I hear. Perhaps he'll find some Emma or other in Annabel's – or wherever it is that type of lad kicks people to death outside these days.'

'I was hopin' that meself, Twenty, but it's much more serious than that. We even had to go meet his family. Sickenin' it was.

'They live in a big house in Blackrock, garden the size of Sundrive Park, yeh know the type: stinkin' rich they are. Not as rich as me, but still stinkin'. And they're all so fuckin' posh. "Ooh, would you like some more 1967 Chateau Neuf de Pape, Tony? Another smoked salmon mousse?" and in me head all I can think is, fuck yiz and yiz's Chateau Neuf de Pape. Yiz can't just call it wine? Yiz have to tell me what make it is and what year it's from? And salmon mousse? Get to fuck. Chocolate mousse, fine, but who ever heard of fish mousse? Only fuckin' cunts would eat that shite.

'Anyway, that's why yiz're here now. Picture the scene: we're just finished dinner. I'm having a cup of scald, hopin' for a bit of fuckin' peace and quiet, and I can see them both lookin' at me. I knew somethin was up. "Tony," says Imelda, sprayin' crumbs of mini-battenburg down her front, "Tony, Cynth has some news for yeh."

'"Oh aye?" I say, "what's that then?" thinkin' she'd gotten a new job or was going on holidays with the girls. Well, yeh can imagine the reaction when she says "Coleman has asked me to marry him!!" with a big smile on her face. "And what did yeh say?" I asked, thinkin', Please let it be no, please let it be no, in me head. "Oh Daddy, what d'yeh think?! I'm going to be Mrs Coleman Darcy-McNeill!" and she came over so delighted, so full of joy that I could only hug her as the blood drained from me face. "Are yeh sure you want to get married, love?" I asked. "Yer still only twenty-two, and there's a whole big world out there. Yeh could travel and meet lots of people then settle down when yeh've experienced a bit more of what life has to offer," but she says, "Daddy, I know what I want, it's Coleman. He's me soulmate." I didn't say another word because I was tryin' to swallow some of the sick I'd burped up so I just smiled. And it was painful.'

'Can't blame you there, Tony,' said Jimmy. 'And here's the worst part,' Tony continued, 'that was months ago. The wedding is in two weeks' time, and it's driving me mental.'

'That's a difficult situation all right. I'm pretty sure I'd be as protective if I had a daughter,' I said.

'It's not just that though. Everythin' about it is drivin' me mental. I'm father of the bride, right? So I'm the one payin' for it all – which I can just about live with – but Twenty, they won't fuckin' leave me alone.'

'How do you mean?'

'It's constant. The talk about the weddin'. Every single dinner conversation is about fuckin' seatin plans, or the menu, or flowers, or dresses, or what car we're going to use, or should the bridesmaids wear green or emerald or jade or . . . excuse me a sec,' he said, stopping to answer the phone that was ringing on his desk. 'Hello? Ah, Imelda. What's wrong? I'm kinda busy here . . . What? . . . OK . . . OK . . . Well, I don't know, do I? Seriously, how would I know that? What? . . . What tone? Jesus, I'm trying to work here, love . . . Right, look, can yeh just decide? Yeh know more about this kind of stuff than me. Yeah, I'm sure . . . OK . . . OK . . . yeah, I'll talk to yeh later. Bye.' He hung up and put his head in his hands. 'See what I mean? Not a fuckin' moment's peace. Wantin' to know did I think we should have linen or muslin tablecloths. What the fuck do I care about fuckin' tablecloths, lads? I swear, I'm at the end of me fuckin' tether here.'

'Couldn't you just have him taken out, Tony? I mean, you're Tony Furriskey. With the greatest of respect, this isn't exactly uncharted terroritory for you,' said Jimmy.

'Look, there's nothin' I'd rather do, but Imelda knows I hate the little fucker, and if anythin' happened to him here she'd know I had somethin' to do with it. And that makes my life at home awkward, and seein' as life outside the home is awkward enough given me line of work, I want peace and fuckin' quiet when I'm there. So I've had to bite me tongue and watch me little girl get closer and closer to marryin' this up-his-own-arse cunt.'

'And imagine all the time you'll have to spend with them.

The wedding, Christmases, family parties and, dare I say it, christenings,' I said.

'Don't fuckin' say christenin's,' Tony roared. 'It's bad enough she's marryin' him, I don't want livin', breathin' proof they're havin' sex. I hope the fucker is a Jaffa.'

'Jaffa?'

'Seedless, Twenty. Get yer head straight, lad.'

'So where do we fit into all this, Tony?' asked Jimmy.

'Right, well, as I said, I'm stymied, so what I was thinkin' was that as yerself and Twenty owe me this favour, yiz could take care of it for me.'

'But surely you getting someone to sort it out for you will just look like you got someone to sort it out for you.'

'That would be true under normal circumstances, but the plank and his mates are goin' away on a stag weekend, and that would be way beyond me own manor, so to speak. If somethin' happened there that meant the weddin' couldn't take place then I could hardly get the fuckin' blame, could I?'

'I suppose not. Where are they going and when?'

'Barcelona, and it's this weekend.'

'Oh, Barcelona. Know it well. I used to live there,' I said.

'Revisit the scene of the crime, wha'? Or should I say crimes? Wha'?! Ha ha ha.'

'Ha ha ha,' I laughed, not just because it was prudent to laugh when Tony laughed but because he'd come a little close to the bone there. It wasn't so much that I had a calling to return to Dublin as much as I had a need to get out of Barcelona in a hurry. But that was all in the past.

I was sure everything had settled down by now. Reasonably sure. Sort of.

'Now, Tony,' said Jimmy, 'when you talk about something happening that might prevent the wedding taking place, what exactly do you mean?'

'I mean you boys have to bring somethin' back from Barcelona I can show to my little girl which will make her call off the weddin'.'

'Right. It wouldn't be enough that he just didn't come back then?'

'Oh fuck no. That would break her heart, and I couldn't inflict that kind of pain on her.'

'Isn't showing her something that will make her call off the wedding going to break her heart too?' said Jimmy.

'Has he lost his mind, Twenty? There's a big difference between a bit of breakin'-up heartbreak and the buryin'-the-corpse-of-the-man-yeh-love heartbreak. Jaysus.'

'OK, so no killing. What if he were to come back a paraplegic vegetable or something?'

'No good either. What if she decides to marry him out of some sense of loyalty then? I'm not havin' her waste her fuckin' life on a capper.'

'Right then, that doesn't leave us with too many options.'

'Well, yiz're smart fellas. I'm sure yiz'll think of somethin'.'

'Do you have any details of where he's staying or anything?' I said.

'No, and I can't ask. All I know is that he's leavin' on Friday.'

'Got a picture?'

'Yeah. I'll get it to yeh later. I know Ron's is still the best place to find yeh.'

'Grand.'

'Might have a pint while I'm down there. Haven't been in Ron's for years now. Me auld fella used to drink there back in the day. Always went on about the fuckin' Guinness. Stopped drinkin' there for some reason though. Anyway, boys, once yiz have that picture I'll leave yeh to it. Don't let me down now, hear?'

'Don't worry, Tony,' said Jimmy, 'you can count on us. Right, Twenty?'

'Not a problem,' I said, with far more confidence than I actually felt.

'OK, yiz have me number but don't fuckin' use it unless it's an absolute emergency. Otherwise I'll talk to yiz next week,' Tony said, turning his back on us to let us know he had given us as much of his time as we were going to get.

'Righto. Cheers,' I said, and we left the office. In the reception area the burly man gave us an almost imperceptible nod, and we saw a nervous, shaking man who was obviously waiting to see the boss. I couldn't blame him for being nervous, as I've said, Tony's ruthlessness is legendary.

Once, when he got unconfirmed reports that a minor player in his crew had been talking out of turn, he had him tied to a chair in his office, his hands and feet bound, his head held steady by two others, and cut out his tongue with a pair of kitchen scissors to make sure he never spoke again. When word got around what had happened people became even more reluctant, if that were possible, to talk about Tony Furriskey. 'But I saw you with him,' the garda might say.

'No, you didn't,' the interviewee would say.

'Yes, I did. And I took some photos. Here, look. There's you. There's Tony.'

'I've never seen that bloke before in my life.'

'You're obviously sharing a joke and shaking hands.'

'No, I'm not.'

'You have one hand on his shoulder.'

'No, I don't.'

And so it would go. Men did their time if that's what it took. Tony was like Fight Club. The first rule of Tony Furriskey was you didn't speak about him.

When Tony actually set up a fight club in 2003 it actually caused some people to go properly mute, such was the intensity of the not talking about it.

I didn't envy the man sitting in the waiting room, and it occurred to me that although Tony and Jimmy and I went back a bit, unless we did what he expected of us we'd be the ones sitting there trying not to cack our pants – if we even made it that far.

Jimmy and I had lots to discuss, and the only place to do that was Ron's.

4

Assembling the troops

Lunchtime in Ron's is merely a time. The concept of lunch being served in his bar is as ridiculous as somebody getting timely and effective hospital treatment in Ireland. With the hangover acids burning a hole in my stomach after the previous night though, I had to stop somewhere on the way back to pick up a couple of sandwiches. It's a fucking chore these days though, isn't it? Everywhere you go you can get oak-smoked pastrami with halloumi on wild rocket with caramelised red onion, or organic salmon with lemon mayo, lettuce and cucumber on white rustic bread, or any other manner of fancy ciabattas, wraps, tortillas or paninis. But fuck me if you can find a simple ham and cheese on Brennan's Bread. You know society is heading for the fucking toilet when the sandwiches become that fancy. It was far from those kinds of things that any of us were reared. Maybe a bit of a recession might help the classic sandwich. See, there's always a silver lining.

Eventually I found a delicatessen on Camden Street, and, after assuring the charming-and-not-at-all-pig-ignorant Chinese girl behind the counter that all I wanted was some fucking ham and some fucking cheese on some fucking buttered white bread, we strolled back to Ron's bar. When we got there Ron was behind the bar, cleaning a glass with a rag that looked like it had been made out of Dirty Dave's underpants. The place was empty apart from old Charlie sitting in the snug, doing the Simplex crossword in *The Irish Times*. At his feet lay McGillicuddy, his faithful mongrel. McGillicuddy was the replacement for the old dog, Slattery, who died last year. Charlie and Slattery had been inseparable; it was the same with the new fella. Charlie was the only one allowed bring a dog into the bar though. Stinking Pete tried some years back, but Ron wouldn't have it. 'Get out of here, Pete, and bring Madonna with you,' he'd roared.

'Howdy, Ron,' said Jimmy. 'A couple of pints, if you please.'

We sat in our usual spots at the end of the bar, furthest from, and in plain sight of, the door. That way we can see whoever comes in. Usually it's just one of the usual reprobates but you can't be too careful. I unwrapped my sandwich and began to eat. My mouth was still very dry so it was like gargling with sand and then trying to eat a hundred moths, but I needed the sustenance. When Ron put the pints down I drained half of mine in one go and felt

some of my vim and vigour return. 'So, whaddya reckon?'
I asked Jimmy.

'Well, on the plus side we get to go to Barcelona, the
sun will be shining, the beer will be cheap, and the girls
will be wearing very little.'

'But . . .'

'The downside is that we have to first think of a way of
bringing something back that will convince Tony's
daughter she doesn't want to marry this guy. I mean, what
are we talking here? A pair of his spunk-crusted jocks? I'll
tell you what, it's a pain in the hole that we can't just push
him off the top of the Sagrada Familia or something . . .'

'I hear ya,' I said.

'So, what do we do?'

'Well, first we need to find out when all the flights from
Dublin arrive in Barcelona on Friday. So that means
checking Aer Lingus, Iberia, British Midland,
Spic'n'spanair and Ryanair—'

'Ha ha!'

'What?'

'Ryanair! They don't fly to Barcelona. They'll go to an
airport in the general vicinity of Barcelona, but it'll be
the usual crack of having to take a bus ride that's longer
than the flight to get to the city. Those cunts once flew me
to "Paris", and, instead of viewing the Eiffel Tower and
the lights of the city as we came in to land, we set down
in a field with a manually operated baggage carousel and
one French airport official to mutter "Eeenglish cunts" at
us as we came through customs. Then, when I eventually
got to the city, I had to put up with all those French

wankers. Jesus Christ, I thought it was just a stereotype about them being as ignorant as fuck, like the thick Irishman, the stingy Scot or the incestuous cellar-loving Austrians, but fuck me, the French really take the biscuit. Pardon me if I don't speak your beautiful language accent-free and with one hundred per cent correct pronunciation. I just asked you the fucking way to the Moulin Rouge not to lick dog shit off my shoes, and if you don't stop sneering at me I'm going to gouge your eyes out with my cock. Fucking Ryanair.'

'Erm . . . right, well, I'll check out the flights when I get back home. So, assuming we get the flight info, we're going to need to get there before him so we can wait at the airport and follow him to his hotel or whatever. Now, I don't think I'm understating it when I say that could turn out to be the biggest pain in the arse of all time. What if he's on the last flight of the day? We can't stand around like chumps in the arrivals area. Tony's a fierce bastard, but I'm not spending all day in the airport for anyone – even him.'

'I see what you mean,' said Jimmy. 'There's got to be a way of sorting something out. And what about Barcelona? Will everything be OK for you there?'

'Yeah. I'm pretty sure it will. It's been years now. It's got to be all forgotten.'

Just then, in came Stinking Pete and Dirty Dave in the middle of a heated discussion.

'What are you on about, Pete?' shrieked Dave. 'You can't be serious, that's the most stupid thing I've ever heard.'

'So's your face!' roared Pete.

'You can't hear my face, you stupid billy.'

'Silly.'

'What is?'

'Billy.'

'Who the fuck is Billy?'

'Your mum.'

'My mum is called Freda, and anyway she's dead. You bastard. How could you?'

'I didn't kill her.'

'But you know who did, don't you? Who was it? Don't hold out on me, you bastard, or I swear I'll throttle the life out of you.'

'She was run over by a milk float thirteen years ago, Dave.'

'Oh Mammy, what a creamy end you had! Waaaaaah!'

'Jesus, calm down. You're a grown man.'

'Unlike your stillborn lovechild!'

'Oh, you bastard. Waaaaaah! Hold me, Dave.'

They held each other, sniffling and weeping, as Jimmy and I looked at each other, sighing deeply. Both of them had been instrumental in foiling the Folkapalooza plot, and had it not been for Dave befriending the Ginger Albino, who had suffered a most hideous and painful death at the vocal cords of crazy Spanish diva and mastermind Mariposa Cachimba, we might not have saved Dublin and, less importantly, the rest of the country from the creeping menace of Damien Rice and his ilk. That said, they both make teenage beauty-pageant competitors look like Einstein but, like it or not, we're stuck with them. The good thing was though that we could usually get them to do all kinds of stuff for our amusement. One time, Dirty Dave spent a week in a coma with Toxic Shock Syndrome after eating a load of tampons for a bet, and, on another occasion, we convinced Stinking Pete that punching a pony in the face three times while its owner was looking at you meant they were legally obliged to pay you twenty guineas. It took him three arrests, a court appearance and the payment of compensation to fix broken pony snouts before he realised we were having him on. For the most part though we could still get them to do what we wanted them to do, and while you had to factor their stupidity into everything you did, they were great for doing the stuff you didn't want to do. Like, for example, waiting around an airport all day for some rugby-playing cunt and his mates.

'Dave, Pete, stop your keening. It's most unbecoming.'

They stopped and pulled up stools at the bar.

'Would you like a pint?' I asked them.

They said nothing, just looked at me suspiciously. 'Are you struck dumb or what?'

'Yeah. I'll have a pint of Guinness,' said Dave.

'Mine's a Satzenbrau with ice,' said Pete until Ron coughed and gave him the 'I will kill you for even thinking I'd have that shite in my bar' look. 'Erm, Smithwicks with a Guinness head then please.'

'How're tricks, Dave?'

'They're fine, Twenty. Like not much different since we saw you right here last night, you know?'

'And you, Pete? Keeping well? Nothing strange or startling to report?'

'Not a bit of it.'

'And have either of you got any plans for the weekend?'

'Not me,' said Dave, 'I was just going to drink some beer, watch some Japanese pornography, masturbate furiously, eat some food and perhaps bring some of my clothes to the laundry. My underwear is due for its annual wash.'

'Well, I don't have anything planned for Saturday and Sunday, but on Friday night I'm going to meet up with an old friend that I haven't seen for years. It's taken months to arrange, and I really am looking forward to it. It's going to be quite capital, I can tell you,' said Pete.

'Ahhh, I'm afraid you're going to have to cancel that,' I said.

'I am? Why?'

'You won't be here on Friday night.'

'I won't?' said Pete.

'He won't?' said Jimmy and Dave at the same time.

'Where will I be?'

'Barcelona!'

'Are you sure you mean me? I don't think I remember anything about making plans to go to Barcelona.'

'You haven't made the plans. I'm making them now. You and Dave are going out on Thursday at some stage—'

'I'm going too!' shrilled Dave.

'Yeah.'

'Awesome! I've never been to Madrid!'

'You're going to Barcelona, not Madrid.'

'Isn't Barcelona in Madrid, or something? Or Madrid

owns Barcelona? That's why all the locals hate Luís Figo because he sold them out for thirty million pieces of silver.'

'Yeah, something like that. But don't you worry about it.'

'Are you sure about this, Twenty?' said Jimmy.

'Friday could be a long day, remember?' I said.

'Right enough.'

'So, why are we going to Barcelona? And where are we staying? And what are we supposed to do there? And what exactly is the purpose of our visit? And what is our motivation for going there?'

'Too many questions, Dave. Too many questions. I'll have more answers for you tomorrow. Just make sure you dig your passport out from whatever pile of crap it's lying in.'

So, while Dave and Pete spoke giddily about going away somewhere foreign for the weekend, like real people, and Jimmy sat looking slightly nervous at whatever it was I was planning for the two of them, I got another pint in before heading towards home. There was a lot to find out and a lot to organise, and that fell to me. I'm very much of the school of thinking that if you want something done right you have to do it yourself, or pay somebody really good money to do it for you, but I wasn't paying any fucker.

I strolled from Ron's back to my house, on autopilot, the summer wind rolling in from across the sea. It smelt like burning. Then I realised it wasn't the summer wind at all but an old folks' home that was on fire. The screaming of the terrified elderly people was just awful, their plaintive wails were so filled with fear and sadness I could hardly bear to listen. So I put on my iPod for the rest of the walk home.

5

The park and such

I got back to the house and let the dog in. He was full of
energy, which meant I was going to have to bring him out.
I had been looking into the purchase of a golf buggy
which I can use to fly around in while the dog is leashed
to the back of it, but one wouldn't fit through the front
gate. Leaving a golf buggy parked outside on, or close to,
the South Circular Road would just be asking for trouble.
It'd be hot-wired and raced up and down on the very first
night. So, the traditional method of exercising the great
beast was the only choice I had. It was still just late afternoon; I could check the flight stuff when I got back in. I
made myself a little joint to smoke while I went with the
dog and set out into the summer sunshine. We walked up
the South Circular Road, past the National Stadium,
where it seemed an entire townful of itinerants were wait-

ing to take part in some kind of boxing tournament, turned left, crossed the canal and up towards Sundrive Park. Bastardface is a very big dog and loves to be out in the fresh air. Sadly, he loves to eat people's faces off, so I can't let him off the lead. This meant I was being pulled at great pace towards the park, which, when we got there, was full of other people walking their dogs. Some of them I was on nodding terms with, regular walkers who recognised the giant hound. There was one lady who made a hasty exit with her Pomeranian as soon as she saw us. It did hurt my feelings somewhat as I had bought that dog for her. Granted, it was a replacement for the one that Bastardface had cannibalised a couple of years previously, but still. Once bitten, and all that, I supposed. I let him stop and sniff and wee and produce an enormous stool, which I, like a good owner, picked up in a plastic bag. There were no bins in the park at all so I'd have to throw it in the canal on the way home, but at least nobody would get their shoes dirty. As we crossed over the football pitches towards the cycling track, I noticed a pretty lady walking a basset hound. Those dogs always make me laugh, what with their enormous ears and low bellies, like overfed midget Prince Charleses.

From behind a hill then appeared a man wearing a long coat, and he looked like he was trying to engage the lady in conversation of some kind. She, quite rightly, was ignoring him as he was a suspicious-looking bastard, but when she looked around to call on the basset, who had stopped to have a smell of something terribly interesting, the man whipped open his coat and started to play with his chopper. Well, that was not the kind of behaviour any lady should be subjected to, and I, as a gentleman, would not stand for it. She walked away, but he came closer, all the while tugging away at himself like a teenager with a copy of Hustler.

If I yelled at him, he'd run off, and that would hardly be any kind of punishment. There was only one thing for it. I unclipped Bastardface's lead and said 'Bastardface: sausage. Go get the sausage.' He doesn't need telling twice to go and get a sausage, and he bounded across the park looking left and right for the delicious treat he'd been told to go and procure. When he caught up with the man in the coat, he took a look, continued for a moment, then realised where the sausage was, slammed on his brakes and went straight for it. Coatman was shocked at the sight of this massive dog run past him and twice as shocked when it came drooling straight for his groin. He shrieked and began to run but had hardly gone three or four paces when Bastardface knocked him flying. He landed face first with an incredible scream, which I thought at first was just fright.

I whistled at Bastardface, and he stepped off the man's back and sat down to wait for me. When I got there, the man's screaming continued.

'Ooooooooh, Jeeeeeeeeeeeeeeesus Chriiiiiiiiiiiiiiiiiiiist!' he yelled.

'Shut up, you perverted cunt,' I said. 'You just fell on your face. The dog has been called off.'

'Noooooooo! I fell. It hurts. Oooowwww! It really hurts!'

'Stop being such a baby and get the fuck up and get out of here before I call the park warden, that most fearsome of authority figures.'

'Can't! Hurts! Ouch! Ouch! Oooowwww!'

'Well, if you're not going to get up, I'll make you.' I said and dragged him up by the collar of his coat. It was then I noticed the blood and let go, dumping him on his back. He sat up gingerly and looked down at his groin.

'Oh fuck! Oh no! Oh fuck! Jesus! Oh no! Oh no!' he said as he inspected the damage, getting more panicked with each utterance and with each look at what I assume was previously a perfectly functional penis. What was there seemed to be almost snapped in half. He must have landed erection first when the dog knocked him over, causing a hideous open penis fracture.

'Oh, that's why you're screaming. You'd want to get that seen to.'

'Help me!' he wailed.

'Yeah, right,' I said as I put the dog back on the lead and headed towards the park exit. We were just going through the gate when the lady with the basset came over. I told Bastardface to sit, and the two dogs looked at each other. The basset was old and realised there was to be no sniffing of the other dog's anus. His ears went forward like an Indian elephant.

'Thanks for your help,' said the lady, who was even prettier up close. I felt a stirring in my stomach, something I hadn't felt for quite some time. Indigestion again. Damn, I knew I'd wolfed that sandwich too quickly.

'You're welcome,' I said. 'Can't have ladies out being

bothered by sickos like that.' I explained the extent of his injury to her, which seemed to delight her immensely. We said our goodbyes, and I watched her go down the road with her dog. Maybe I'd see her again in the park one day. I hoped so. She made indigestion feel quite nice.

I took the dog home, his energy sated for a little while, and I thought about how much he meant to me. Since rescuing him from a scumbag who beat his litter mates to death, Bastardface had been my constant companion. He was loyal, not stupid and didn't answer back. A proper example of man's best friend.

I went into the room I use as my little office. I have a desk against the wall and above it are shelves with hundreds of vinyl records. To the side of the desk is a Technics SL1210 running into an amp into which I have connected a series of speakers. I love vinyl. Now, I love technology as much as the next man, I have my iPod and a hard drive full of MP3s and what have you, but you just can't beat the sound of a record. Every crackle has character. It may not be as clean as a CD or other digital version, but it's just got more balls. On the wall behind me is a series of bookshelves containing, erm, books. I like books. I have too many. I should throw some of them out, but I just can't bear it. I like to hoard.

I flicked through the vinyl, and, as I was feeling a bit stoned, I slapped on 'The Man Who Sold the World' by David Bowie. As the music kicked in and David crazed on about crazy blackbirds quoting Kahlil Gibran, I turned on my Mac and started checking out the flights to Barcelona. Aer Lingus went early in the morning then one in the late afternoon; KLM had a flight in the afternoon, while Clickair, whoever the fuck they were, went at about 11 a.m.

If we got lucky – rather, if Dave and Pete got lucky – they wouldn't be waiting all day, but if the lads weren't arriving until the late Aer Lingus flight, then they'd be spending all day in Arrivals. Waiting. And waiting. And waiting. Oh well, that wouldn't be my problem. Anyway, as I thought to myself, I was the one paying for them to go in the first place. Hanging around an airport was not much to ask for a free trip to one of the best cities in Europe. With that in mind, I booked four flights with Clickair for Thursday. The Aer Lingus flight was too early. There really is no call to be up at 5 a.m. to get a 7 a.m. flight.

After that, I had to sort out accommodation. Having lived in Barcelona in the past I knew which part of town I wanted to stay in, so I booked the Gran Hotel Havana on the corner of Gran Vía Corts Catalanes and c/Bruc. A room for me and a room for Jimmy. For Dave and Pete, I reserved a room each in a hostel around the corner. You might think that's a bit unfair, but a good hotel would just be wasted on them, the pair of half-witted reprobates. Anyway, it was on Passeig de Gràcia, the poshest shopping street in town. A hostel there wasn't exactly like making them stay in one of those kips on Amiens Street or anything.

With all my online purchasing complete, I kicked off my shoes, lit what remained of my joint, opened up the French doors into the garden and let the music wash over me like I was an actor in a German watersports video.

Wednesday

6

Photo

I woke up around lunchtime after spending the previous evening in Ron's. I had filled in the lads on the travel plans, made sure that Dave and Pete had their passports and assured our Italian friend Lucky that we'd bring him back something from Spain. He was most upset that he couldn't come with us: his domineering wife, being slightly pregnant with triplets, wouldn't even consider the possibility of him going away. That he was so hen-pecked always amused me, due to his profession. Lucky was the world's only compassionate assassin. Most other contract killers didn't want to know anything about their target other than who they were – personal details complicated things. Not so with Lucky Luciano: he would only kill people who he felt deserved to be killed. To be fair, he generally found some reason. I think it was

Absinthe Makes the Heart Grow Fonder

because Elisa, his beautiful but typically fiery Italian wife, wouldn't let him turn down work. In the past, he claimed to have killed Benazir Bhutto, Heath Ledger (apparently his unconvincing performance as Casanova was all the justification for Lucky to carry out the hit) and a load of Juventus fans at the 1985 European Cup Final at the Heysel Stadium. So cunningly brilliant was Lucky – a fan of his hometown club Livorno – he made it look like Liverpool fans were to blame. It was a shame he wasn't coming with us.

I shook my head slightly – this was how I checked to see if I had a headache or not. While there had been some drinking, it wasn't too hectic – perhaps subconsciously we were preparing ourselves for the wonder of cheap booze on the Continent. Conserving our energy, almost. While the head-shaking didn't produce too much in the way of pain, I lashed back a couple of Ibuprofen anyway. People often told me they were very bad for your liver. My theory was that drinking was bad for your liver too, and, as I once read on the back of a crime novel, sometimes, just sometimes, two wrongs do make a right, so I was banking on the pills cancelling out the damage the booze was doing. I grabbed a shower, then I fed the dog (a frightened goat tethered to the apple tree).

There was still no sign of the cat. I pish-wished him from the back door and hit a knife off a tin of food, which generally brought him back if he was in the vicinity, but he must have been too far away to hear. I wasn't too worried though: he was a hardy beast. The last kitten alive in a litter dumped into the canal at Kilmainham, I found him while out walking the dog one night. He had-n't used up all his lives yet.

I locked up and headed into town. I had a few things to pick up ahead of the trip to Barcelona. A couple of new T-shirts and some sunblock – so I didn't repeat the mistake I'd made some years previously. On one of my first sun holidays to Spain I managed to drag myself down to the beach the morning after a heavy session. I lay down and promptly fell asleep. When I woke up, a couple of hours later, my chest looked like it had been given a good coat of Dulux Flames of Hell so red was it. The skin felt tight, and it was beginning to hurt already. I asked for advice from the people in the hotel, having never experi-enced this kind of thing before. They asked me to show them my chest.

'Holy fucking shit!' they said, in Spanish, putting their hands to their mouths and making the face people make when they see 2 Girls, 1 Cup for the first time. A trip to a pharmacy and some after-sun later I thought I had beaten the worst of it. Sadly not. As the afternoon became early evening I felt myself getting hot. Not just my chest. All of me. I decided the best thing to do was to cool myself down by immersing myself in a cold bath. I positively siz-zled, and I felt most queer when I got out. I decided to lie down in bed for a while, which wasn't necessarily a great idea but I couldn't do much else. I sweated, yet I was freezing cold; I shivered, although I was absolutely roast-ing. I lay under the covers alternating between the two states for hours.

Then the hallucinations started. My holiday reading

had been a Hitler biography, and soon there were dozens of Hitlers walking past the end of my bed. They came from the left-hand side of the bedroom and walked out the doors onto the little terrace. They were very, very real-looking. Certainly more real than any mushroom- or chemical-induced hallucinations I had had. I heard noises and voices. I had to close my eyes because staring at the blank wall was like watching one of those crazy Bulgarian cartoons they used to show on RTÉ 2 when they couldn't find any *Tom and Jerry*, and my senses generally suffered a full-on assault until I fell asleep what seemed like twenty-four hours later (it was only eight or ten though, I think).

So, since then, I have ensured no such burn would ever happen again. Boots had Factor 900 which was for people holidaying on the Sun itself: that'd do. I could be safe, and I would point and laugh at all the pale-skinned Irish, English and Scandis we'd see wandering around looking like lobsters. The main purchase though had to be footwear. To my mind, there was only one thing to be wearing on the feet, and that was flip-flops. And not just any flip-flops. Brazilian flip-flops. It took me some time, but I managed to find a place that stocked Havaianas and got myself a couple of pairs of the original style, one with a black toe bit and the other with a blue toe bit. Classy, I have to say. People's feet need a good airing. In Ireland we don't really get flip-flop weather so people have sweaty, gnarled, slightly albino feet with corns and bunions and heels that look like they're made from dried-out old plastic and papier-mâché.

I grabbed a bite of lunch in a Japanese place behind Brown Thomas – I'm a sucker for sushi – then headed to Ron's for a post-meal digestif.

'Guess who was in here looking for you earlier?' said Ron as he pulled the pint.

'Interpol?'

'Nah.'

'The Edge? Because if it was I am so going back to my solicitor, the fucker won't leave me alone.'

'Nah. Tony Furriskey.'

'Ah, he said he'd call in actually.'

'Yeah, haven't seen him in a while. Used to know his dad, back in the day. What a nasty cunt he was.'

'Oh aye?'

'Yeah, he was mean as they come. I barred him out of here after an incident with a customer.'

'What happened?'

'Tony Senior was in here with a couple of mates and took offence to something Cretinous Colin said to him.'

'Who's Cretinous Colin and what did he say?'

'Cretinous Colin was a young fella, around twenty-one at the time I reckon. He was probably the stupidest bastard I've ever met. He was so stupid he thought Johnny Cash was what you used to buy condoms. Seriously, he once tried to tell me that a myth was a female moth. Not a bad lad though. Just thick as bottled shit.'

'What did he say to provoke Old Tony?'

'"Hello".'

'Hello?'

'Yeah. Tony was a mean drunk, and even when sober

everyone knew you didn't speak to him, look at him or acknowledge his presence in any way.'

'And what happened?'

'Cretinous Colin said "hello" to him as he was going to the toilets. Tony followed him in. When he came out and there was no sign of Colin after about fifteen minutes, I went in to find him face down in the cubicle. He'd been drowned in the toilet bowl then raped in the face. I couldn't stand for that. Drown someone by all means, I mean we've all done it, but there's no call to be raping corpses in the face – certainly not in my bar. So I barred him. He and his mates went to drink in Lynch's down on Thomas Street from then on.'

'That's a bit nasty all right.'

'I'm told Young Tony didn't get spared the beatings either. His old man wanted to make sure he was toughened up. Toughened him up a bit too much though.'

'How's that?'

'You don't know? It was Young Tony who killed his father.'

'Really? The story I always heard was that he got done by the Ballyfermot Toolmen for knocking off a truckload of hash. Young Tony then stepped up and took over. And didn't he take out Deco Murtagh as revenge?'

'All a cover. Notice how Tony and Ray Doyle managed to broker a truce so easily after those killings? Tony wanted to get his old man, Ray wanted to get Deco Murtagh out of the picture so he could take over. A quick pow-wow meant Young Tony could kill Old Tony, blame it on the Toolmen and then make a public show of revenge by having Deco beaten to death outside The Harp while they spread the story about the drugs. That suited both of them down to the ground,' he said, putting the pint of creamy Guinness in front of me. 'Jaysus, it's like *The Sopranos* crossed with *The Godfather* crossed with *Fair City*.'

'Look, Tony's beatings from his old man made him vow never to treat his own family that badly. But don't think for a second his loyalty to his own family means he's a soft touch. He's still a very dangerous man, make no mistake about that, Twenty.'

'I know, Ron. But he helped us out of a hole that time. Remember that situation involving those fellas from that place? He's just calling in his marker now. We've got to go to Barcelona and—'

'Enough, Twenty. I don't want to know the details. I've been behind this bar long enough to know it's best to not know stuff most of the time. Just take care with this. I know you and Jimmy and Tony go back a bit, but you don't get where he is and do what he does without being an ice-cold bastard. Friendships mean nothing.'

'Fair enough.'

'And don't start thinking I'm saying this to you because I care about you two or any shite like that. You cunts are my best customers, I find you all reasonably tolerable, and I don't want to have to get used to new clientele. Anyway, he had a pint, we had a chat. He gave me an envelope for you, said you'd know what it was about.'

'That's true.'

'And when you're out in Barcelona, look up my cousin.

He's got a bar there.'

'Oh yeah? What's it called?'

'Ronaldo's.'

'I should have known.'

'That you should. Tell him I sent you, he'll look after you,' Ron said, handing me the envelope and going to the other end of the bar to serve the two old men sitting there. The Stadler and Waldorf of Ron's, they came in every single day and drank pints of stout with Jameson chasers. What they still had to talk about every day of every week was beyond me, but they were always locked in conversation. Well, it was a bit one way: Old Paddy had a mouth like a Jewish wife – it never stopped – and Old Tom, who sat beside him, had big ears, so I suppose it worked out well enough for them.

I took a big gulp of my pint and opened up the envelope. Inside was a picture of a young guy, about twenty-three or twenty-four years of age. He had that weird hair that youngsters these days have. I remember when someone with spiky hair had it spiky at the top, but there don't seem to be any rules about that any more. His hair was spiky at the top and the sides and, I guessed, spiky at the back too. He wore a suit jacket and a casual shirt underneath. Although his legs weren't in the picture, I imagined him wearing faded or 'distressed' denims, possibly with a couple of pre-made rips, that cost a couple of hundred quid in Brown Thomas. He was smiling at the camera.

'Look at him,' I thought, 'the poor cunt thinks he's going off on his stag weekend and he's going to have a great time. Little does he know that the very reason he's going over there is what's going to cause his weekend to be not as great as he expected. Mwa ha ha ha ha!' Then I stopped twiddling my moustache and went back to not being a cartoon-evil-villain-type character. I finished my pint, gave Ron a nod, threw my black cape over my shoulder, stalked out the door and headed home.

When I got back in, I took a nap then packed my holdall for the trip abroad. Flip-flops: check. Underwear: check. Pants: check. T-shirts: check. Toothbrush: check. Sun cream: check. Cartons of delicious Major: check. Passport: check. Skimpy Speedos: check.

Ahhh, I'm joking. I'm not a Speedos man at all. Not that I have concerns about the size of my package. It's just that I have a really, really hairy arse, and wearing skimpy red Speedos makes it look like someone has cleaved Gerry Adams's face in two with an axe every time I bend over. I prefer long shorts anyway. If they stop just above my knee then they're perfect. The way good old-fashioned football shorts used to be.

After ordering an Indian takeaway from Bu Ali on Clanbrassil Street, I rang the lads to make sure they knew the arrangements for the morning. Everyone was to meet at my house and we'd get a taxi from there to the airport. Speaking of which . . . I rang and ordered a taxi to pick us up at 8.30 a.m. Still quite early, but when you consider we might have had to be up at 5 a.m. to get the 7 a.m. flight then it wasn't so bad.

When my food arrived and I'd washed it down with a couple of large bottles of Czech lager, I got to thinking a bit about when I lived in Barcelona.

It had been a glorious time in my life – until the incident. Since then I hadn't been back. It just never seemed right, and I knew that certain people wouldn't have appreciated it if they'd known I was in town. There was no time to dwell on things like that though. Like it or not, I was going back to Catalunya.

Thursday

7

A phone call

Have I mentioned before I hate alarm clocks? There are lots of things that can wake you in the morning – the sun beaming through the curtains the one night you've neglected to put on your eye mask, a dog barking, next door's alarm going off, somebody banging on your front door to tell you your cat has broken into their house and eviscerated their rabbit – but nothing is quite as annoying as the old-fashioned alarm clock. Which is what mine is. You wind it up and then, in the morning, the bell goes off, rousing you from the wonderful sleep you're in. I keep my alarm clock on the far side of the room. There are two reasons for it being there. The first and most obvious reason is that I have to actually get out of bed to make the awful sound stop. I learned from the many times I just turned the clock off. Once I even picked it up and fucked it straight out the bedroom window before falling back asleep.

The second reason is because it's an old-fashioned clock and it ticks. I hate ticking clocks. Once I hear the ticking I can't stop hearing the ticking and then the ticking amplifies itself in my brain to become less like ticking and more like bonging, and I don't mean smoking hash out of a water-filled vase.

On the far side of the room I can't hear it ticking.

Of course, I could have just gone to Argos and gotten myself a new fangled digital alarm clock with a radio and stuff on it, but I never listen to the radio while I'm in bed so I don't see the point.

But there are worse ways of waking up, as I was soon to discover. That morning, I was having the most wonderful dream. I was playing football against all the footballers in the world that I hate most, and every time I tackled one of them their legs would break and they would fall shrieking to the floor. Even if I took the ball fairly their femur would snap in two. It was brilliant.

As I crept towards awakedness, I became aware of something. You know that feeling you get when you're sitting on a bus and you can feel someone looking at you? It was like that. And imagine my surprise as I removed my night-time eye mask, cracked one eye open and saw a big head staring down at me.

'Mornin', Twenty,' said Tony Furriskey.

'Jesus fucking Christ on a leper's bike!' I said, sitting up in the bed. 'What the fuck are you doing here? And how did you get in?'

'Don't worry about that, lad. I just wanted to make sure yeh understood what was expected of yeh before yeh left this mornin' on the 11.00 a.m. Clickair flight CA154B to Barcelona.'

'How did you know I was leaving this morning?'

'Let me ask yeh this, Twenty. Is how I have that information in any way relevant to what yerself and Jimmy have to do when yiz get there?'

'I don't suppose it is, no.'

'Well then, let's just leave it at that. Anyway, no pressure or anythin', just wanted to make sure yeh understood the seriousness of this. I can't have that little cunt marryin' me baby, Twenty. I don't care how yeh manage to do it, just make sure this weddin' doesn't happen. Because as much as I like the pair of yiz, I won't have anyone else to hold responsible if it goes ahead. Do yeh understand what I'm sayin'?'

'Loud and clear, Tony.'

'Good man. Enjoy the sunshine. I'll let meself out.'

After he left I sat there for a bit, and, I have to say, my heart was a-racing. That was very unexpected. My home was always my fortress. I've got a motion-sensor alarm system and a huge dog out the back who normally barks at people on the other side of the road to let them know they're getting too close for his liking. How did Tony get in?

I lit a cigarette and smoked it down to the filter. When I was relatively calm, I went for a good slash and let the dog in. I stuck the kettle on to make coffee and then went and got ready. I was having my second cup when Jimmy arrived at the door.

'Morning,' I said.

'Ugh,' he said. He's not much of a morning person either.

'Late night?'

'Ugh.'

'I see.' I gave him a cup of coffee and went out the back to feed the dog. There was still no sign of the cat. I was a bit worried now, but there wasn't much I could do except hope he'd turn up. I put a plate of dry food on the back wall in case he did. Anywhere else and the dog would just eat it.

As Bastardface got tucked into his twenty-four gammon steaks I rubbed his head and said 'goodbye'. I had arranged with Ron to come in and give him his food while I was gone. He was one of the only people Bastardface would allow near him. I once had to go away on an emergency trip, and with nobody else around I asked one of the young lads in the shop just up the road to pop in to the house and throw some chunks of meat out the window to the dog. Unfortunately, he misheard me and opened the back door and became the chunks of meat himself. The gardaí did come looking, but I'd already burnt the clothes while Bastardface had left not even the slightest fragment of bone as evidence. I did feel bad for that boy's parents when I saw them on the news begging for anyone to tell them where their son might be, but I thought they'd be better living with the hope that he'd gone off to join some sinister cult, like Fianna Fáil, rather than being food for an enormous, grumpy dog the size of a small horse. I think I got that one right.

I went back inside and locked up the back door. Just then the doorbell rang. I wandered out to find Dirty Dave and Stinking Pete standing before me. I stood looking at them, speechless for a few moments.

'What the fuck are you two cunts wearing?' I said.

'Holiday clothes!' said Dave.

'Yeah, holiday clothes!' said Pete.

Dave had on a pair of denim shorts so short that not even Pamela Anderson would wear them, a sleeveless lemon T-shirt, a sombrero, a pair of purple-tinted John Lennon glasses and a pair of sandals with white socks on underneath. His milky white legs were almost glowing beneath the thick, matted hair that covered them. Pete was in a suit of some kind and a panama hat. I'm sure the material of the suit was supposed to be linen; it might have been linen a number of decades ago but now it just looked like a well-worn dishcloth, except scummier. He had a pair of black, patent George Webb brogues on, and under his arm he carried an inflatable crocodile. Inflated, obviously. Because that's the most convenient way to transport it.

'Jimmy,' I said, 'come here and look at this.'

'Fucking hell,' said Jimmy, who had regained the power of speech after the coffee. 'If you two cunts think I'm going to even acknowledge your presence for the duration of the journey you are sadly mistaken. Why the fuck did we have to bring them, Twenty?'

'Dirty work, Jimmy. Remember?'

'Yeah, dirty work!' said Pete. 'Wait a minute . . . dirty work?'

'Shut up, Pete,' I said. 'Have you got everything now? Passports? Whatever medications you might need?'

'Yeah, definitely.'

'And you, Dave?'

'I'm as sorted as a bloke who has just gone out to get his drugs on a Friday night and bought an extra wrap just in case.'

'OK, I'll take your word for it, but I don't want any hassle at the airport, right? You know how much I hate airports.'

'Yeah, we know. You've only told us about four hundred times while sitting in Ron's.'

'Yeah, well, now that's four hundred and one, you sassy-mouthed cunt. The taxi should be here any minute,' I said, looking at my watch.

I looked over their heads and cocked my ear. In the distance I could hear a car engine screaming and the screech of tyres as it went around a corner. 'Ah, that'll be it now!'

Twenty seconds later, a car skidded to a halt outside the house and the horn blared. I gave a thumbs-up to acknowledge we'd seen it, went inside, grabbed my bag and double-checked the house was locked up.

'Hello Beardface,' said Grace Jones Taxi Driver when I jumped into the front seat beside her.

Grace Jones Taxi Driver was the fastest driver I'd ever seen in my life. Donald Campbell had nothing on this woman. Her love of speed was matched only by her complete disregard for the safety of her passengers, other road-users or pedestrians.

'Hello, Grace Jones Taxi Driver,' I said. 'To the airport!'

'You got it!' she said, spinning the car around on the pavement, hitting the Muslim bloke who goes up and down on his crutches. 'Bwa ha ha ha ha!' she laughed, 'his legs're fucked anyway!'

And so it was we hit the road. The journey had begun.

8

Driving and flying

'Where you going?' asked Grace Jones Taxi Driver as she hurtled through town, weaving in and out of traffic on Dorset Street. 'Barcelona,' I said.

'I was once there. Had sex with a man at the top of mountain with a funfair . . . then I cut his head off!'

'What?'

'Bwa ha ha ha ha! Joking! I didn't have sex with him!'

'Watch out for that,' said Jimmy from the back seat, sandwiched between Dave and Pete.

'What?' she said turning around to face him.

'That truck turning there!'

'Oh, don't worry,' she said, swerving hard to her left, drifting onto the footpath, narrowly avoiding a lamp-post before getting back onto the road. 'Anyway, I didn't think you social worker, Beardface.'

'Social worker?'

'Social worker. Special-needs supervisor. Whatever. Nice of you to bring two retards on holiday. Like one of them trip-of-a-lifetime things they do for little kids who have cancer. We take you to Disneyland. You still going to die of cancer but at least you get to see mouse with high-pitched voice!'

'Hey!' said Dave, 'we're not retards.'

'Looks like a retard, smells like a retard, talks like a retard, is a retard for me! Bwa ha ha ha ha!'

'For your information, we've got very big responsibilities, isn't that right, Twenty?'

'Oh yeah,' I said, winking at Grace Jones Taxi Driver, 'just you wait.'

Eventually, after nearly rear-ending a school bus, side-swiping an old-age pensioner, who I'm sure I saw clutching her heart as we went past, and taking a number of traffic lights at the very moment amber became red – 'Is a different shade of red, bwa ha ha ha ha!' – we got to the departures drop-off point at the airport.

'How much do we owe you?' I asked.

'For you, Beardface, special price: one hundred euro!'

'Bwa ha ha ha ha,' I said, 'you're such a joker—'

'I'm not joking,' she said, stone-faced.

'Oh. Well, one hundred euro is pretty expensive for a taxi ride to the airport. Even with four of us and with luggage.'

'Look,' she said, getting obviously angry, 'you ask me price, I give you price. One hundred euro. Now either pay me or I call cops.'

'OK, OK, relax,' I said, taking out my wallet and handing her two fifty-euro notes.

'Thank you,' she said, before handing me one of them back and bursting into that paint-stripping, infectious laugh of hers. 'Got you. Irish people so stupid!'

'You sure did,' I said. 'I'll give you a shout if we need a pick-up on Sunday.'

'OK Beardface, byeeee,' she said, speeding off, leaving the tourist couple who had just put their luggage in the boot standing there looking most confused indeed.

'Right you cunts, let's get checked in. I need a drink.'

There wasn't too long a line at the Clickair desk, and the young woman sorted us out very quickly. We put our luggage through and went to the security check-in point. There was the usual rubbish of taking off your shoes, your belt, putting your change and anything vaguely metallic into a tray then walking through and having the thing go off anyway. After being frisked by a rather-too-enthusiastic, heavy-set guard I put myself back together, followed by Pete, Jimmy, then Dave. We were just waiting for Dave to get his stuff together when we noticed a couple of armed guards arrive, the woman who was doing the scanning, looking quite panicked, having called them over. They looked at the screen, looked at Dave, who was obliviously putting on his belt, much to the relief of the young woman behind him who was getting a generous view of his builder's cleavage, then looked at the screen again. One of them came over.

'Excuse me, sir. Can you come with me?'

'What seems to be the problem?'

'Just come with me.'

They took Dave over to the far end of the security checkpoints, brought over his bag and very carefully emptied it, before holding up what looked like two handguns.

'What the hell is this, boy?' said the lead bloke.

'Cap guns,' said Dave.

'Cap guns?'

'Yeah, you can shoot caps, and they go "bkeewwww!"'

'I know what cap guns are.'

'Then why did you ask me what they were?'

'Are you being funny with me?'

'No.'

'Do you not know anything about airport security? You can't bring cap guns into an airport!'

'Why not? They only shoot caps. I can understand you not allowing real guns, what with them being dangerous, but I never heard of anyone getting shot to death with caps.'

'It's not that they're completely harmless, it's that they look like they're real.'

'Ah. So I shouldn't have brought my grenade lighter then?'

'What?!'

'This time I'm joking with you!'

'Have you travelled at all since 9/11?'

'Yeah, we left Twenty's house at about half eight, and it took us forty-five minutes to get here, so yeah, about four minutes after 9.11.'

'What?!' said the bloke, looking thoroughly confused.

I felt it best if I intervened at that stage.

'Look,' I said, 'I'm . . . er . . . a special-needs supervisor, and we're taking these two retar— erm . . . mentally deficient chaps on a holiday of a lifetime.'

'I'm not special-needs, Twenty.'

'Shut up, Dave. Look, keep those things. He's got what they call mega-autism. At times he appears lucid and normal but he's living in a different world to you and me.'

'You don't say.'

'I'll make sure he stays out of trouble.'

'Yeah, well, do that.'

'I will, thanks.'

They handed me Dave's bag, and I grabbed him by the scruff of the neck and dragged him away. When we got far enough away from the security point I twisted the skin as hard as I could.

'Ooooooooowwww,' he whined. 'What's that for?'

'Jesus help me. What the fuck were you doing bringing two lifelike pistols in your hand luggage?'

'I just thought if we got bored in Barcelona me and Pete could play *Cagney and Lacey* like we do at home.'

'*Cagney and Lacey*?'

'Yeah, I'm the blonde one, and he's the fat one.'

'Sometimes I'm Harv too!' said Pete.

'Shut the fuck up Pete.'

At this point, Jimmy had wandered off to the bar, and I thought that was a much better idea than having to talk to those cretins.

I had been expecting something to happen: no trip anywhere with those two is without incident.

I remember once being at a funeral of a close friend of

Ron's, and we'd all been out on the batter the night before. We were in the church when Stinking Pete realised he had to fart. Even though he is more stupid than a drink-driving Leeds United fan, he understood that letting rip at high volume was not appropriate given the circumstances, so he leant forward a little bit and tried to squeeze it out as quietly as he could. Unfortunately, due the overconsumption of pints and a dodgy kebab on Aungier Street, there was a certain amount of what you might call 'follow through'. As it trickled down his leg, the stench began to waft forth, and, while most of us were able to cope, Dirty Dave, feeling similarly unwell, retched, heaved and then vomited all over the back of the woman in front of him. Who just happened to be the wife of the man lying in the coffin on the altar.

Dave tried to get out of the pew but stood in the pool of his own vomit, slipped and fell out into the aisle, dragging Pete down on top of him. Pete's rancid inner-leg juice had made his trousers damp, and it was the damp patch that rested against Dave's nose and mouth, causing him to throw up even more. Now, Pete is one of those people who can't even see puke without it making his own stomach turn. The idea that Dave had covered his pants with his sickly, lamby barf caused a torrent of his own sickly, lamby barf to erupt and cover the aisle. All the while, people were looking on, horrified, while the weeping widow was hysterical at the fact that someone had made what was already a difficult day for her beyond insufferable. They received a two-week ban from Ron's, which was more for their own safety than anything else.

A couple of fake pistols was hardly a big shock really, when you considered their past form, but I still needed a drink. And not just because of those two: I hate flying. Hate it more than I hate folk music, Cristiano Ronaldo, Gypsies begging by thrusting babies under your nose, celebrity culture, Big Brother and selfish bastards who take up most of the pavement when you're trying to get past. Oh, it's all right for them in their wheelchairs; they just sit there and zoom along, but they don't think for a second about the busy pedestrian. Fuckers. I hate flying more than I hate dolphins, and I really fucking hate dolphins.

The whole concept is ludicrous to me. Thirty-six thousand feet in the air in a metal tube. It's stupid. People say they don't mind flying because if something happens there's nothing you can do anyway so they don't worry about it. That is also stupid. You could have not gone on the plane in the first place. Then you wouldn't be hurtling towards the ground at five hundred miles an hour. Also, you cannot express your fear of flying without some absolute fuckwit telling you that 'statistically you have more chance of being involved in a car crash, you know?' Those people are fucking cunts who need to be repeatedly punched in the throat. While that statistic might well be true, the fact is you can survive a car crash.

In fact, I did survive a car crash once. A drunken Chinese man turned right across me and Jimmy as we were going through Terenure Cross one night. 'Oh, look at that,' I said as I got out of the car, 'I appear to have another elbow in my upper arm.' While I spent the next six months picking glass out of my forehead and the whole thing was a painful episode, I would much prefer it to slamming into the side of a mountain in a Boeing or an Airbus.

So, flying requires drink. Not a huge amount – I have two gin and tonics per hour of flying time. This is an absolute requirement or I will not get on the plane. Once, at Heathrow Airport, the bar had no gin. Which is possibly the most stupid thing I have ever heard. I then had to go to the duty free, buy a bottle of gin, then buy tonics with ice and a slice at the bar before adding my own gin. Hey, I got home in one piece, so it worked out OK. I once flew to LA. Twenty-two G and Ts were a bit of a stretch at 9 a.m., but needs must. At least I had no problems sleeping.

I ordered a couple at the bar and wandered over to where Jimmy was sitting with a pint.

'Fucking hell,' he said, 'those two are getting worse.'

'I know, but they'll save us hanging around the airport tomorrow waiting for that lad to arrive.'

'You realise that they'll probably both go for a piss at the same time which will be the exact time yer man comes through the departure gate.'

'I have thought about that. But we have to weigh up the likelihood of them fucking it all up against us wandering around the city eating and drinking and not being on our feet all day in an arrivals hall.'

'Do you reckon this kid can be persuaded not to go ahead with the wedding?'

'I know we're persuasive chaps, but I think this might

be a bit beyond us. I mean, how do you persuade some-one you've just met not to go and get married without using intense violence – or at least the threat of it. And as Tony has made it quite clear he doesn't want the bloke harmed, then we need to go at it a different way.'

'Yeah, you're probably right.'

'I think we probably need to provide . . . What's her name again?'

'Cynthia.'

'Jesus. Cynthia. As classy as a knacker's Communion. Anyway, we'll probably have to give her something that will make her call things off so it doesn't seem suspicious at all.'

'The clap?'

'Ha ha, yeah, something like that. Anyway, I have to get these gins down me, not long to flight time.'

And so I downed the two gin and tonics. No, one dou-ble gin and tonic is not the same. I got a couple more, downed them, and soon it was time to put my life in the hands of some stranger who called himself a pilot.

9

Arrival

After two hours, eleven minutes and sixteen seconds in the air we landed in Barcelona. I had a pain in my knuckles from gripping the armrest, much to the amusement of Jimmy, who is one of those 'que sera, sera' flyers. I'd love to say the flight was uneventful, but sometimes when you cross the Pyrenees there are pockets of turbulence due to the mix of the hot and cold air. This time there weren't so much pockets of turbulence as great satchels of the stuff. The plane was bumping along like an old Ford on a cobbled street. Do you ever get that thing when you're nearly asleep and you feel like you're falling? That happened about four times, but I wasn't nearly asleep. I was listening to music on my iPod and desperately trying to concentrate on my book to take my mind off it all. And all the while the cabin crew went about their business as if we weren't going to die at any second. They are consummate actors, I'll give them that. We made our way to the luggage carousel where I lit up a smoke and inhaled deeply. Even though I don't believe in God, I thought I'd say thanks to Him anyway for answering my prayers and getting me down safely.

'You can't smoke here,' said a busybody Irish woman who had been on the same flight.

'Lady, your belly is so large you can't see your toes,' I said, 'but I don't give you a hard time about it.'

'How dare you? I'm going to get security to make you put it out.'

'Go right ahead,' I said, knowing fine well all the security guards would be puffing away on their Fortunas or Ducados. This was Spain after all. She frantically tried to find one who didn't have a cigarette hanging out of his mouth. I think she knew she was fighting a losing battle. The belt started moving, the bags came, and, unlike when you fly with Ryanair, they hadn't ended up in a completely different country. The joys of paying that little bit extra.

We went out into the arrivals hall where we hired a car from Hertz – a nice people carrier. The bloke gave us the keys to a black Seat. We stepped out of the revolving doors of the airport into what I can only describe as a blanket of heat. It is one of my favourite feelings in the whole world. You never get heat like that Ireland, and I used to really enjoy leaving somewhere nicely air-conditioned and getting smacked in the face with the heat of a Barcelona summer.

Jimmy was driving. Show the slightest bit of fear on the Spanish road and they'll destroy you. You have to drive like a native. So, obviously, Jimmy drove like a drunken, blind, crack-smoking lunatic intent on causing his own death as quickly as possible. Taking the motorway out of the airport we headed towards the city, swerving and changing lanes, and, when we nearly hit somebody because of our own careless driving, we blasted them with the horn and called them hijo de puta. When in Rome and all that.

We dropped Pete and Dave off at their pension and parked in the underground car park at the Gran Hotel Havana before checking in. The plan was to meet in the lobby of the hotel in an hour, so that gave me time to get showered and changed. Flying always makes me feel somewhat grubby afterwards. It's probably all the terrified sweating I do. I got changed into a pair of shorts, a white shirt and my new flip-flops, and, as I was early, I took the elevator to the roof.

There was a swimming pool there with chairs and tables scattered around the garden. I ordered a beer from the waiter guy who was standing around and went to the edge of the roof to have a look down. I watched the mid-afternoon traffic speed down Gran Vía towards Plaça de Tetuan. It was like real-life Mario Kart but without any exploding turtles. The waiter brought me a bottle of Estrella, for which I paid there and then, and I took a good slug from it. The taste – so many memories. Estrella was the bottle of choice when I lived in Barcelona all those years ago. I thought about the reasons why I left briefly but pushed those thoughts from my brain. I took my time with my beer and wandered down to the lobby when it was finished. I found Jimmy, Dave and Pete sitting there already.

'Right,' I said, 'we need to get some food and a couple of thinking beers down us. I know just the place, come on.'

We left the hotel and wandered down Gran Vía, the wide boulevard that dissects the city, towards Passeig de Gràcia, taking a left down the main shopping street. Dave was still in his teeny-tiny shorts, and he drew amused and often aroused glances from passers-by. I was just praying he didn't drop anything because if he bent over to pick it up I'm sure he would be arrested for a breach of public decency or for exposing one's anus in a manner which might cause old people's hearts to stop. We came to El Corte Inglés, the big department store, and took a left, wandering down to a bar-café I used to frequent. We sat up at the bar, and I ordered us beers while the lads looked at the menus and the plates of tapas behind the glass at the bar itself.

'What the hell are those?' asked Dirty Dave.

'Snails,' I said.

'And they eat them? What's the green stuff, is that snail poo?'

'No, you twat. Some kind of garlic sauce.'

'And what's that?'

'Squid.'

'Ewww. Regular squid or colossal squid?'

'Regular.'

'Ewww. And what's that?'

'Octopus.'

'Yak. And that?'

'Artichoke hearts.'

'Those poor artichokes. It's bad enough that they get chased across the plains by lions but then we devour their hearts? Don't they have any normal food in this country?'

'Yeah, see those?'

'Sure.'

'They're kitten legs; those things there are deep-fried anteater snout; the things to the left of them are pickled squirrel balls; and beside them are the slugs covered in parsley and goat-urine sauce.'

'Oooh, I'll have the slugs!'

To shut him up, I just went ahead and ordered a sandwich for each of us. That particular bar made the very best sandwich on the planet. It's basically an omelette with little bits of serrano ham served on a baguette which has been rubbed with fresh tomato. The man with the very deep voice behind the bar called out the order to one of his colleagues who got working on them.

I used to live on these sandwiches. The hangover killer. The stomach settler. The tasty bastard. All my pet names for this wonderful food. I've often tried making them at home, but it's just not the same. It's like trying to make home-made Big Mac sauce – you can nearly get there, but not quite. You just lack the additives and ultra-cheap ingredients that McDonald's uses.

It seemed to take him ages to make the sandwiches; I was like a child waiting for Christmas. Eventually they came, and we ate, and it was good. I ordered some more beers.

'So, what's the plan for tomorrow then?' asked Stinking Pete.

'Right, well, we don't know what time this Coleman Darcy-McNeill is arriving so that means you and Dave have to be at the airport before 9 a.m., that's when the Aer Lingus flight arrives. The Clickair flight arrives the same time as we landed today, and the late Aer Lingus flight comes in at about 7.30 in the evening.'

'And how will we know him?'

'I've got a picture back in the hotel, you can take that, but here's what we're going to do. You know the way when you land at airports there are people standing around holding pieces of card up with people's name on them?'

'Yeah.'

'Well, that's what you and Dave are going to do. We're going to get you a couple of chauffeur uniforms, and you're going to wait there for him, then drive him to whatever hotel he and his friends are staying at. When they have settled into the hotel you will pick them up and bring them to a bar of my instruction.'

'Won't he be wondering who's organised that for him?' asked Stinking Pete.

'If he says anything, just hint at it being from Tony – he'll think his soon-to-be father-in-law has arranged it. He knows Tony has loads of money, but he doesn't know Tony hates his guts, so there's no worries there.'

'OK, gotcha.'

'Right then, Dave: repeat back to me what you have to do tomorrow.'

'OK, we get up in the morning, go to the airport dressed as chauffeurs, stand around with a sign with his name on it, and, when he arrives, we drive him to the hotel. Then we ring you and Jimmy and tell you where he's staying. Then we bring them to a bar of your instruction.'

'Unreal. That is absolutely perfect.'

'I'm not as stupid as you think I look I am, Twenty.'

'Eh?'

'Never mind.'

'That was too easy,' said Jimmy finishing his beer. 'Too easy.'

'It wasn't too difficult to understand, Jimmy,' said Pete. 'I know you think Dave and I are hapless morons but it's not necessarily true.'

'Look, the last time we sent you to do something you nearly lost the Ginger Albino going down Pearse Street moments after we had to tell you what a Ginger Albino would look like. I mean, it was a fucking Ginger Albino. Not a man of average height and average build with short dark hair wearing nondescript clothes. Then you both got nosebleeds at the same time and nearly got us killed. Dave, are you crying?'

'No, I have something in my eye.'

'What is it?'

'Tears!'

'Then you are crying. What are you crying for?'

'I miss the Ginger Albino. He was my friend. I had a

connection with him, a deep spiritual connection, and now he's dead.'

'You should get something to replace him,' said Stinking Pete.

'Like what?'

'A puppy. Or some other kind of pet like a pony or a Vietnamese.'

'I don't have a garden overgrown enough to keep a Vietnamese.'

'Jesus, shut up.' I said. 'We've gone way off the point here. Just remember what you need to do. I'm going to buy a mobile phone next door so you can contact us in case of emergency. I'll be back in a few minutes.'

I wandered off, leaving them in the bar, and went into El Corte Inglés to buy three pay-as-you-go phones. Despite them seeming to get the instructions first time, there was no doubting their ability to get separated and fuck things up in a way that not even the greatest minds on earth working with the most powerful probability-generating computers could predict. I went upstairs, bought the three phones and headed back towards the bar.

On the way out the door I thought I caught a glimpse of a familiar figure. My heart skipped a beat. Could it be? So soon? As the person slipped away into the crowds I thought about following, but I just couldn't. I didn't want to anyway. That was a confrontation I didn't have time for this particular weekend.

I went back to the bar, gave Dave and Pete their phones and ordered another beer. After they were finished and we settled up the bill, we went to one of the costume shops on Gran Vía. I know, you're probably thinking, That's handy, isn't it? A costume shop right around the corner from the bar you were drinking in? Sounds a little bit like you're making stuff up just to make life easier for yourself – and I can fully understand why you'd think that, but I promise you these places are real.

Spaniards love to dress up in costumes. Each town has its own carnival every year, where there are travelling sideshows run by the most Gypsiest Gypsies you ever did see. There are fairground rides that look like they're made out of Meccano, rigged games like 'Throw the Hoop Over the Bottle' and 'Burst the Balloons with the Wobbly Darts,' bingo, that game with all the coins where you put more coins in and it should knock a load of coins for you to win but they somehow just spread out and don't knock any out at all – the usual rip-off stuff. But the costumes are what make the carnivals. Of course, kids dress up, and it's quite fetching to see toddlers going about the place in their all-in-one cow/puppy/lion suits, but the adults do it as well. Masks, outfits, wigs, hats, capes, staffs, tridents, swords and everything else you can think of. They love it. Costume hire is big business, and there are two big shops on Gran Vía.

As I was the one who could speak Spanish, I had to coordinate everything. Well, when I say I can speak Spanish, I can hold a perfectly acceptable conversation, but verb conjugation has always been a bit of a tricky one. I speak mostly in the present tense but do that gesture where you point your thumb over your shoulder to point out that you're talking about the past. And the old

'I am going' when it came to talking about the future was always a godsend. As for third conditional subjunctive perfect, you might as well ask me to speak Martian. Still, my vocabulary is good. I even know the Spanish for 'anteater'. (It's *oso hormiguero* in case you're wondering.) That literally means anty bear. Spanish is cool.

Thankfully Dave and Pete had both taken a shower when they got to their pension, so the nice lady in the shop wasn't at all concerned about letting them try on the chauffeur costumes they had. Pete was particularly taken with a large womble outfit but understood when I told him the lads might be slightly suspicious if they were collected by Great Uncle Bulgaria. Soon we had our costume-hiring done: dark suits, shiny hats, the whole lot.

I sent them back to drop off the costumes and to pick up some stationery supplies on the way. A large piece of white card and a permanent marker to write on it with was surely not beyond them. We arranged to meet back in a bar on Passeig de Sant Joan called the 55. It was called this because the number of the building it was in was 55. We sat outside at a table, and the owner came out to take our order. Despite the fact I hadn't been there for a good number of years, he remembered me, and we spent a few minutes chatting. There's nothing quite like sitting outside drinking in the warm weather and if you can have a crafty smoke then all the better. I asked around and bought some hash from a chap a couple of tables up. I rolled up, and we all drank and smoked and smoked and drank. Dirty Dave gets a bit funny when he gets stoned, and his 'Twenty, who would you rather be? An astronaut, a brain surgeon or that monster that's coming out of the cracks in the wall to eat my brains?' question was no real surprise.

We did a bit of bar-hopping for the rest of the evening, ending up in a strange place with red velvet couches and a big TV screen showing music videos. The bar owner was a flamboyant Argentine who looked like a cross between Picasso and Kenny Everett. He wore the striped top of a cartoon Frenchman and had painted a small tear with a mascara pencil beneath his left eye. When he discovered we were there to drink and not to engage in the usual Catalan custom of sitting around one cup of coffee or bottle of sparkling water for the whole night he became a very hospitable host, and I blame him entirely for the hangover I woke up with the next day.

Friday

10

Morning

Despite the fact that I wasn't required to go to the airport, I decided it would be best to go over things with Dirty Dave and Stinking Pete first thing in the morning. This meant dragging myself out of bed much, much earlier than I would have liked. They had to come by the hotel anyway to pick up the car so I took the lift down to meet them in the lobby, drawing some snooty stares from the Welsh couple who were also on their way down. Ignorant fuckers, like they've never seen an unkempt, scruffy, stubbly, topless man with wiry grey hair on his chest in a pair of shorts and flip-flops stinking of booze and cannabis looking like he could vomit on their shoes at any moment. What a pack of up-their-own-arses cunts the Welsh are. When I got down there, I got a coffee at the bar and picked up a copy of the *International Herald Tribune* that was lying on one of the tables. It's a strange newspaper. Generally speaking of course. I mean, does anyone ever actually buy it? All the news seems strangely out of date, even though it isn't.

I lit up a delicious, refreshing Major, took a drag, then hocked up a lump of phlegm so large my cheeks bulged. I looked like Lionel Richie just before hibernation. I spat it into my coffee, which made the coffee spill over the sides onto the saucer, and put the cup down on a nearby table. I thought about ordering another one but didn't. Thankfully Dave and Pete arrived shortly afterwards.

'Right, are you all set?'

'Yes, one hundred per cent. Don't you worry.'

'And you know what you have to do.'

'Yes, we have to go the airport, hold up the sign with his name on it, drive him to his hotel then ring you and tell you where he is.'

'Superb. And you've got the sign.'

'Yes indeed.'

'Gimme a look, just so I can be sure.'

'Here you go!'

I looked. And sighed. I closed my eyes really tightly and breathed deeply for a few moments. 'Are you taking the piss?'

'No! Why?'

'Look at it.'

'I don't need to. I made it.'

'And you think this is going to do the trick, do you?'

'It is exactly like you told us. Don't get all stroppy now.'

'Dave, I swear one of these days I am going to break in to your house while you're sleeping and smother you where you lie. It will cost me, but, by Christ, I will fuck-ing do it.'

'Jesus, what's up with you, man? I just did what you said.'

'You are more stupid than Bertie Ahern thinks people are when he says he won the money to buy his house on the horses. And he must think we're a pack of drooling vegetables to even try that one. When I told you to write a sign with his name on it I meant his actual name.'

'Right?'

'Not a sign with the words "HIS NAME" in big fuck-ing letters, you leather-headed mong.'

'Ahhhh . . . yeah, that would make more sense all right.'

'Give me fucking strength. Turn it over and write "COLEMAN DARCY-MCNEILL" on it right now. Come on, do it. I don't want to fucking leave anything to chance now. Jesus, I thought you had actually fully understood a set of instructions for once. I should have known better.'

'But Twenty—,' started Stinking Pete.

'Shut it, Pete. You're just as bad.'

'Hey—'

'I said shut it. Now, when you see him, you say, "Hello, we're your chauffeurs. We'll take you to your hotel." Then you bring him and his friends and their luggage to the car – the machine with the wheels and the engine – and then you drive them in this car to the hotel they tell you to go to. There's a Sat Nav in the car, just type in the street address when they give it to you. Dave, you're good at computers, you do that bit.'

'Right.'

'And let them know you know the city, right? That you know where the good bars and clubs are. That way, they'll look for you to bring them somewhere after they check in. So, as soon as you drop them off, you ring me with the mobile phone I gave you last night. You use the number pad to dial the number of my phone and then you speak to me and listen when I'm talking, is that clear?'

'Yeah, I mean, I know how to use a phone, Twenty.'

'I'm just making sure. At that stage, I'll give you directions to the bar Jimmy and I will be waiting in. Now, here are the keys of the car, here's a picture of him. He'll be travelling with some of his pals. Don't fuck this up. Because if you fuck this bit up then the whole plan is fucked, and if the whole plan is fucked, then sooner or later I'm going to be fucked, and if I'm going to be fucked, I will make sure you two are double-fucked. Now get the fuck out of here and for the love of all that is holy just don't do anything stupid. OK?'

'OK!' said Pete, like an eager-to-please puppy. 'Don't you worry, Twenty, we won't let you down. Will we Dave?'

'That's only because we won't pick him up in the first place! Ha ha ha!'

'Ha ha ha!'

I watched them as they made their way out of the hotel towards the underground car park, and I held my head in my hands. Sure, some of it was due to the hangover, but mostly it was because I couldn't for the life of me understand how such a pair of witless clits had ever made it to the age they had without dying in some ridiculously avoidable accident. I went upstairs, took a handful of painkillers and went back to sleep for a while.

11

An old friend

I woke up around lunchtime with a knocking on the door.
It was Jimmy wondering what the plan for the afternoon
was. I told him I'd meet him in the lobby, took a shower,
took some more painkillers and went downstairs. I found
Jimmy outside the hotel on the far side of the road reading the instructions for the public bike rack.

Basically you joined up to the scheme, got a card, and
then you could, for a small price, take a bike from any
rack in the city, go where you needed to go and drop it off
at any of the other racks. In a relatively small city like
Barcelona it's a brilliant idea. 'Can you imagine them trying to introduce something like this in Dublin?' he said.
'If the bikes weren't stolen within weeks you just know
some drunken cunt would spend an evening stabbing
holes in all the tyres.'

'How cynical of you, Jimmy. Are we not proud of our city and its amenities?'

'They'd be blown up, set on fire, bashed around, have the handlebars sawn off, the brake cables cut, the bulbs out of the lights would be nicked by Gypsies, the saddles pissed, pooed, sicked on or graffitied by that Maser cunt – I don't give a fuck if you love me or not, just stop recklessly spray painting public property, you lout. If Dublin had the most beautiful statue in all the world and everyone in the whole world admired it, and it was something we could be really proud of, you'd still walk up to it at any time and find a big lump of chewing-gum stuck to it and some pie-eyed wanker round the back having a piss on it. Imagine what they'd do to bikes that nobody owned.'

'You're probably right . . .'

'You know I am. Anyway, where are we going?'

'First I need breakfast. And a beer. So we'll go back to the place we were in yesterday, unless you have any objections?'

'None at all. If that's the Spanish equivalent of the breakfast roll then it's all right by me.'

'Cool. Then we're going to try and find someone I knew when I lived here. I think we might need some help over the course of the weekend, and he's just the man to provide it.'

'Grand. And the other two got off OK this morning, did they?'

As we walked to the bar I explained to Jimmy about the sign. He winced.

'I know this is a phrase that's overused somewhat,' he said, 'but this actually is a matter of life and death. Unless we fix this so yer man doesn't marry Tony's daughter our lives will be replaced by death. And to be honest, Twenty, I'm not ready for death yet. There's so much killing I still have to do myself.'

'I hear you.'

'So it begs the question why have two supposedly intelligent men like ourselves put our lives in the hands of a pair of buffoons with all the intelligence of a "Dancercise" pamphlet?'

'You know, that is a good question. If and when that time came, I think we'd both look back and think that standing around an airport for a few hours wasn't really the worst thing in the world. On the other hand though, we get to spend the afternoon drinking in the sunshine.'

'And there it is.'

'Slaves to the delicious booze.'

We went and got ourselves a couple of sandwiches and some beers. You order one when you come in first, and because it's so hot and you're so thirsty it's gone in about two minutes. So you order another one to have with your sandwich, and that one's gone before the sandwich is finished, so you need one to wash the rest of it down with, and then you need one for the road. It would be rude not to. It just means that a twenty-minute visit to a bar to have a bite to eat ends up with you drinking four beers. And if you think I'm complaining for a second, then you need to think again. I'm just trying to explain things to you.

After that, we wandered down to see the man we were going to see. It was very hot, so naturally we had to stop on the way for some refreshments. After a couple of hours of drinking and about fifteen minutes of walking, all in, we arrived at Plaça Reial, which was full of tourists and people trying as hard as they could to rip off tourists while amused locals looked on. Around the square there were countless bars and restaurants. If you even so much as glanced at a waiter they'd be over to you with a menu and a hand on your back trying to make you sit down and eat. Even if you were standing there with a sign saying, 'I'm full, I've just had dinner', while eating a rotisserie chicken on a lollipop stick they'd still try it.

All manner of street performers rotated from one restaurant to the next doing their juggling, acrobatics, clown tricks, balloon shaping or, most heinous of all, playing the accordion at you. It was non-stop. To be fair to the police they did their best to solve the problem. It was just that their solution was to move the down-and-outs, drunkards, junkies and other miscreants to Plaça George Orwell, a few hundred yards away.

I took a look around me and remembered the many nights I'd spent here robbing tourists myself.

Above a famous restaurant, which people queued outside for ages to get a table, there used to be a brilliant little bar. This was the *penya*, or supporters' club, for Espanyol, the other football team in Barcelona. The great thing was that you didn't have to be a member to get in, but you did have to know it was there. It wasn't obvious. You had to go down the little side street, ring the bell, then tramp up a few flights of stairs before you found yourself in the place. If you got lucky, you could get a table at one of the windows, the old-fashioned shutters pulled wide open, and to sit there for an evening drinking, smoking and watching all the stuff going on down the square was one of the hidden pleasures of Barcelona.

Now though, it was gone. The famous restaurant underneath snapped up the space. Progress, you see. We left the plaça and turned onto c/Escudellers, a narrow Gothic street filled with restaurants, bars, kebab take-aways and shops with windows full of every kind of booze you could ever want and at prices that would make grown men weep in Ireland.

A bottle of Gordon's for nine euro, you say? What's that? Havana Club rum, number 7 no less, for twelve euro, Jameson for about the same, and the absinthe . . . ? Oh, the absinthe. So many different kinds ranging from mega-powerful to stuff that caused hallucinations when you simply looked at the bottle. Like the teenager who can never even smell tequila again after a night vomiting it back up, I had learned my lesson with that particular drink. It didn't really agree with me. Or, to put it another way, it made other people not agree with me, and it was, ultimately, part of the reason I had to leave Barcelona.

Jimmy, almost overcome with the range and price of the goods in front of him, went in and bought a couple of bottles of a green absinthe and a couple of six-packs of beer, all for less than thirty euro.

'Why was it you ever came back to Ireland?' he said, before he remembered. 'Oh. Sorry.'

We drank a beer each as we walked past the great unwashed in Plaça George Orwell. They sat drinking, trying to roll joints and to not pass out, while some police stood around not caring what they did so long as it meant they didn't have to move. The best thing about them being all in the one spot in this particular place was the CCTV camera that overlooked them. Who's that watching, George? And who says the Catalans have no sense of humour?

Eventually we turned into a kind of horseshoe-shaped street, and in the bottom of the curve was a bar. To the right was an apartment building, which, given the filth of the front door, looked like it was home to zombie itinerants. There was graffiti all over the door, which appeared to be covered in a film of dried scum. The intercom buttons had things growing out them. I'd like to be more specific but I don't know what they were. Maybe some kind of plant, some kind of animal or hybrid fungus or a new species altogether. It was hard to tell, but it did seem to have some kind of tentacles. I summoned up all my courage and pressed the buzzer for the top floor. It was amazing that even with all the stuff growing out of it and the generally dilapidated state of the building that it still worked, but there you go. I buzzed. And waited. Eventually a voice crackled through the intercom.

12

Terrace

'Si?' said the voice.

'Open up, it's me.'

'Me who?'

'Twenty.'

'Twenty? Twenty facking Major?'

'Yeah.'

'Twenty Major from Dublin?'

'No, Twenty Major from fucking Timbuktu. Open the door you big cunt.'

'Well, fack me with a pirate's septic cock. This is a surprise. Come on up.'

The door buzzed, I kicked it open with my foot, and we went inside. Unlike some apartment buildings which have lifts, this one had barely lit stairs, and we had five flights to get up to reach the ático, our final destination.

When we got there, somewhat gasping for air due to our fitness levels not being what they once were, I knocked on the door at the top of the landing. It opened, and out came Big Ian.

'Well, Twenty, me old mucker. How the facking hell are you?'

'I'm tired from walking up your stairs.'

'Ha ha ha, that'd bring you back a bit, eh?'

'Aye. Big Ian, Jimmy the Bollix. Jimmy the Bollix, Big Ian.'

The two shook hands.

'Come on in, I see you brought some beer. How very sociable of you.'

We walked inside. The difference between the outside of Big Ian's place and the inside was something you never really got used to. While beyond his front door existed grime, grot and gunge, the interior was immaculate, modern and almost shiny in places. There was a flat-screen TV, a nice leather sofa, shelves with books, a large Mac laptop, a drinks cabinet and sliding doors that opened out onto a terrace that caught the sun most of the day during the summer.

Big Ian was, as you might have gathered, a big bloke called Ian, originally from North London, but he'd been in Barcelona for years. He was round of belly and of face, and the face was covered with a wild, bushy beard. I'd never seen him without it, and, although it got trimmed about twice a year, it was always mighty. It was the sort of beard that would have made ZZ Top feel pre-pubescent. He wore a pair of three-quarter-length pants, a chequered shirt open to his belly button (an outy in case you were wondering) and a battered pair of old Adidas Roms, which, given the heat, must have smelt like a zombie's impacted arsehole when he took them off.

I met Big Ian not long after I arrived in Barcelona, me a relatively young man, scratching around not quite knowing what to do with myself. One of the things I did want to do was play football though, and I found a team that played in a mixed league of natives and ex-pats. Big Ian was the manager. As a nippy winger I fitted into the team well, scoring regularly and picking up my fair share of yellow cards. It took me a while to get used to the fact that the slightest touch on a Spanish opponent would see him crash to the ground wailing and praying to God to save his leg which would surely have to be amputated such was the ferocity of the challenge he'd just been subjected to. For a while I thought the referee's cards were magic because the moment I got booked the injured lad would have a miraculous recovery. It was like the ref got them at Lourdes or something.

Big Ian was also an English teacher, and, when I began to run short of the money I'd arrived with, he got me a job working in his school.

'Don't I need some kind of qualification?' I asked. 'Look,' he said, 'you could go and spend a grand or two doing some TEFL course which will give you a piece of paper at the end of it, or you can simply facking save yourself that money and just lie about your background. You know how to lie, don't you?'

'No,' I said. He looked shocked. 'See,' I said, 'that was a lie.'

'Oooh, you're good!'

So I winged it. I spent a year teaching English to teenagers and troubled adults, and I can honestly say, hand on heart, that I would rather sit down and listen to Damien Rice's albums fifty times each than ever teach English again. I hated it. Hated having to be in front of a class of people all staring at me. Hated having to prepare lessons, and truly hated MWT, the disgusting ginger bastard who worked in the school.

Like Daryl Hall before him, he became one of my mortal enemies. I called him MWT (Minge With Teeth) because he had this perfectly triangular goatee beard and enormous horse teeth. I'm sure somebody in Hollywood saw him in the recent past and decided to make a horror film with exactly the same concept, except this time the minge with teeth was actually a real minge.

Some of the students were quite amusing though. One was a very strange young man called Carlos, part of a pre-intermediate class of adults, who would listen intently then ask you about something completely unrelated. You might be teaching the past perfect and he'd ask you about some random piece of grammar. I used to try and elicit as much vocabulary as possible from the students in every class. One day we were doing the past continuous and in the book there was a pictures showing people performing various actions in a park: 'She's in the park. She's walking her dog.' There were just four in the class, so I asked each of them to give me three words. We had all the usual park stuff like 'tree', 'grass', 'lake', 'bench', and so on. It came to Carlos, and he was a bit stumped.

'Erm . . . tree,' he said.

'Good,' I replied. 'Any more?'

'Erm . . . children!' he said.

'Good. Now, one more.'

He was struggling at this stage. So I decided to give him a bit of help. 'You find them in trees,' I said.

Silence.

'They have wings.'

More silence.

'They fly and they sing.'

A look of understanding crossed Carlos's face, and he proudly gave me the answer.

'Monkeys!'

But those kinds of moments were sadly too few and far between to put up with the sheer, mind-numbing tedium of the job. I couldn't understand how people did it, but, apart from bartending, it was the easiest work for 'foreigners' to come by in Spain.

As I said, I lasted a year before I couldn't hack it any more. A life of petty crime and defrauding the Spanish welfare system was a much better idea, despite being slightly more risky.

Big Ian still taught – although that wasn't his forte. Big Ian was famous around town for being able to get stuff. Whatever you needed he could find it. That was every-thing from drugs, documents, fake driving licences, ivory-handled toothbrushes, hard-to-come-by food from back home, like Heinz strawberry sponge pudding that you boil in its tin, and pretty much anything else you could think of.

For the weekend ahead I figured we'd need some stuff, and who better to get it for us? We adjourned to a table out on the terrace where Big Ian sat and rolled a large joint from the smelliest grass I think I've ever smelled. Jimmy cracked open the beers, and I felt a huge wave of nostalgia wash over me. How many times had I sat at this table, drinking, smoking, having a laugh? I couldn't count, and, at that moment, I missed it and felt sad that I'd never had a chance to say my goodbyes properly when I left.

'So,' said Big Ian, 'what brings you back here after all this time? Considering the way you left I wasn't sure we'd ever see you round these parts again.'

'I wasn't planning it, to be honest, but we've found ourselves in a bit of a bind.'

'Is that right?'

'Yeah, pretty much a life-or-death situation, right Jimmy?'

'Too true. And the death part could be us if things don't go right.'

'Shit, that's not good. What's happened?'

I filled Big Ian in on what had happened back when Tony Furriskey had done that favour for us and told him that now he was calling in his marker.

'Jesus, he did you a good turn there, no doubt about it. Given the circumstances there are plenty who wouldn't have helped you out the way he did. How the fack did you get involved in something like that in the first place?'

'Oh, that's a long story, eh Twenty?' said Jimmy.

'It certainly is.' So I proceeded to tell Big Ian the long

story, and by the time I'd finished we'd almost gotten through all the beer. Jimmy volunteered to go out and get some more – reasoning very wisely that it was rather too early to start on the absinthe – leaving me and Big Ian to talk some more.

'Have you thought about what happens if you run into you-know-who? I know you well enough, Twenty. You're a creature of habit. You'll go back to all the same bars, the same hangouts, and I can tell you he hasn't forgotten. They say he burns inside with the need for revenge. Some say that even if he had terminal cancer his desire to see you would fight it off until he got payback. Do you need that hassle with everything else that's going on?'

'No man, I just want to get this stag thing over and done with. I can certainly live without any more hassle. You know, I thought I saw him earlier, but I only got here last night. He couldn't have found out already, could he?'

'He is very well connected, don't forget.'

'Don't I know it.'

'Well, don't let your drunken head lead you. You know what your drunken head is like. A bit sappy and sentimental. You think it's a good idea to call up people you haven't seen in ages. Like last facking Christmas when you rang me up and told me you missed me and all that.'

'I did?'

'Yes, you did. Don't you ever check your phone after you go out drinking to see who you sent text messages to or who you might have rung?'

'No way. I prefer not to know. Ignorance is bliss and all that.'

'Well, Jimmy seems like a sensible enough chap. I'll make him aware of where you shouldn't be. Hopefully he can keep you in line if you decide to go scratching itches that have no need to be scratched.'

'He can try.'

'Hah, you haven't changed a bit. Apart from being older, hairier and a bit chunkier than you were.'

'Same goes for you, pal. So, I reckon we're going to need some bits and pieces for this weekend.'

'What exactly are you looking for?'

I told him, and he went back inside, opened up a floor safe covered by a rug with the crest of his beloved Arsenal FC on it, and took out what was needed. Jimmy arrived back with some more beer and a couple of shawarmas each. All the afternoon drinking and the smoking had given us all the munchies, and we ate in contented silence until my phone rang.

'Hello?'

'Twenty, it's me. Dirty Dave.'

'Well?'

'No sign of him yet. I just thought I'd give you a ring to let you know we're staying vigilant and on our toes keeping our eyes peeled and a close lookout for the chap in question.'

'Good man.'

'It's very boring out here, and Stinking Pete is complaining that his arms are really tired from holding the sign up all day.'

'He only has to hold it up when the flights from Dublin arrive though.'

'Oh yeah. That makes sense. I'll tell him. He's gone off to have a poo and a sandwich.'

'At the same time?'

'Yeah. Killing two birds with one stone or something.'

'All right,' I said, looking at my watch which read 5.30 p.m., 'the next flight is due in in a couple of hours. He's got to be on this one, so make sure you get it right.'

'You don't even worry about it. We're on top of things. You can trust us, Twenty.'

'Famous last words, those. All right, call me if there's any hassle, and as soon as you drop him at his hotel you let me know where they're staying.'

'Will do. Oh, here comes Pete and he's got half a sandwich for me. How thoughtful! Talk to you later.'

I put the phone down and turned to Jimmy.

'Well, they haven't managed to fuck up completely yet.'

'That's only because there's nothing for them to fuck up.'

'Hmm, good point.'

Now we just had to wait and keep our fingers crossed that when the time came they'd manage not to make a complete hash of it. I was beginning to worry that I really should have handled this part myself instead of trusting two blokes who made the characters from *Dumb and Dumber* seem like Mensa and Mensa-er. If we grabbed a cab there was still time to get out there before the Aer Lingus flight arrived and make a hundred per cent sure everything went smoothly. Then I remembered the cans of beer and the joints and thought, 'Fuck it, if it all goes wrong we'll figure something out the way we always do.'

Beer really is my one character flaw.

13

Waiting . . .

The afternoon passed easily. There's really nothing like sunshine to make beer, which is already the most delicious thing on earth, taste even better. As usual when people who work, or have worked together in the same field, get together the conversation turns to that topic, and we swapped stories from our English teaching days. Big Ian told us about some of his students, I recalled some tales about mine, and Jimmy had the good manners to laugh. I have to say, with the drinking all day and the smoking, I was beginning to feel just a bit woozy.

'You heard about MWT, didn't you?' said Big Ian.

'No, what happened?'

'Dead!'

'Get out!'

'Seriously.'

'How?'

'Well, remember that facking little scooter he had that he used go about the place on?'

'Yeah.'

'Well, one day he was doing a private lesson up in Les Corts, and the gas main outside the building exploded and killed him and about seven other people inside. They said the corpses were like cow pats – all crunchy on the outside but all squashy and stinking once you poked through.'

'Fucking hell. What's that got to do with his scooter though?' I said.

'Nothing. I was just asking if you remembered it.'

'Hah. Well, the main thing is MWT is dead. Do we know if he was killed instantly or if he spent his last agonising moments completely on fire with the skin dripping from his limbs and his eyes melting out of his head?'

'You and your imagination. If you think that's the way he went then go for it.'

I was quite happy to do that. I've never been one for post-death revisionism. It always gave me a pain in my arse the way somebody was a 'great fella' after he died, that what he did during his life didn't seem to matter any more. I always felt like shouting, 'But he was a cunt when he was alive. He stole, he cheated, he lied, he killed his children, then his wife, set their corpses on fire then killed himself. What's with all this "the poor fella, you can't speak ill of the dead" shit you're going on with?' If Hitler had been Irish there'd have been people down the local saying, 'Well, he might have killed a load of Jews, and I'm not here to judge whether that's right or wrong, but he always got his round in, and you can't argue with that,' as if someone who didn't kill a load of Jews but didn't get their round in was somehow worse. So I sat for a while thinking about MWT's last moments, ensuring that, in my mind at least, they were as horrible and frightening as I could possibly make them.

I glanced at my watch and realised it was coming up towards 9 p.m. If the flight arrived on time then they'd surely be at their hotel by now. I got that feeling in my stomach you get when you think you've got your head caught between some railings. Maybe the flight was delayed though. Perhaps the luggage took ages to come out. Traffic back into the city was very heavy. All good reasons why I hadn't heard from the lads yet. But that part of me which said 'They've fucked it up' was louder than the part of me that considered reasonable explanations. You can imagine my relief then when the phone rang, and Dirty Dave said hello.

'Where the fuck have you been?'

'Ah, just got a bit lost on the way into the town. The Sat Nav thing is speaking in Spanish, and when I tried to change the language, it went into Japanese, and my Japanese is rudimentary at best so we took a wrong turn or two.'

'But did you not just follow the line on the display that tells you where you were going?'

'Never even occurred to me, but what can you do?'

'Jesus. Right, what hotel are they are at?'

'Some place called the Hotel Majestic on Passeig de Gràcia. Not far from where me and Pete are staying actually.'

'Right, here's what you do. You pick them up from their hotel, I assume they're all freshening up, and you drive them to the bottom of Via Laietana. It's a big wide road that even you can't miss. On the right-hand side you'll see a turn for the Post Office, the Spanish name is "Correos", take that turn and let the lads out there. Tell them to go under the arch and into a bar on the right-hand side called Milk. Me and Jimmy are going to be in there, and the fun and games will begin. Got that?'

'Yeah, Via Banana, find the Koreans, underneath the arches, some milky bar, you and Jimmy playing fun games.'

'Fuck me. Close enough. Ring me if you have any problems.'

He hung up. I lit a cigarette: it was time to sober up a bit because now the mission was under way. Big Ian wasn't coming with us – he claimed he had some kind of early class and would catch up with us at some stage tomorrow – so Jimmy and I bade him farewell and headed out into the gloriously warm and rain-free Barcelona night.

Milk was a quite a happening place which served good cocktails and would be just the kind of bar the lads would be looking for. It would only take us a couple of minutes to walk there.

'What's your thinking on all this, Twenty?'

'I reckon we get in with these lads. They're here to have a mad weekend. What better than to meet somebody who knows the city, who knows where all the good clubs, bars and strip joints are and who can get his hands on the one thing that young, trendy Dubliners want on a night out?'

'Kebabs?'

'No! Coke.'

'Where do you get that then?'

'Right here,' I said, pulling out a small plastic bag with wraps of coke in it. 'Big Ian can get anything, and you know what the kids today are like. They're all mad for the coke. They won't even leave the house until someone has sorted out a few grams.'

'I may set up a septum repair clinic, you know.'

'Here's what I'm thinking. We act as their "guides" for the weekend, getting them all, and more importantly Coleman himself, out of their tiny little minds on booze and drugs. Then we try and compromise him or get him involved in situations which may prove prejudicial to his marriage. Seeing as we can't hurt him, kill him, make him disappear or anything else, it's about the only thing we can do.'

'Good plan. I suppose we'll need some kind of camera to get the evidence. I mean, it's all well and good that it happens but without something to show Tony we're wasting our time.'

'True, but it's a bit late to sort that out now. You know, we really should have thought of that before now.'

'Yeah, but we had beer to drink and joints to smoke,' said Jimmy.

'This is true. Anyway, what we'll do is tease them a bit with a small amount of drugs tonight then make sure we can meet up with them tomorrow to sort them out with more. Gives us an in and time to buy a camera.'

'Sounds entirely reasonable to me. We'll just have to

remember not to get carried away ourselves and to keep focused on the task in hand. We have been drinking since earlier.'

'If I find myself enjoying myself too much I'll picture me watching you being tortured to death by Tony Furriskey. That'll keep me on track.'

'Ha ha, yeah. Fuck. I do not want to be Tony's next video star.'

And with that sobering thought fresh in our minds we went inside, pulled up a couple of seats at the bar and ordered a couple of double mojitos. As you do.

14

Kick-off

After we'd finished our third mojito I was beginning to think that Dave and Pete had fucked it up, that the lads wouldn't be coming at all. But, remarkably, about ten minutes later the door opened, and in came Coleman and his three mates, all dressed in three-quarter-length pants that looked like they came from the most expensive shelf in BT2, with designer T-shirts, sunglasses on their heads (which I had to admire because I assumed they were planning on being out all night) and each one reeking of expensive aftershave. I caught the scent of Cool Water, Fahrenheit and two kinds of Hugo Boss. I have a very good nose. My phone buzzed, and it was a text message from Dave asking me to meet them outside. Jimmy said he'd monitor the lads, and I went out.

'Good work, lads. You're doing all right so far this

weekend. Apart from the getting lost and nearly getting arrested in Dublin airport.'

'Ups and downs, Twenty,' said Pete.

'Look,' said Dirty Dave, 'they said they didn't need us any more tonight. I'm tired, filthy – even for me – and hungry. I need some food and a shower and some beers, so can we knock off now? Do our own thing?'

'Yeah, no problem. Me and Jimmy have the rest of this night covered.'

'I think I'm going to go see the Camp Nou,' said Dirty Dave. 'I've always wanted to do that.'

'It'll be closed, what with it being 10.30 at night.'

'Ah, fuck it, I'll just go up anyway. Admire it from the outside. Who knows if I'll get a chance in the daytime due to all the crime fighting we're going to be doing.'

'Crime fighting . . . ?' I began, but decided against pursuing it. God knows what he thought we were here for.

'I'm going to KFC,' said Stinking Pete.

'I heard that in Barcelona it's not chicken but pigeon and that the pigeons all come from Plaça Catalunya because there's an endless supply of them,' said Dirty Dave.

'It is not pigeon,' said Pete.

'Is too.'

'You're a pigeon!'

'Right lads, have fun,' I said before this went on too long and became too irritating. 'I'll catch up with you tomorrow.'

'OK Twenty. Cheers!'

And off they went into the night. Or, more correctly,

off I went leaving them standing there still arguing about whether or not they were pigeons or KFC was made from pigeon or God only knows what else.

I walked through the arch of the post office and down the alley back towards the bar. I sat down with Jimmy again, ordered another drink, and waited. The lads had ordered rounds of beers and were in good spirits. I was plotting with Jimmy about how to make our opening move and how we should approach them when fate gave us a little helping hand. Their first round of drinks had been served by a pretty Irish waitress who they had a great time chatting up, but she got called into the back for something so one of the lads came up to the bar to get the next round.

'Erm,' he said to the barman, 'kwatre . . . kwatro . . . erm . . . four' – at this point he held up four fingers – 'erm . . . beers!'

'No problem,' said the barman, well used to the influx of foreigners to the city. As the guy stood there waiting for them to be poured I knew it was an opportunity to break the ice.

'From Dublin then, eh?'

'Oh . . . yeah.'

'Whereabouts?'

'Southside, like.'

'Ahh, me too. Which part of town?'

'Blackrock, Dun Laoghaire, Foxrock, that kind of way.'

'That's a fairly wide area you've covered there. I'm closer to town than you.'

He didn't look remotely interested, as he was really far

too cool to be talking to a beardy old shite at the bar, no matter where he came from.

'Just over for the weekend, are you?'

'Yeah, our mate is getting married so we're here on a stag weekend, y'know?'

'You picked a good town for it,' I said, 'loads to do here, if you know the right places. Ever been here before?'

'Nah, I was in Malaga once when I was fifteen though.'

'I see. Well, I used to live here, and if you want a bit of help with places, restaurants, clubs – any kind of club, if you get what I'm saying – I'd be more than happy to help out some fellow Dubliners.'

'Oh right, yeah, well, look, I'll say it to Coleman. It's his party, so it'd be down to him.'

'Of course. And I could also sort you out with a few party extras, know what I mean?'

'Oh yeah?' Now he looked interested. 'Yeah. You go talk to your mates. I'll be right here. I'm Twenty, by the way. This is Jimmy.'

'Diarmuid,' he said. 'Right, I'll go chat with the lads.'

So off he went with the drinks and over to the table.

'I was in Malaga once,' mimicked Jimmy. 'Fuck me.'

Jimmy and I had our backs to them, not looking like we were too interested but in the mirror behind the bar I could see Diarmuid telling them something and pointing in our direction. I could only hope it wasn't 'I met these weirdos at the bar, let's get the fuck out of here quick!' I needn't have worried though. About fifteen minutes later another one of them came over. He was a tall fella with a shock of platinum blond hair and unsettlingly blue eyes that put me in mind of Limahl crossed with some kind of Eastern European hitman. Eyes that blue always put me on edge, there's just something wrong about them. Like the paleness of the eyes is directly proportional to the coldness of the heart.

'Hi there,' he said confidently. 'I'm Kyle. I'm the best man at the wedding of our mate so I'm the one that has to do all this kind of stuff, you know.'

'A pleasure,' I said, holding out my hand. 'I'm Twenty.' He made no attempt to shake, just looked at my hand as if it was diseased.

'I hear you were talking to Diarmuid.'

'Yeah. He's been to Malaga, you know.'

'So he never stops telling us. So, you used to live here then?'

'Yeah.'

'And Diarmuid mentioned you might be able to provide us with some stuff to keep the party going, shall we say?' he said.

'I can do lots of stuff. Tell you what, how about I buy you lads a round of drinks and join you at the table. We can talk a bit more.'

'Yeah, great. Beers all round then.'

I ordered the drinks from the barman and went over and sat down at the table. I nodded at Diarmuid and introduced myself as Twenty to the other two.

'Hi. Breffni,' said one.

'I'm Coleman,' said the other. The one whose fault it was we were here in the first place. As much as I was enjoying the warm weather and the cheap booze I couldn't quite shake the whole 'We could die thanks to this little bastard.' I found myself looking at him and wishing his father had had just one more wank so Coleman had ended up dry and crunchy in a tissue and not here in front of us.

'Stag then? Who's the poor fucker.'

'Ha ha, that'd be me,' said Coleman. 'And you wouldn't be saying that if you saw my moth. She's a total lash, right lads?'

There was clinking of glasses as they agreed whole-heartedly with him, although Kyle couldn't quite disguise the look on his face. As if he'd tasted something that was on the cusp of going off. Interesting, I thought to myself. Jimmy noticed it too.

'So, first time in Barcelona?'

'Yeah,' said Coleman. 'Diarmuid was in Malaga though.'

I gave Jimmy a swift kick under the table as I could feel him about to make some kind of comment.

'Well, I know you lads are here to do your own thing and such, but we can show you about the place, show you the cool bars, the ones where you won't get ripped off, the good clubs, clubs with . . . ladies . . . and all that. Plus, as I was saying to the other lads, we can definitely help keep you going, you feel me?'

'Cool,' said Coleman, 'what can you get?'

'What do you want?'

'I suppose some charlie, you know. Chaps?'

The rest of them nodded, along with the odd utterance of 'Tops' or 'Deadly'.

'That shouldn't be any problem at all. Just need to give the man a shout.'

'Can you get any tonight, like?'

'I'm sure we can manage that, can't we Jimmy?'

'Oh, I'm sure we can,' said Jimmy, trying to smile a friendly smile. This time I did give him a bit of a kick. Jimmy's not much of a smiler, and he's not that friendly, so when he does try it looks a bit like someone grimacing in intense pain as they contemplate the way in which they're going to kill you. Oddly though he's quite the charmer with the ladies, and he can flash them the kind of toothy grin that would make Tom Cruise jealous.

'Tell you what, how about we finish up these drinks and I take you to another bar. I can go make a phone call, pick up some stuff, and we'll take it from there.'

'Wicked!' said Coleman. 'That sounds great, right fellas?'

'Sure!' said Breffni.

'Of course, Coleman,' said Diarmuid.

While Kyle, the best man, said nothing but finished his pint with a strange look on his face. But they all went along with Coleman. Perhaps it was just because it was his stag night that they were doing what he wanted, but I got the impression that even if we were back in Dublin and I offered to rape them all with a red-hot poker and Coleman was into it the rest of them would be too. He was definitely the leader of the gang, he made the decisions, and I figured that if we got properly onside with him then the others wouldn't prove to be any hassle. So we finished up and went out into the night.

15

Black Sheep

We walked up the Ramblas, the wide, tree-lined boulevard that runs from the statue of Christopher Columbus
by the sea right up to Plaça Catalunya in the centre of
town. It is filled with kiosks, street performers, weird pet
shops where you can buy all manner of animal by simply
pointing and saying 'that one', terraces where you can
buy the most expensive beer in Barcelona and artists dis-
playing and trying to sell their wares. Traffic is restricted
to one lane on each side, and on both sides of the street
there are souvenir shops, bars, restaurants, hotels, strip
clubs and video-game arcades. It is always teeming with
life, whether it's people strolling after dinner, tourists
(being spied on by various pickpockets and other
chancers) taking in the incredible collision between
beauty and tacky, young people zipping their way through

the crowds on their way to somewhere important, or people streaming out of the metro station and into the night.

The people milling up and down were in good spirits, enjoying the summer and the start of the weekend. There were girls in tiny skirts and T-shirts handing out flyers for the various nightclubs around town. There were Nigerian grifters who looked for tourists or anyone that might show the slightest bit of weakness. Their trick was to try and sell you some drugs, which, even if you said you didn't want them, they'd try and slip into your pocket. In so doing, they'd attempt to relieve you of your wallet, your phone or your cash. And if you did decide to buy something from them you generally found yourself in possession of a little baggy or wrap of flour or baking soda. All the way along were the 'beer monkeys,' as I called them. These were guys who sold cans of beer for a euro each. They were very handy when walking between bars, so I bought a six-pack from one of them and handed them out to the boys on our way up the road.

As we swigged our beers I told the lads how to watch out for pickpockets and beggars and generally regaled them with tales of the city. I was at my charming, effervescent best. We arrived at the front door of the bar about fifteen minutes later. The Black Sheep is a bar just off the top of the Ramblas, on a little street called c/Sitges. You'd nearly miss it – the door is almost hidden and you kind of have to stoop down going through – but when you go inside you step into another world. Not a particularly awe-inspiring world, but a great one in which to drink lots and lots of beer. The tables are long with benches each side, bar a couple of round tables, and the clientele, for the most part, are what you might casually call 'rockers'. Young guys and girls with chains and steel-capped boots, black pants, long hair and badly applied make-up. But amongst them are normal folk as well who come for the beer, which is the most potent beer in the whole of Barcelona.

Now, the draught beer is the same as nearly every other bar: Estrella, the local brew. Most bars in Spain don't have the wide range of draught beers like we do in Ireland. It's generally one tap, maybe two if it's a bit posh. So I was always very used to drinking that particular brand. However, for some reason or other, the beer in the Black Sheep is particularly puissant, as John Banville might say. Drinking four pints in there is the equivalent of drinking 28.4 pints somewhere else. You go in, drink some beers, then try and stand up and you realise it's more difficult than trying to find an Irish barman in a Dublin pub.

As Jimmy and I had had a bit of a head start in terms of the drinking, I thought this would be the perfect place to get the lads caught up, so to speak. They sell the beer in tankards or in pitchers, as well as selling pitchers of sangria too. I went to the bar, got a round of six tankards in and brought them back over to the table. I told them I was going out to make a quick phone call about the stuff, and Jimmy walked out with me.

'Why are you telling them you need to make a phone call? You have the stuff on you.'

'Yeah, but if we say we have it and give it to them they

might just say "Thanks very much" and bugger off. We need to butter them up a bit, get them a bit drunk, and then we can give them some drugs. At that point they'll be well oiled and us hanging around them won't seem so strange.'

'Any plans for the wedding boy?'

'Not really, as I said, tonight it just a bit of recon. Tomorrow is when we try and set something up.'

'Righto. I'm finding it difficult to cope with them, what with them being complete arsewipes and all.'

'I know, but think about it: if you can put up with Dave and Pete then you can put up with anything.'

'But I can tell Dave and Pete to shut up and punch them and thrash them to within an inch of their lives. I can't do that to these guys. I have to pretend to be nice and to enjoy their company.'

'Them or death,' I said.

'Gah.'

'Aye, but there you go. Right, let's get back inside.'

We wandered back in, expecting to find them sitting around the table, but they were all standing around a table-football table with Coleman and the one called Breffni taking on a couple of local boys. Now, the local boys were a little on the rough-and-ready side and were trying to get the two Irish lads to put some money on the game.

'Apuesta! Apuesta!' said one of them, rubbing his thumb and index finger together in the universal 'money, money' gesture.

'What? WHAT? I DON'T UNDERSTAND!' said

Coleman, as if shouting really loudly would cross the language barrier.

'Apuesta!' the lad said again, looking at his friend in the vague hope that he knew the English word he needed.

'He wants to bet on the game,' I said.

'Oh, right. Why didn't he just say so then?' said Coleman, swigging from his beer which was almost gone. I gave Jimmy the nod, and he headed towards the bar to stock up.

'He did. Except in Spanish.'

'I thought they only spoke Catamaran here?' said a puzzled-looking Diarmuid.

'Catalan. And they speak both.'

'HOW MUCH?' roared Coleman at Local Number One, who looked a bit shocked at this Brian-O'Driscoll-looking Irishman yelling at him. I translated. He wanted to play a euro each for the game, which, when I told Coleman, sent him into hysterics of laughter.

'A euro each? A whole euro? Talk about last of the big spenders. Tell him twenty euro. TWENTY, Twenty!'

'No. No. Demasiado,' said the local lad.

'He says that's too much.'

'Ha ha! Twenty euro is too much? Where are we? Africa?'

The rest of his mates laughed like he'd just told the world's funniest joke.

I spoke to the local lad in Spanish. 'Look, play him for twenty euro. I know it's a lot for you, but Irish people are absolutely rubbish at table football. We have no coordination, trying to spin one of the arms is work enough, but two, plus a keeper, is a nightmare. And we have no pedigree in this game. The only time we ever play is when we're on holidays and pissed. Like these cunts. You're going to thrash him.'

He seemed reassured by that, if still a bit suspicious, but went ahead with the bet anyway. The table was old school. The players were not your moulded plastic like they are today. These were cast-iron footballers. One team in the white of Real Madrid (Coleman and Breffni) with Locals One and Two with the Barcelona clad players. The balls were wooden, and the game was on.

The locals raced into an early one-goal lead which made Coleman very cross indeed. I could tell he wasn't the kind of guy who enjoyed sport or games for the fun of the game. It was all about winning. 'Come on, Breff, you gimp,' said Coleman as ball two of seven entered play. Breffni didn't look like he was enjoying himself much at all, the pressure of having to be on Coleman's side, knowing he had to win, looked like it was too much for him. Still, after a few seconds, the ball broke to him, he turned the arm containing the midfield players and smashed it home to make it 1–1.

'Good goal,' said Local One.

'What did he say?' asked Coleman.

Sensing the chance for some mischief, I replied, 'He said you were jammy cunts.'

'Did he now? We'll see about that.'

Miraculously, Coleman and Breffni went 2–1 up when a long punt from the back clanked off one of the Barcelona defenders and deflected in.

'Ha ha. Now who's jammy?'

'What did he say?' asked Local Two.

'He said you're terrible at this game, possibly because you're retarded.'

'Piece of shit.'

The locals soon came into their own though and scored two quick goals to go 3–2 ahead, needing only one goal for the win.

'Vamos! Vamos!' they cried as they slapped each other's hands in a display of comradeship and team spirit.

'He says you look like an abortion,' I told Coleman.

'Oh yeah, well, tell him I rode his sister and she loved it.'

'He says you two are typical Catalan insurrectionists, unable to accept that Madrid is now your master.'

'Hijo de puta!'

'He says your mam's a streetwalking slutbag.'

Jimmy looked at me quizzically, I gave him a quick wink. With tensions now really high, the game continued, and there was an epic battle for the next goal. You could see Coleman and Breffni didn't have the same skill or technique as the other two, but Coleman's sheer desire to win and Breffni's outright terror at somehow preventing Coleman from winning kept them in it.

Eventually, having stopped one on their own goal line, the Irish lads scored to make it 3–3. It was all down to the final ball. The Spanish lads looked a bit nervous: there was twenty euro each riding on this, and, while it was not a big sum to affluent Dublin southsiders, it was much more than they wanted to lose.

'You're going down! You're going down!' taunted Coleman, which, after I translated, became 'You both want to suck the cock of Raul.'

The Spaniards' typically incensed response was given back to Coleman, who couldn't really understand why they were getting so irate over some fairly typical mind games but his competitive spirit helped him gloss over it.

The ball was dropped into the middle of the table, and it rolled towards the Spanish goal. Some clever midfield play saw the central player hold it up and play a lovely pass up to the striker. He shifted it left to his striking partner who shot on goal, but the Irish defence stood firm. The ball was swirling towards the Spanish half, the Irish winger picked it up and hoofed it at goal, but it was an easy save for the goalkeeper who rolled it out to the centre-half. His pass into midfield was intercepted though, and the Irish striker hammered one that hit the left-hand side of the goal, rolled right across the gaping chasm, hit the right-hand side and came out.

Breffni held his head in his heads in despair until he realised he needed his hands for the game.

Spain took the ball and didn't risk the short pass this time, it was pure route-one stuff. They clogged it up to the striker, and, in an instant, Local Two shimmied one way, then the other, before slamming it home to win the game. The Spanish were delighted, hugging each other, while Coleman looked disgusted. The two Irish lads handed over the money, and Coleman took a drink of his beer before speaking.

'Tell them I want a rematch, double or quits.'

'Are you sure?' I said.

'Yeah. I hate losing, and I hate losing money.'

'Right enough then. I'll say it to them.' This was too much for me. I knew that Coleman wasn't supposed to be harmed in any way, but this was too good to pass up. If they did beat the crap out of him and leave him in a permanently vegetative state it would be enough for us to call it quits on Tony's scheme. I didn't share his fears. No girl, no matter how much she loves a man, is going to marry someone whose nappies she has to change while he drools on her head. And a bar fight, well, that would hardly be our fault, would it? 'Oi chicos, he says that your mothers took turns sucking Franco's cock.'

The jubilation of the two local lads was cut very short indeed when they heard that.

'Look, don't blame me. I'm just telling you what he said.'

Local Two, the biggest and most aggressive of the pair, turned to face Coleman, stood right in front of him, face to face almost, and said, 'Tell him if he ever says anything like that again I will kill him, the pig.'

'What's he saying?' asked Coleman, confused that a request for another game would spark such anger.

'He says you cheated in the last game and he won't play with cheats.'

'Cheated? How did we cheat? We lost, like. I don't like being called a cheat. Tell him to take that back or there's going to be trouble.'

'He says not only did they suck Franco's cock, but your

dad watched, and then he licked Franco's balls before the great dictator fucked him right up the arse,' I said to Local Two, who paused for a moment to take this in before landing a head-butt out of nowhere on Coleman. I stepped back as Coleman held his face in his hands.

'Owwww, Jesus. What's the problem with this guy? Talk about a sore loser.'

'Now who sucks Franco's cock?' the local roared as the blood began to trickle from Coleman's nose.

'He says you English are afraid of fighting,' I shouted over from a safe distance. Well, that did it. Coleman charged at Local Two, picking him up around the waist in a perfect rugby-style tackle before slamming him down on the table-football table. I winced – that must have hurt, the heads of the solid metal players going directly into the soft flesh of the back. Local One decided he'd get involved then and threw a punch at Coleman, who ducked and knocked him clean off his feet and into unconsciousness with an uppercut to the chin. He then picked up Local Two by the collar and began to slap his face back and forward until he himself was grabbed by a couple of hefty bouncers who had come running in from the front door.

'Fuera! Fuera!' they yelled, telling us to get out. With the adrenalin and the beer flowing Coleman struggled with them and, in a move straight out of a *Die Hard* film, cracked their two heads together like coconuts. The bouncers slumped to the ground while Coleman looked around to see if there was anyone else he could fight. The watching crowd backed away as a great big stalagmite of saliva hung from Coleman's mouth. OK, getting him beaten into a hospice wasn't going to work. Not to worry. It had been fun all the same.

'Erm, I think we had better get out of here,' I said to Breffni, who was watching with something between astonishment and pure hero worship. 'OK, I'll grab him.'

We made our way out of the bar, turned onto the Ramblas and onto Plaça Catalunya.

'Sorry about that,' I said to Coleman, vaguely afraid he might blame me for the fight. We needed to keep him sweet until we got something that we could bring back to get the wedding called off. I shouldn't have worried though.

'No problem, man. That was AWESOME! Thank God we met up with you two, we'd never have known what they were saying otherwise. Woooo, yeah! Come on!'

He was hyped up like a kid who comes out of the cinema and asks 'What was your favourite bit? Mine was when the hero got in that fight and he was all "pow", and stuff.' He went over the various conflicts in great detail, the others standing open-mouthed, listening to him prattle on and on and on.

I looked at Jimmy, he rolled his eyes. I rolled mine back. This was going to be a long weekend.

16

Mojitos

After the violence and excitement I needed a good mojito – its delicious combination of rum, mint and sugar is good for the nerves, you know. Forget Prozac, mojitos are the far superior and much more alcoholic alternative. Now, they are ten a penny in Barcelona, in any city really, but as a connoisseur of the minty cocktails there was only one place we could go. It was slightly out of the centre on c/Roger de Llúria at the corner of c/Diputació. Else's Bar was a small place, but Else made the best damn mojito in town. All the way up Coleman talked about the fight he was in and told us about a few more for good measure. It was hard going trying to pretend to be interested when a twenty-four-year-old is telling you about how he knocked the 'shoite' out of some guy who he'd played rugby against and who had grabbed his balls during the game.

Apparently he couldn't do it on the pitch because that would be letting the side down, but later that night when he saw him in Krystal he battered the head off him in the jacks because nobody was allowed touch his balls that way without express permission.

I told them we were going to get some more drinks in a quieter bar where I'd pick up the stuff. Diarmuid started to moan about wanting to go to a nightclub, but I explained to him that it was so early in the evening that nightclubs would be empty at the moment.

'But it's like 11.30,' he said.

'Yeah, but it's like open till 6 a.m. here so nobody goes this early. Unless you want to and stand on your own. Is that what you want to do?'

'Yeah, is it? Is that what you REALLY want to do, like?' joined in Coleman, eager to reassert his position as leader of the pack. 'Everyone knows they party late here, Diarmuid, you great big fanny. Just because you went to Malaga once doesn't mean you know everything. Pffft.'

So Diarmuid kept his mouth shut, and we arrived at Else's. She runs the bar with her eccentric mother, who, as we came through the door and stepped down into the place, took one look at me, looked away, then the recognition kicked in, and she came running over.

'Ohmygod, is Twenty! A long time I have not seen your head.' She has a unique take on the English language, having lived in Carlow for six months as a teenager – (long story, but it involves a man, another man, two more men and their wives and some pitchforks) and learned the rest from the English-speaking tourists who frequent the bar.

'Well, hello Rosa,' I said. 'You are looking as beautiful as always.'

'You snake charmer!' she said fluttering her eyelashes. 'Anyhowway, this is a bad night to see me.'

'Why?'

'I have a pig's house.'

'A what?'

'I look in dictionary, and it say I have pig's house in my eye.'

'You've lost me, Rosa. What do you mean?'

'Look!' she said pointing at her eye, 'pig's house!'

'Ahhh, a sty.'

'Yes, a pig's house in my eye. Is disgusting. Who is this?'

'This is Jimmy the Bollix. He's kind of like my sidekick.'

'Oooh, is psychic.'

'No, he is my sidekick.'

'Can see into the future or not?'

'No, he's just my friend.'

'Oh, friend. Why you don't just say? Welcome, Jiminy!'

'Erm, it's nice to meet you,' said a rather nonplussed Jimmy.

'Else! Else! Look who is,' said Rosa, ushering me towards her daughter who was busily mixing drinks behind the bar.

'Well, hello there,' she said, greeting me with a kiss on

each cheek, such was the Spanish way. 'I didn't think we'd ever see you again after what happened.'

'Things change, eh? You never know what's going to happen or where life leads you.'

'Actually, I must ask you something about this,' she said.

'Tell you what, we need a round of mojitos, six please, and then I'll tell you all about it.'

When she went off to prepare the drinks, I sat down with the lads at the end of the bar and handed Coleman three wraps of cocaine. 'Right, that's all I can get tonight, but there'll be more tomorrow. They're fifty euro.'

'Where did you get them? I didn't see you meet anyone.'

'You didn't see because you weren't supposed to see.'

'Ahhh, I get you. You are one slick mofo, dude,' he said tapping the side of his nose. 'Right, I'm off to the Goldman Sachs for a bit of a toot. Kyle, pay the man!'

He left the others sitting there all looking like bold schoolboys who weren't quite sure how they were supposed to behave. Jimmy was up at the far end of the bar, as far away from them as he could possibly get, talking to Rosa and Else. I couldn't really blame him there. The lads weren't much fun.

'Thanks,' I said to Kyle, as he handed over three fifty euro notes. 'So what kind of pranks do you have lined up?'

'What do you mean "pranks"?' he said, looking at me as if I was a utter moron. I was beginning to not like him very much.

'Well, this is a stag weekend, right?'

'Yeah. So what?'

'Well it's fairly typical that on a stag weekend the rest of the lads play a prank or two on the groom, you know? Like shaving his eyebrows off when he's passed out from drinking all day or making him walk naked through the city centre, perhaps wearing only a policeman's hat or giving him a large dose of Rohypnol, wrapping him in clingfilm then putting him in a large crate with only some dry crackers and drinking water and posting him via a dodgy cargo ship to Malaysia. See?'

'Oh yeah,' said Diarmuid, 'that's normal, but we can't do anything like that.'

'Why not?'

'Coleman would kill us.'

'You what?' I said.

'Yeah. He'd go batshit mental if we did anything like that. He plays centre for Blackrock, you know.'

'I see. How is that relevant?'

'That's just not how you treat someone that plays centre for Blackrock.'

'He's right,' said Kyle, 'Coleman just would not like that, and it's his weekend.'

'Let me ask you this. If one of you were getting married, would you expect Coleman to carry out some kind of prank on you?'

'Sure,' said Breffni, scratching his prominent Roman nose, 'but it's kinda different.'

'How?'

'None of us play centre for Blackrock. It is a role which merits respect and an amount of hushed adulation, even from one's closest friends.'

I sighed. These boys were fucking pussy-whipped. They weren't Coleman's friends, they were his entourage, there to tell him just how incredibly awesome he was at all times. Whatever he did was brilliant, marvellous and hilarious even if it involved him doing the Ricky Gervais dance from *The Office* to a David Gray tune. In a way I felt sorry for them, sad cunts that they were, destined to spend their whole lives living in this bloke's shadow just because he was good at rugby, the game that provided the banking sector with the majority of its staff. The best players from the private schools didn't have to worry about their Leaving Certs or colleges; the connections – the knowing people who know people – ensured they all got nice jobs in a bank or in insurance or something equally easy on the brain.

'Look,' I said, 'this is a stag weekend in Spain. The possibilities are endless. Even if it's something relatively harmless you have to do something, right?'

Silence.

'Come on lads, it won't be that bad, and, when he looks back on it he'll have a good laugh. He'll be able to tell the "Did I ever tell you what these fellas did to me on my stag weekend?" story while drinking pints after rugby matches. And I guarantee you he'll respect you more.'

'You think?'

'Yeah. I'm positive. Trust me, I've been around the block a bit—'

'More than once, I reckon,' said Diarmuid.

'Haw haw haw,' guffawed Kyle. That was an irritating laugh.

'Good one, Diarmuid,' I said, shooting him a look

which told him I was going to give him at least a Chinese burn at some stage, 'but the point is I know people. I've met guys like Coleman before, and I'm telling you he'd be disappointed if you didn't do something. Not just disappointed, thoroughly let down, I reckon. You know the lads on his team are going to ask him what delicious caper was played upon him, and if he doesn't have something to tell them he's going to look a right chump.'

'Yeah,' said Kyle, 'that all sounds well and good, but I'm not convinced. If he says he doesn't want a prank then I'm not getting involved.'

'Yeah, me neither,' said Breffni.

'Well, if those two think it's a bad idea then I also think it's a bad idea. No thanks. Keep your tricks to yourself,' said Diarmuid.

'Really?' I said.

'Yeah, really,' said Kyle, and I could tell that some of the groundwork had been undone here. This wasn't good. We needed to stay onside with the lads. 'And don't take this the wrong way,' he said, 'but I'm certainly not going to get involved in anything that someone like you is trying to set up.'

'Someone like me?' I said, thinking that the groundwork could go well and truly out the window, along with Kyle's teeth.

'You know, someone from, like, the inner city, with your kind of accent, "yore a reel Dublinah, reet!",' he said in the worst impersonation of a 'Dublin' accent I ever heard.

'Oh, so you'll take the drugs I get you but because of my accent and where I live you won't entertain my ideas?'

'Well, let's face it, you people are more known for your drug-dealing and shooting each other than for your meaningful contributions to society. You don't hear of people being mugged around where we live but you probably can't walk down your road without having to blast someone or stab them or whatever. As I said, it's nothing personal, that's just the way society has made us.'

'OK, well, you guys know best then,' I said, picking up my drink and standing up. I really wanted to glass him but I wouldn't have done that in Else's bar and left her with the mess to clean up.

'Damn, that's some good stuff there man,' said Coleman, slapping me on the back and nearly sending me out the front door. He was one strong fucker. I saw him pass the other two wraps over to his mates while I made my excuses and went up to the other end of the bar, seething at Kyle's snobbery.

I'd met people like him before, of course, but a cunt doesn't become any less of a cunt the more often you meet him. I was a bit worried they might say something to Coleman about the prank idea, but, from the way the others took turns going to the jacks to use the stuff I'd got them, it didn't look like they'd said anything to him.

'So, I wanted to ask you about why you left,' said Else, who had just deposited the drinks to the stag chums. I took a good sip of mine and told her all about the reasons why I left and why it had been so hard for me to come back until now.

17

Hatching a plan

'Wow,' Else said when I'd finished, 'no wonder you left so quickly.'

There wasn't too much I could say to that so I ordered another round of mojitos and a couple of shots of whiskey for me and Jimmy. He drummed his fingers on the bar and downed his shot the minute it was put in front of him. 'Twenty,' he said, 'this is fucking hard work.'

'All the drinking in the warm weather? Yeah, I know.'

'You know what I mean. Those lads. Seriously. We are chalk and cheese. They're suburban trendies, I'm an inner-city grifter. They say "like" all the time, and I hate people who say "like" all the time. And that Diarmuid one is stupider than Dave and Pete combined. I don't know if I can cope with a whole weekend of them.'

'Yeah, I know what you mean, but what if we didn't have to spend all weekend with them?'

'Go on . . .'

'Well, I was down there talking to them while Coleman was in powdering his nose, and it turns out they're not planning any kind of stag-party prank.'

'Really? Why not?'

'They say he wouldn't like it because it wouldn't be becoming to treat someone who plays rugby for Blackrock in that way.'

'Ha ha, you fucking slay me, Twenty.'

'I'm serious.'

'Get . . . to . . . fuck.'

'Honestly, what a pack of fannies they are.'

'He does seem like that kind of humourless twat, in fairness. So, what are you thinking?'

'OK, when I heard that, my little brain went "click", which is quite impressive when you consider how much we've had to drink today. I told them, as a man of great experience, that Coleman might say he doesn't want any stag pranks played on him but that ultimately he'd be disappointed if they didn't do something.'

'And?'

'I was thinking that if we get them to play some kind of trick on him, something that makes him look a bit stupid, he'd lose the rag, and, with a little bit of patented Twenty and Jimmy mischief, we could get him to ditch them and then have him to ourselves. Now, ideally you wouldn't want to inflict that kind of thing on yourself, but, given the fact we have to try and put a stop to this wedding, it'd be much easier for us to get him into trouble without those saps around.'

'You sly old fox.'

'Yes, indeed I am. However, the problem is that they're not for moving. They don't want to get involved. If Coleman says he doesn't want a prank, then nothing is going to happen.'

'Jesus. What are these boys like? The stag-party caper is an integral part of the whole thing. It'd be like having a stag without booze, some kind of fight, someone touching a stripper on the minge then getting beaten up by the bouncers but not feeling a thing because he was so drunk.'

'I know, but they seem quite adamant, and that one Kyle is a proper little cunt. So far up his own arsehole he could eat the shit from between his teeth. He actually said "you people" to me, as if we were some kind of different species.'

'Right, that's it. I say we kill them all. Fuck Tony.'

'I'm really not sure that's the approach we should take.'

'Argh. I've only known these cunts a couple of hours, and I already hate them so, so much.'

'Jaaaaysus, Twenty,' said Coleman on his way to the toilet again, 'this stuff is, like, mega-strong. The first line always makes me want to . . .' he sniffed '. . . lay cable, know what I mean?!'

'Ha ha, well, you enjoy yourself in there,' I said.

'I sure will, better run though. The turtle's tail is sticking out!'

'Look,' I said to Jimmy when Coleman had gone, 'we're going to have to think of something.'

'Yeah, well, I'm fresh out of ideas right now.'

I ordered some more mojitos from Else, shot the breeze with her a bit more, saw Jimmy giving her the classic 'the Bollix' eye and figured we'd better get out of there sooner rather than later. Once he gets his eye on a lady he's almost impossible to shift. It doesn't matter if what he has to do will save his life, he just focuses on the prize, and, to be fair to him, he is one charming motherfucker. If I were a girl I know I'd do him.

As it was getting later, it was about nightclub time, so I brought the lads down to Razzamatazz, an enormous nightclub not too far from the beach. It was like a massive old airplane hangar with many different rooms and types of music. The place was packed to the rafters with locals and tourists, all of them shouting and roaring and dancing and drinking.

The Irish boys took to it like ducks to water, flitting about the place, flirting with girls who were more than happy to flirt back. Coleman himself didn't pay too much attention to the tight-bodied, scantily clad young ones, but the others were trying their luck with anything that moved. Diarmuid and Breffni seemed to have some success as I noticed them dancing with some girls then standing there, necks craned at forty-five-degree angles, tongues halfway down the throats of said girls. I found myself a nice dark corner to sit and drink and watch the people throwing shapes on the dance-floor.

There was no sign of Jimmy or Kyle, but, at that

point, I was quite content to sit on my own and just drink and think about how we were going to orchestrate a situation in which we could get Coleman on his own. It took me another two beers to realise I was too drunk to think of anything that might even be a vague possibility. This was not good.

Just then, Jimmy came back over. 'Oh Twenty,' he said with that familiar bollix twinkle in his eye. 'I think we may have found the weak link – the Achilles heel, if you will.'

'Oh yeah?'

'Yeah, I was having a piss and yer bloke Kyle was beside me.'

'He loved your cock, did he?'

'Hah, who wouldn't? But no. I was thinking about smashing his face off the wall but given the sensitive nature of our mission I didn't and actually talked to him instead.'

'Fucking hell,' I said, 'I know how much you dislike talking to people.'

'Right, well, you're not wrong about him being a stuck-up little prick, he could barely disguise the fact he found talking to me as much fun as eating the dangleberries off a homeless person's matted arsehole.'

'I see, but what's your point?'

'It turns out he's not a fan of the wedding.'

'How do you mean?'

'Well, it's not the wedding so much as the bride-to-be. He fucking hates her. Called her a "Crumlin whore" and a "jumped-up knacker".'

'What a charmer he is.'

'Here we were feeling offended that he hated us but we lost sight of the fact that Coleman is marrying Tony's daughter.'

'So, despite the fact that Coleman is his best friend, he can't get past the fact he's not marrying one of his own. He wouldn't care if the girl came from Foxrock, her parents had a nice house and all that, but because Cynthia comes from Crumlin he's against it.'

'Exactly.'

'So, what are you thinking?' I asked.

'What if we tell him what we're up to? That we're here to get the wedding called off and we'll need his help to do it?'

'Isn't that a bit risky? I mean, what if he gets an attack of conscience and tells Coleman? They are best friends, after all. He might also be just a bit pissed and mouthing off. Maybe he doesn't hate her that much.'

'I think that's a risk we're going to have to take. It's not like we have a plethora of options, is it?'

'True enough. Right, let's give it a shot.'

So we tracked down Kyle who was at the bar, standing looking around at the people in the nightclub. I sidled up beside him.

'I hear you're not a fan of Coleman's fiancée,' I said.

'That's putting it mildly,' he said with a sneer. 'I can't stand her. I don't know what he's doing marrying her.'

'Maybe he loves her,' I said.

'What's that got to do with anything? She's a knacker, who looks like a knacker, from a knacker family.'

'I see, well, now is not the time or place, but meet us

tomorrow morning. We've got something that might interest you.'

'What?'

'Not now,' I said. 'We people like to hold our counsel for more appropriate moments. Let's just say it has something to do with the "knacker" your friend is about to marry.'

I told him where we'd be at eleven in the morning and left it up to him. I hoped he remembered, that the booze and the drugs didn't render his memory as useless as one of those 'Let's all turn our lights off for an hour' things that they do to try and save the planet.

At about 4 a.m., I looked at Jimmy and made the archetypal 'Fuck this for a game of soldiers, I've had so much to drink my heart is sloshing in my chest and I'm fucking wrecked' face. It had been a long day, and he didn't need telling twice. After reminding Kyle about our get-together and a brief conversation with Coleman who was insistent, jaw clenched, that I get him more of that 'rooty-tooty' for the following night, we headed for the exit and grabbed a taxi back to the hotel.

On the way, I realised the mobile phone I'd bought was ringing, and I have a vague recollection of talking to a very excited-sounding Dirty Dave, who was telling me that at last he'd finally met someone who understood him and who was more beautiful than he could possibly have imagined. I hung up midway through his inane ramblings, and the last thing I remember is the fountain in the middle of Passeig de Gràcia and Gran Vía which was close enough to the hotel for the blackout to take over fully.

Saturday

18

Great enormous pain

You would think that after many years of drinking lots and lots of delicious alcohol that you would, in some small way, get used to the hangovers. Not true. There was a time one summer many years ago when I thought I'd cracked it. I was living in Barcelona at that time, now that I think of it. It was a carefree summer, with little or no work to trouble me, and I found myself drinking a lot and starting much earlier in the day. I certainly built up a resistance to the booze, meaning I had to drink more to get drunk, but that was good fun in itself. I would get up, wander down to the beach, passing by a supermarket on the way. I'd pick up some cans of beer, or a bottle of Cava, or two bottles of Cava, and I would lie on the beach and smoke and drink while reading detective novels which were my brain food back then.

Let me tell you something: there really is nothing like sitting on the shore in the early evening with the water lapping up to your waist, reading Joseph Wambaugh, smoking a big fat joint and swigging from a bottle of Cava wrapped in a brown paper bag. I'll admit, it's certainly not classy, but I guarantee you that when my life flashes before my eyes that is going to be right up there with the most vivid memories.

Anyway, there was this one night when I got really, really, really drunk, in Else's bar now that I think about it. I think I popped in for a mojito or two to quench my thirst at around 4 p.m. At 2 a.m. I was still there, having progressed from mojitos to Havana Club and coke to Hendrick's Gin and tonic with a slice of orange in it. I spent my time talking to strangers, falling off stools, being quite loud, and I have a vague memory of inviting some lady walking a dog into the bar and then going back inside, picking up Rosa and bringing her outside to introduce her to my new friend and her hound. The lady and dog enjoyed a drink or two, and, after that, I don't really remember too much. Else told me the next day that I was there until 3.30 a.m. before staggering off in the general direction of home.

I woke the next morning with my legs on the couch and my head on the ground, and it took me some time to get my bearings. At first I thought I'd been run over (what else would explain being upside down?) but when I remembered I'd been out drinking I braced myself for the onset of the pain. Almost like when you really hurt yourself and at first there's no pain but then it hits you. But it never came.

'Aha,' I thought, 'I know what this is. I'm still so fucking pickled that the hangover hasn't even begun yet', and all day I waited for it to get me but it never did. Sure, I was a little more loose of bowel than usual, but that was easy to cope with. The hangover never happened. And I had been drunker than I can ever not remember being.

Well, I was chuffed, as you might imagine, thinking that not only had I built up a resistance to the hooch, which could always be countered by simply drinking more, I had built up a resistance to hangovers, which was a far superior achievement altogether. I spent the rest of the day looking forward to a life without dry mouth, sickly stomach, headaches, squirty arse, aching limbs, heart palpitations and a reluctance to eat because everything seemed so dry and tasteless and sure to make me vomit.

To celebrate, I went out that day and got absolutely shit-faced, and the next day I woke up and thought I was going to die as I had obviously been poisoned and somehow violated by a dinosaur. It was the kind of hangover that would make a man truly mean it as he groaned 'I'm never drinking again.' Well, for a few hours at least.

So it was with much fondness that I recalled that wonderful, blissful day when I woke up on the Saturday morning feeling like a bag of leper's shit. I reached for the bottle of water I hoped was beside my bed and found nothing. My mouth felt like it had grown a coat of badger's fur so I had to get up and make my way to the bathroom where I stuck my head under the tap and drank greedily. They say you're not supposed to drink the tap water, but there are Africans drinking out of dirty puddles so in comparison this was probably as pure as pure could be. As I lapped at the water, like a Labrador licking peanut butter from his owner's balls, I became aware of the phone in the bedroom ringing. It had to be Jimmy or the other two, so I ignored it until it stopped.

I wandered back into the bedroom, opened the curtains, wincing as the sunlight burnt my eyes, and lay back on the bed. I scrabbled around for the remote control and put on BBC World News to try and distract me from the horrors I was in. The phone rang again, and, sighing deeply, I picked it up.

'What?' I croaked.

'What indeed,' said Tony Furriskey.

'Ah . . . Tony. How's it going?'

'Oh, I'm fine, Twenty, in grand form. In fact, I'm in such good form that I'm willin' to overlook the fact yeh didn't pick up on the first fuckin' ring.'

'Well . . . yeah . . . I was—'

'In the bathroom. I know.'

'How do—'

'Don't worry about how. How is for Red Indians, Twenty, not blokes from the South Circular Road. Anyway, do yeh wanna know why I'm in such good form?'

'Sure.'

'It's because me old pals Twenty and Jimmy are out in Barcelona with me soon to be ex-soon-to-be-son-in-law, and I know that they're goin' to have good news for me when they arrive back in Dublin. Isn't that right?'

'Yeah, no problem. Excuse me just a sec, Tony,' I said,

holding my hand over the mouthpiece before vomiting into the bin beside the bed. I wiped my mouth and came back to the phone. 'We've got it all under control. Christ, he's one pain in the fucking hole though.'

'Yeh do not need to tell me this, Twenty. Anyway, just thought I'd call to give a bit of encouragement, not that I think yeh'll need it. I'm quite sure yiz're well aware of how very pleased I'll be when yiz pull this off.'

'You're too kind, Tony.'

'Always been my trouble, that.'

'Yeah, I often hear people say that about you.'

'Yeh should be careful who yeh listen to. Anyway, I hope it all goes well out there. It'd be terrible for a man to come home from his holidays and find, let's say, his beloved dog shot in the back of the head, wouldn't it?'

'That it would,' I said, trying not to react. I wanted to tell Tony if he went anywhere near Bastardface I'd fucking kill him and I didn't give a fuck who he was. However, that would have been counter-productive with me here and Bastardface back at home.

'Right so, I'll leave yeh to it. Woof-woof, Twenty.'

And with that he hung up. Not even a goodbye, ignorant old cunt. I felt my heart racing in my chest at the thought he might shoot my dog. As if threatening you with your own death wasn't pressure enough, anyone who'd let you know they'd kill your dog first was just pure scum. Bastardface was as tough as they come but even he couldn't do much about a bullet to the back of the head. I vomited into the bin again. I necked a few painkillers and jumped in the shower, hoping the jets of water would help. They simply made me wet. I got dressed and rang Jimmy's room.

'What?' he said.

'We've got to meet Kyle. Come on.'

'Fuck off. I'm dying.'

'Fuck you, Jimmy. You got me out of bed the other morning, now it's your turn to be on the end of the irritating phone call. Meet me downstairs in fifteen minutes.'

I wandered down to the lobby and drank a coffee without hocking up any phlegm into it. Maybe this was going to be a good day.

Jimmy came down later, his bloodshot eyes well covered by his shades, but I could tell from the tiny beads of sweat that dotted his forehead that he was suffering. I was sure if you sponged it off and squeezed it into a glass you'd have the most potent drink known to man.

We walked in silence to the bar where we'd arranged to meet Kyle. It was a little café on the corner of Rambla de Catalunya and c/Mallorca which served fantastic hotdogs. I needed some food to settle my stomach and a beer to settle my headache. Jimmy just drank beer. A short while later, Kyle arrived, looking none the worse for wear. He'd been out all night drinking and snorting coke yet he looked like he'd had an early night and eighteen hours' sleep. The joys of youth. I felt a little jealous for a moment, not of Kyle himself, because he was obviously a twat, but of his tender years.

'Good morning,' he said. 'You look rough.'

'Yesterday was a long day. And night,' I said. 'Want something?'

'Sure. I'll have a beer.' At least he wasn't too much of a fanny not to have a pre-noon beer. When the beer arrived, we got down to business.

'So, what's your problem with Coleman's fiancée then?' I said.

'It's not that she's not a nice-looking girl, because she is, but she's just so . . . like . . . common.'

'Common?'

'Yeah, I mean, she's a bit of a knacker, you know? She comes from Crumlin or Rialto or something, and, while it might be, like, southside and preferable to northside, it's still scummy.'

'You have a problem with people from Crumlin or Rialto?' growled Jimmy, his hangover making his voice about two octaves deeper. It was like the question came from the movie-trailers guy but with much more menace. I gave him a little kick under the table. We needed Kyle onside. Any reaction to his snobbery would have to wait.

'Look,' said Kyle, 'I've got no problem with anyone from Crumlin or any of those kind of council-house places as long as they're not going to marry my best friend. Because then I don't have to have anything to do with them.'

'Apart from get your drugs off them?'

'Haw haw haw, yeah. Look, Coleman can do better than her. And I hear her dad is some kind of layabout, doesn't even have a real job. There are loads of girls from the right part of town – and with, like, the right kind of parents – who Coleman could pull any time he wanted. He plays rugby for Blackrock, f.f.s.'

He actually said 'f.f.s.' I wanted to throttle him.

'OK, hypothetically speaking, what if the wedding was called off?' I asked. 'Would that be a good thing, in your opinion?'

'That would be totally sick, to be honest.'

'Sick? I thought you would want it to be called off.'

'Yeah, I do. "Sick" means good, like.'

'Young-people-speak makes my head hurt,' said Jimmy. 'Why can't something just be good if it's good. Sick is not good, sick is vomity and stinking.'

'So, if we were to tell you,' I said, 'that there is somebody who shares in your belief that it would be better if this wedding didn't take place, what would you say?'

'I'd say whoever that is has the right idea.'

'And would you be willing to help out people who might be charged with making sure it doesn't happen?'

'Well, I dunno . . .'

'Do you want him to marry her or not?'

'No.'

'Right, so do you want to do something about it, or do you want to sit there and moan and bleat like a blogger who talks a lot but get him out from behind his keyboard and he does fuck all?'

'I suppose . . .'

'Even if it meant going against your best friend? Because that's what it's going to take.'

'How do I know I can trust you guys? You could be winding me up or something.'

'Look Ryle, or whatever your name is,' said Jimmy, 'I like a good wind-up as much as the next man, but I can tell you I wouldn't get out of bed with a hangover like this to play a trick on some cunt I just met.'

'He's right, Kyle. Here's the thing: you hate us, we hate you, but like it or not we have something in common. Unless we actually work together, much as it pains us – and believe me I'm in a lot of pain right now – none of us are going to be happy. So, will you do it?'

He pondered for a few moments. 'All right. But on one condition.'

'What's that?'

'That Coleman never finds out I was involved in this. I don't want him to marry her, but I don't want to lose him as a friend.'

'You have our word on that. Right, Jimmy?'

'Right,' said Jimmy.

'OK then,' he said, still a bit cautious. 'So what do you need from me?'

'We need to play a prank on Coleman so foul and disgusting that he dumps you lot and goes off on his own. Then me and Jimmy swoop in, get him fucked up and arrange for some incriminating pictures to find their way back home which will make his bride-to-be call the whole thing off.'

'How sneaky. But how can I help?'

'You need to help us convince the other two that taking part in a prank would be a good idea. There's a tapas bar on the corner of c/Consell de Cent and c/Bruc called Don Tapas. Be there at six. We'll just happen to pass by, and we'll take it from there.'

'OK, cool. But, like, nobody can ever know I've helped

you, and you should know Coleman is a serious drinker. You're going to have a long night ahead of you.'

'I think we're more than capable of keeping up,' I said with what turned out to be rather misplaced confidence. We finished our beers, paid the bill and left the café. Kyle promised to be at the tapas place on time. Jimmy wanted to go and drop pennies off the top of the Sagrada Familia, so I arranged to meet him back at the hotel. In the meantime, I had some thinking to do.

19

An unexpected meeting

I figured another beer was in order as the first one hadn't quite cured me. I went as far as Passeig de Gràcia, where I sat up at the counter in a big tapas place, filled with tourists, ordered a large beer and thought about what it was we were going to do to get Coleman pissed off enough with his mates that he'd go off without them. That would leave him in the clutches of Jimmy and myself, and then it would be easy to get him properly wrecked.

It occurred to me I'd better buy a camera too. I'd forgotten to bring mine with me, and the crappy quality on the cheap mobile I'd bought wouldn't be nearly good enough. Given that there was so much riding on this thing it'd be better to spend a few quid on something that took pictures that didn't look like the lens had been smeared with a goat's afterbirth.

I sat, ate, drank and just watched people for a while. It really is an entertaining thing to do. The couple on holidays who are obviously in a complete grump with each other and neither of them is giving an inch so they sit and eat in near silence, shrugging at each other occasionally; the elderly couple in comfortable silence; the guy just dropping in for a quick lunch before heading back to work – the variety of people was always interesting. If you watch long enough you can sometimes get a good insight into the human condition. Other times you realise you're sitting there slack-jawed and drooling slightly because you're hungover like a cunt.

And so, when I felt my own spittle hit my knee, I realised I'd been staring at a man and his girlfriend for rather too long and I was setting myself for a barrage of angry Catalan unless I moved on. I paid the bill and strolled down the street, lost in my thoughts a bit. I was thoroughly enjoying the sensation of being warm, the wind blowing up my shorts and giving my goolies a good airing, the flippity-flop of my flip-flops as they flip-flopped along. How nice it all was. Until a hand grabbed me by the shoulder. I spun around, my lightning-fast ninja reflexes kicking in, ready to face my attacker, whoever it might be.

'Hi!' said Dirty Dave.

'Oh, you. I thought it might have been someone else,' I said, looking around suspiciously anyway.

'Twenty, this is Gloria,' he said, pointing at the person beside him. I craned my neck to look upwards, and there was a lady in a dress. And what a lady. 'Amazonian' was the first word that came into my head.

'Hello, Gloria,' I said, holding out my hand to shake.

'Hola!' she said before grabbing me by both shoulders and planting a kiss on each cheek. Jesus Christ, this was some strong lady. Oh shit, this was no lady. Oh shit.

'We met up at the Camp Nou last night,' said Dave. 'I went up to see the stadium, but it was all closed—'

'I told you it would be.'

'Yeah, well, Anyway, I had a walk around the outside of the stadium. It's massive! Jesus, Tolka Park it ain't! Then I walked around it the other way because I was feeling a bit dizzy. I stopped for a couple of beers and a pizza, and then when I was trying to find a taxi I met Gloria on the road and offered her a lift back into town. Twenty, it's amazing. We just have this connection, you know?'

'Erm, I suppose so,' I said, looking at Gloria, who was doing her best to follow the conversation.

'We stayed up all night talking and talking. Her English is not good, and my Spanish is not as good as that, but when you meet the right person you don't need anything as mundane as language. So much of how we communicate is non-verbal, isn't it? Body language, pointing, drawing pictures of things on napkins.'

'Right . . .'

'I think she's "the one",' he whispered to me. 'Last year, when I realised I was never going to find true love and I thought about killing myself I don't mind telling you it was the lowest I'd ever been in my life. Worse than my tortured artist Emo period even. But then I just accepted it and got on with life. Now though, this is like a wonderful gift from the heavens. A beautiful woman, and she really likes me, Twenty. She really likes me.'

Gloria fluttered her eyelashes and rummaged around in her handbag. I couldn't take my eyes off her enormous hands.

'Gloria, excuse us just a moment, por favor?'

'Oh, si, si.'

I took Dave a little bit down the street. 'Erm, are you sure she's "the one", Dave? You know what they say about holiday romances . . .'

'No doubt about it, Twenty. You just know, isn't that the way it goes? It's like your guttural instincts telling you this is your perfect mate. And that's what's happening.'

'And you stayed up all night, just talking?'

'Well,' he blushed, 'I did Frenchie the gob off her for a while, but we're taking it slow. It'll be special that way.'

'Oh, it'll be special all right—'

'I knew you'd be happy for me!' he grinned, his stupid little face lit up with absolute pleasure. I didn't have the heart to tell him. I just couldn't. How was he to know that the area close to the stadium was where transvestite streetwalkers hung out? Anyway, I didn't have the time or the energy to deal with this. I had to keep my focus on Coleman and the fact that Tony Furriskey was going to kill me, Jimmy and Bastardface if I didn't sort this out. That he would probably, out of some misguided notion of friendship, do it quickly instead of in his usual protracted and very painful way was of no real comfort to me.

'OK, well, you have fun. I've got to get going.'

We wandered back up the street where Gloria was waiting, and I could see the question in her eyes as we came back. 'Did you tell you him, you pig?' it said.

'Nice to meet you, Gordon,' I said.

'Gloria, Twenty,' said Dave.

'Sorry, silly me. Nice to meet you, Gloria.' I grabbed one of those giant hands and gave it a good shake, making sure I didn't break eye contact with her. She knew I knew. I knew she knew I knew. Dave didn't know. Which was probably just as well. He was going to find out at some stage anyway – if it was to be as he was trying to insert his mickey into Gloria's Jap's eye then so be it.

I bid them both farewell, shaking my head at Dave's uncanny ability to get mixed up in things like this, and made my way to the camera shop. For a moment, I got the sense that somebody was watching me, but I figured it was just the hangover. After buying a digital camera there were still hours to go before I'd arranged to meet Jimmy, and I still had to think of a joke they could play on Coleman. Whenever I was in Barcelona and I needed to do some thinking, there was only one place for it.

Tibidabo is a mountain overlooking the city. There's a church, an amusement park (with some of the rides looking as if they date back to when dinosaurs first thought of amusement parks), an observatory and the telecommunications tower you can see from nearly everywhere in Barcelona. I took a taxi up to the end of the tram line. I could have taken the tram itself, but it was always full of tourists. When I got out, I made my way over to a bar called the Mirablau. It was a trendy spot with a nightclub, and at night it was always packed to the rafters. In the daytime though, especially in the intense heat of the summer, it was generally quiet. The best thing about this bar was the incredible view it gave you over the city. You could sit at a large window and see most of Barcelona spread out in front of you. The Olympic towers, the incredible surreal shapes of the Sagrada Familia, the new Torre Agbar, which, in the daytime looked like a giant tampon applicator but at night-time was lit up with the most amazing colours, making it look like a giant, fluorescent tampon applicator. You could see down to the cable car bringing people from the port over to Montjuïc, the green strip of the Ramblas, and cruise ships coming and going as the Mediterranean spread out like a shimmering blue blanket on the horizon. You could almost feel the city throb with activity. But from up here it was silent, quiet and just rather wonderful.

I sat up on a stool at the window, ordered a mojito and snapped a few pictures of the incredible view. There was the very faintest of breezes, probably because of the height, and I sat for a while just watching the planes arriving at Barcelona Airport. From where I was sitting they seemed to skim over the top of Montjuïc, and I could follow them practically all the way to the runway. Every two minutes or so, one would land, a non-stop stream of people arriving from all over the world.

I ordered another drink and began to think about what sort of prank I could get the lads to pull on Coleman that would make him so angry, so outraged, that he'd ditch them, playing perfectly into our hands. The problem was that most of these things relied on the groom to be absolutely shit-faced so you could pull them off. It's very hard to shave off his eyebrows when he's stone-cold sober. You can't really strip him naked and handcuff him to a lamp-post after just a couple of pints. It is just not possible to write 'cockface' on his forehead in permanent marker and draw mickeys and balls on his cheeks while he's conscious. And we needed to make this happen relatively early in the night so we could then bring him out and get him wasted to the point where we could then take advantage of it. We could get him a stripper of some kind, but, really, what would be so outrageous about that?

I was struggling a bit, I have to say, until the couple next to me ordered a couple of B52s from the waiter. It didn't quite register with me until I saw them brought to the table: the dark body, the Baileys head on the top of the glass. That was it! B52s! Talk about a flash of inspiration. Satisfied I had the perfect prank for all concerned, I relaxed, sipped my mojito and looked out over the city. There was a big night ahead.

20

Convincing

'You want us to what?' said Diarmuid.

'You heard me,' I said, Jimmy sitting next to me. We were sitting outside the tapas bar on the corner of c/Consell de Cent, and the boys were uneasy. When they told Coleman they were leaving him in the hotel he'd become a bit suspicious, warning them they had better not be planning any jokes or 'high jinks'. They assured him they were just going out to make some arrangements for the night ahead, which is what Kyle had told the other two. Then they just happened to bump into us. What a coincidence. Coleman, with a nose full of crusty coke-powered snot, was happy enough to laze around in his bedroom, readying himself to do it all over again.

'No way,' said Diarmuid. 'There's a line, right, and if you cross that line then the line is crossed, you know?'

'I'm not sure I do,' I said.

'What he's saying is that this is pretty disgusting, and Coleman already said he doesn't want anything like this,' said Breffni.

'Yeah,' said Diarmuid, 'why do we have do anything at all?'

'What the fuck is wrong with you lads?' said Jimmy.

'What do you mean?'

'How old are you?'

'I'm twenty-four, he's twenty-four, he's twenty-five. Why?'

'Because you're acting like a pack of uptight seventy-year-olds. Your twenties are the time when you can do all kinds of mad stuff. You have the youthful energy, the lack of experience, the trouble distinguishing between good ideas and bad ones – and you lot are like prissy old women. You know what I was doing in my twenties? I was drinking, smoking, taking drugs, having sex with as many girls as possible, doing stupid things like stealing traffic cones, smashing things, having "Who Can Headbutt the Wall Hardest" competitions, vomiting in girls' handbags, breaking and entering, shoplifting, grifting, losing loads of money gambling one night, winning it back the next, getting into fights, jumping off things, committing acts of genocide, smuggling, muling, robbing cars to order, dancing in chains in Howard Jones videos, cutting off people's fingers as a warning at being late with repayments made to loan sharks, handing out cigarettes to kids and pocketing cash from tobacco companies for doing it, absconding with champion racehorses, pledging hundreds of thousands of pounds to Live Aid and never paying it, taking the ferry to Holyhead and back so we could keep drinking, eating dead jellyfish for a bet, identifying rogue Arab terrorists and sending the information to Mossad who would kill them in the most outrageously painful ways you can possibly think of, punching owls in the face and, above all else, playing jokes on my mates.'

'What kind of jokes?'

'Well, there was the time – remember this one, Twenty? – when I kept ringing up Stinking Pete, pretending to be a doctor from the Mater Hospital to tell him his parents were dead, having been crushed in a horrific car crash. Eventually he copped on and didn't believe us, and then when we cut the brakes on his parents' car and they did actually get crushed to death when they slammed into a wall, he told the real doctor to fuck off, and their corpses lay unclaimed for days.'

'Ha ha ha,' I said, 'good times.'

'Jesus Christ,' said Kyle.

'Look,' said Jimmy, 'nobody's saying you have to cause the harrowing death of his parents, right?'

'I suppose so . . .,' said Breffni.

'And what we've suggested to you is nothing at all compared to that, right?'

'Yeah, but still—'

'Come on lads,' said Kyle, speaking for the first time. 'They have a point. Are we men or what, like? This is the only time Coleman is getting married. It would be wrong of us, as lads, not to do something.'

'I hear what you're saying,' said Diarmuid, 'but this is, a bit, you know . . .'

'No buts. And it's unique, right? Have you ever heard of anyone doing this on a stag weekend?'

'No,' said Diarmuid, 'and my brother's cousin's mate was on a stag there last year and did this thing to the groom where they got him to sexually assault a bargirl in a toilet and he went to prison for eight years!'

'Breff, come on. How awful would it be to sit around when we're older and have regrets? Why didn't we do that one thing? We've got to grasp the day.'

'But he'll be so angry. And yesterday you were totally opposed to doing anything at all. Why have you changed your mind?'

'I just had time to think about it. We're all best friends, right?'

'Right,' said Breffni.

'And friends are supposed to do their best for each other. If he comes back and doesn't have a cool story to tell, won't we, like, have failed him?'

'I suppose, but he's definitely going to be angry,' said Diarmuid.

'Hey, even if he is, he's got our own stag nights to get his revenge. And ask yourself this: do you think if we said we didn't want pranks on our stag nights that it would stop him?'

'You have a good point there,' said Diarmuid. 'OK, I'm in!'

'Breff?'

'All right then,' Breffni said, 'but I'm a bit worried

about it all the same.'

'Three amigos!' said Kyle, holding out his fist, which the others bumped with theirs.

'There you go then,' I said, still cringing at the 'three amigos' line. 'Honestly, this is going to be brilliant. And afterwards he's going to have a great story to tell the rest of the lads on his rugby team, right? Even now, from time to time, Stinking Pete will have a good old laugh at the thought of his parents' bodies lying in the mortuary for days until a policeman actually came to the door to tell him they really were dead. In ten years' time you'll all be sitting in a bar somewhere, drinking pints and talking loudly, like your kind do, and someone will mention that great trick in Barcelona, and, by God, your braying laughter will have decent people wincing and covering their ears.'

'Well, when you put it like that . . . How are we going to do it though? It's a bit messy,' said Kyle.

'It's easy,' I said, 'you just need to go to the pharmacy and pick up a couple of things. I've written them down on this piece of paper and spelt them out phonetically so you can pronounce them properly. Before you go out tonight, fill them up and bring them with you. I'll give you the nod a bit later, you can unleash the pranky goodness, and it'll all go perfectly. I promise. It'll be awesome. Right, Jimmy?'

'Oh yeah. This is so good I wish I'd thought of it myself and done it to my own mates.'

'OK then. And you're sure this will have the required effect?' asked Kyle, knowingly.

'It will, no doubt about it.'

So off they went to collect the bits and pieces they'd need for later that night.

'Fucking hell, those lads are painfully dull. When did the youth of today become such a pack of toadying, insufferable little cunts?' said Jimmy.

'I think it happened as soon as we reached something approaching middle age.' I replied, continuing, 'I got a phone call from Tony this morning.'

'Oh, checking in, was he?'

'Something like that. He also threatened to kill Bastardface if things didn't go well.'

'Jesus. It's one thing killing people, but killing someone's dog before you kill them . . . That's snake-belly low. What a nasty old bollocks he is.'

'Ooooh, speaking of bollocks and such, I ran into Dave earlier.'

'So?'

'Well, turns out he met someone out and about last night.'

'A girl?'

'Erm . . . in a way, yes.'

'In a way?'

'I'm not going to explain. Let me phone the fucker up, and let's go meet him.'

So I rang Dave, discovered he was in a little restaurant close by, and we wandered down to meet him. On the way, we stopped in at their pension to look for Stinking Pete, but he wasn't in his room. I figured he'd just gone to the beach for a swim or to have a look around the city. Not to worry, we'd catch up with him later on if we needed him.

We arrived at the restaurant to find Dave and his new love sitting gazing at each other like a pair of smitten teenagers. If they were a pair of dogs, this would be a perfect *Lady and the Tramp* spaghetti moment, even though they were sharing a paella. Not easy to do that sucky thing on a grain of rice. They didn't even see us as we came to the table.

'Good afternoon,' said Jimmy, pulling up a chair.

'Oh, hi Jimmy,' said Dave. 'Gloria, this . . . is . . . my . . . amigo . . . Jimmy.'

'Hola Himmy.'

'Jimmy.'

'Himmy.'

'Jimmy.'

'Himmy'

'Juh—'

'Huh—'

'Juh-juh-Jimmy.'

'Huh-huh-himmy!'

'Never mind. So, how're things, Dave? You've obviously found a real cracker here.'

'Oh yeah. I don't think I've ever felt like this before.'

'What about Gobnait Riordan?'

'That was nothing compared to this.'

'But you stalked her for three-and-a-half years, ignored court orders and spent time in jail, eventually forcing her to move to New Zealand to get away from you.'

'Yeah, but—'

'And then you went to New Zealand, and you drove her so mad she jumped off a mountain and killed herself.'

'This is better.'

'So, Gloria, how do you like my friend Da . . .,' Jimmy stopped, seeing her properly for the first time. He looked at me, raised an eyebrow quizzically and did that 'What the fuck?!' expression, to which I could only smirk in reply. He shook his head slightly. Again, I could see Gloria get nervous because she knew we knew what Dave didn't.

'Well, I for one am delighted for you, Dave,' I said. 'It's great that you've found someone who can appreciate you for who you are and who you can appreciate for who they are.' As Dave turned in my direction – I was sitting to his left – Jimmy gave Gloria a nudge and made a cupping gesture at his own groin.

'Me too,' said Jimmy, 'I think it's marvellous that you've managed to transcend the language barrier. It must take some balls, right Gloria?'

'Is very nice,' said Gloria, pointing to Dave, not really knowing what we were saying but understanding the context only too well.

'It'd be a crying game if this didn't work out,' I said.

'Warm in here, isn't it?' said Jimmy. 'Although I suppose some like it hot.'

'What are you two on about?' said Dave. 'It's too early in the day for you to be that drunk. You're not making sense. Why won't you just make sense?'

'Ah, just messin' with ya,' said Jimmy. 'C'mon, Twenty, let's leave the love birds to themselves.'

'Yeah, we're like a pair of big hairy gooseberries here. Catch you later, Dave.'

'Yeah. OK,' he said, looking at us suspiciously. He might be more stupid than they come, but he knows the pair of us well enough to know there was something going on. He'd find out soon enough. Anyway, to prepare for the night ahead we had to get a good feed into us, so I brought Jimmy to an old haunt of mine. An Argentinean restaurant where they cook great chunks of meat on a wood-fired grill. It really is something else, and once you've had a steak there you realise why Argentinean meat is not allowed in Ireland. It's because the moment people tasted Argie steaks they'd realise that Irish meat was utterly bland and tasteless in comparison. So they make up some stuff about it being 'unsafe' and ban it just to keep our farmers happy. What a fucking swizz.

We ate steaks the size of the plates, and the plates were among the biggest plates I'd ever seen. Washed down with a couple of beers and some chunks of bread to soak up all the blood sploshing around, it was just the kind of soakage you'd need if you were going out knowing you had to drink, like Lionel Richie, all night long.

21

Diversions

I got back to the hotel to freshen up, and the girl at reception passed on a message that had been left for me at the front desk. It was from Big Ian, hoping we could get together later for some beers. I made a mental note to call him – he could be handy just to have around. He knew people and places better than I did. There was a time I knew every bar, speakeasy, private drinking club, mid-morning discotheque and nefarious bodega the town had to offer. God, it had been good back then, and then it had all gone wrong. In just a matter of days, things had turned absolutely upside down. One day, everything is perfect; the next, the routine you've worked so hard to cultivate is gone, dead and buried. And I'm a man who loves routine. I can remember the circumstances leading up to it as if it were yesterday. How just one wrong decision meant I had to leave and face the fact that I couldn't come back for a long, long time, if at all. Just as I was about to relive the whole episode in my head, my mobile rang in my pocket. Which was odd – only the lads had the number, and I'd just left Dave and Jimmy.

'Hello?'

'Twenty, it's me, Stinking Pete.'

'What's up, Pete?'

'I've been kidnapped!'

'You what?'

'Kidnapped, like a baby goat.'

'By who?'

'I don't know, do I?'

'Well, what the fuck happened?'

'See, I was sitting in a little plaça enjoying a lovely aniseedy drink called Patxaran and reading a detective novel about some stupid idiot and his Polish friend thinking they're all gangster in Dublin but they're not. Anyway, beside me was an elderly English couple, and I couldn't help but overhear their conversation. Turns out the wife is suffering from terminal cancer, and this is the last trip they'll ever take after so many years together.'

'OK.'

'So, there were these Gypsy girls going around the tables begging. Naturally, I told them to fuck right off. "If you're so fucking poor sell one of those gold teeth you keep flashing, you ugly bint," I said. I think she understood. If she didn't, she certainly got the message when I gave her the fingers with both hands and made a face at her. Anyway, the elderly woman had left a mobile phone and her purse on the table. So the Gypsy girl went over begging, trying to get them to buy a newspaper she was holding, right? But what she did was hold the newspaper over the purse and phone with one hand and, like a sneaky thieving harridan, proceeded to take the valuables with the other. Of course, the couple didn't see it.'

'Right . . .'

'But I saw it. So I got the stuff back for them. I stood up, the girl tried to make an escape by scuttling along like a dirty little hairy-lipped penguin, so I booted her right up the fucking hole, sent her flying, gave her a couple of kicks in the head and took the stuff back. It just got me mad, Twenty. You can't go around robbing people, you can't go around robbing old people, and you certainly can't go around robbing old people who have spent their whole lives together when one of them is about to die soon. It's just wrong.'

'Fair fucking play to you, Pete. I didn't think you had it in you.'

'Yeah, well, now you know. Anyway, I decided I'd better get out of there before someone called the cops. I know they were Gypsies but some pinko-liberal was bound to have some objection to me kicking them about the street.'

'Good thinking.'

'I left the plaça and turned onto a little street. This bloke in a car said "Quick, get in!" So I got in.'

'Why did you get in a car with a complete stranger? Even a kid wouldn't do that.'

'I just thought it was a bit like the movies. That some-

one who approved of my Gypsy-bashing was going to rescue me.'

'You know you don't actually live in a movie?'

'I know. Anyway, the bloke in the car told me he was
going to bring me somewhere safe. Which turned out to be
an apartment somewhere where I am currently being held.'

'Erm, are you sure you've been kidnapped and not just
brought back to someone's place?'

'I'm sure,' he said.

'How so sure?'

'Well, he said, "I'm kidnapping you."'

'But most kidnappers would have the common sense
to check if you had a mobile phone so you couldn't phone
and let people know what had happened,' I said.

'That's the thing,' he said, 'he told me to phone you.
He said he knows you and that if you ever want to see me
alive again you've got to come and meet him.'

'Oh fuck,' I said. This I did not need. I had been hoping to get in and out of town without running in to him,
but obviously I underestimated his desire for revenge. He
was so well connected in Barcelona he probably knew I
was arriving within minutes of booking the tickets. As
Big Ian said, I'm a man of routine. He'd have known
which area I'd stay in, and, after that, it was just a matter
of checking the hotels. He'd had us followed from the airport no doubt. Bollocks.

'Twenty?' said Pete. 'Are you there?'

'Yeah. I'm here. Does he want to speak to me?'

'No, he said that he'd be in touch again but you would
know what all this was about. What's it about, Twenty?'

'It's a long story, Pete,' I said, remembering that day. How good it had been, how much fun I'd been having, how it had all gone wrong when that bottle of the Green Fairy had been produced. I had left, preferring not to deal with the consequences and had, up until now, successfully avoided them. But life drags you in funny directions sometimes, and now I couldn't avoid this confrontation any longer. For Pete's sake I had to face up to it. 'Pete, tell him I'm up to my eyes with something but I will meet him before I leave. I'll get you out of this.'

'OK, Twenty. He said that if you don't he'll make sure you get me back in different parts.'

'Oh Jesus.'

'And that'd be bad, Twenty. Waiting around the airport for one flight is bad enough . . .'

'Hang tight, Pete,' I said. 'I'll sort this out, I promise.'

At that, the phone went dead. Christ, as if there wasn't enough pressure this weekend. So now I had to go through the stuff with Coleman and then sort out the Pete situation.

I went upstairs to the room, half-expecting to open the door and see Tony Furriskey sitting there smacking a closed fist in his palm, just to give me a little reminder. As if I fucking needed it. This whole thing was turning into a bit of a nightmare. If I was the kind of person who believed in signs, I'd be slightly worried that Pete had been kidnapped, Dave appeared to have fallen head over heels for a transvestite, while Jimmy was getting to the point where I could see him ignoring the 'Don't Kill Him' edict, and that would land us thoroughly in the shit.

Rubbing my temples, I could feel a very big headache starting.

We had the night ahead to create some kind of situation whereby we could get a picture of Coleman with another woman. It really was the only kind of evidence that would be sure to have the wedding called off, and even if it didn't, nobody could say we hadn't done our best. It would be entirely up to Tony's daughter to choose to ignore his indiscretion. I glanced at my watch. It was now 9.30 p.m. I needed to get cleaned up and changed and then ready myself for the night ahead, a night which had so much at stake that vampires across town fled in fear without even knowing why.

22

Ronaldo's, but not the Portuguese ponce

Half an hour later, after leaving a message with my mobile number on Big Ian's voicemail, I met Jimmy down in the lobby. He was dressed in faded blue jeans, a white T-shirt with his cigarettes tucked into the arm like a fifties teddy boy and his hair fashionably tousled. He'd just had a shave. This was worrying. This was what Jimmy always did before he did something really bad. He cleaned himself up beforehand to make up for how much he was going to dirty himself later on. I'd have to keep an eye on this. He had that glint in his eye. You know the one we all get from time to time. That 'Oh man, I'm so gonna strangle someone tonight then dump their body underneath a bridge somewhere' glint. The stag lads had gone for dinner earlier. Kyle, apparently, had spent hours researching restaurants via the Internet, and they were now dining at a place called Don Pescado down at the Olympic Port where they served you enormous platters of seafood. On the face of it, this sounds like a very nice thing. The reality is great swathes of shrimp, calamari, shellfish, haddock and other fish are scooped out of a deep fat fryer and then plonked down on your table. The closest I can get to describing the food in Don Pescado is to ask you to imagine what it's like to eat crunchy fish-flavoured scabs. Then imagine the scabs are from a dead hippo's arsehole after he had been bitten by a cobra with serious gum disease. Still, I'm sure it all seemed very 'Med' and haute cuisine to lads whose appreciation of fine dining stretched as far as asking for extra garlic sauce on their kebab in Zaytoon on a Friday night.

I had arranged to meet them at 11 p.m. in a cocktail bar down there, Luigi's, run by an Italian pal of mine and his girlfriend. Before we went down, we decided to try and find Ron's cousin's bar. Ron had given me the address, but the name of the road wasn't familiar to me. I had looked it up on Google Maps earlier on, and so we went down the Ramblas, took a right into the Raval area, down c/Sant Pau, then we took a right and a left, then another right, and there, tucked between a *locutorio* (a place where you can get internet access, with phone cabins to make cheap calls using the various phone cards they sold) and a shop selling only walking sticks was Ronaldo's bar. Not that you'd know it from the outside. According to Ron, as a fiercely proud Catalan and FC Barcelona fan, the owner of the bar took down the sign saying 'Ronaldo's' when the fat Brazilian footballer signed for Real Madrid. It might have been a different Ronaldo, but he wasn't prepared to advertise anything relating to Los Merengues. We pushed the door open and went inside. It was basic: a L-shaped bar with the L at the door end, some rather ancient-looking tapas behind glass cabinets, bright, fluorescent lighting, a couple of round tables and an old TV bolted to the wall, which appeared to be showing something akin to *It's a Knockout*, except this version was dangerous.

The contestants were in these enormous foam suits, with their arms and legs barely sticking out of them, like thalidomide Mary Harneys, standing on podiums in what seemed to be some kind of stable. Then, the host of the show, laughing manically, pulled open a gate at the far end, releasing a very lively and seemingly pissed-off young bull, who charged them, knocking them to the ground with kicks and with his enormous head. From what I could gather, the team who had the last man standing was the one that would win. I'd forgotten how mental Spanish TV was.

Behind the bar was a swarthy, hairy man wearing a khaki shirt which had sweat stains at the armpits and all across the back. He had a pungent cigarette hanging from his lips and the sort of frown that would scare babies. The resemblance to Ron was uncanny.

'Hola,' I said, 'dos cervezas, por favor.'

He plonked two bottles of Estrella in front of us. I continued to speak to him in Spanish.

'We're from Dublin, we drink in Ron's bar. Your cousin?'

'Oh, you know Ron. You should have said so,' he said,

whipping the bottles from in front of us and putting down two fresh ones. 'Those are for tourists. Not that we get many in here.'

'I can't imagine why,' I said.

'So, how is Ron, the son of a bitch?'

'Mean, grumpy and overly hairy.'

'Same as always then. That's good. I keep meaning to go and visit him, but what the fuck do I want to go to Dublin for? It's cold and wet, and who needs that?'

'You've got me there.'

'Do you want to eat something?' he asked, pointing at the withered and slightly furry things on the counter.

'No, we're fine thanks,' I said.

'Right, let me know when you want another beer. I can't spend all day here chatting,' he said and moved down to the far end of the bar where he smoked and watched the telly, grunting occasionally at a bearded chap who was making comments about the TV. It was just like being in Ron's, except a bit sweatier and with more flies.

'What was all that about?' asked Jimmy.

'He said he should visit Ron but our weather is too shit, and he asked if we wanted any food.'

'Christ. I'd rather eat an AIDS baby's placenta than anything on that counter.'

'When are we due to meet the idiots?'

'Well, Stinking Pete has been kidnapped, and Dave is off with his "girlfriend".'

'Not those idiots, the other idiots.'

'Sorry, force of habit. Eleven o'clock down in Luigi's at the port. Then we get a couple of drinks in, and when he slips off for a piss or to do a line then we get the lads to do their thing. After that, we make it look like they're out of order, play up any kind of fight and then hopefully we can make off with him.'

'Good stuff. Then what?'

'I dunno really, let's play it by ear. We'll have to bring him places with lots of girls, nightclubs, strip clubs and try and egg him on to do something with someone. Then the camera does its work, and we don't end up in a mincer in Rialto somewhere.'

'Cool. Stinking Pete's been kidnapped?'

I explained to him what had happened.

'That's not good,' said Jimmy. 'Will he hurt him?'

'Maybe. I would have said no but the fact that he's waited over thirteen years to get even with me must mean he's lost his mind a bit. I mean, get over it already.'

'Of course, this wouldn't have happened if Pete hadn't booted a Gypsy in the gee.'

'Maybe you could say what he did was grime and punishment.'

'Fuck off, Twenty. This is no time for one of your poxy puns.'

'Fair enough.'

'Well, we have to prioritise things,' said Jimmy. 'First we get what we need to get Tony off our backs, then we rescue Pete, if he's still alive.'

'Sounds reasonable.'

We had another couple of beers in Ronaldo's, bid farewell to the man himself after paying him and leaving him a tip (so much for being looked after) and headed down towards the port. We ambled our way down the Ramblas, across Passeig de Colom, named after Christopher Columbus, down past Barceloneta and a football pitch I used to play on (now a lovely Astroturf instead of the packed sand and dirt it was back in my day) and down to the twin towers, built for the 1992 Olympics.

'You know, a man could get used to this kind of thing,' said Jimmy. 'Warm weather, lots of people about without them being roaring drunk, palm trees, the soothing noise of the ocean.'

'Who are you telling?' I said.

'What a shame that what happened here denied you the chance to come back for so long.'

'Yeah, well, that's life. You either just get on with things or you become a bitter, twisted old curmudgeon.'

'And.'

'What?'

'Not "or": "and". You got on with things and became a bitter, twisted old misanthrope.'

'Curmudgeon.'

'A curmudgeonly misanthrope then.'

'A curmunthrope. That's me.'

'Don't ever change.'

We continued our walk. The air smelt of salt and heat and the fragrance of people out for a Saturday night. We went down the steps to the row of bars and restaurants where the tourists flocked and the bar-owners fleeced the tourists. We had bigger fish than them to fry. And hopefully this one would turn out better than the crap you got in Don Pescado.

23

Italian Jesus

Luigi is an Italian from just outside Milan who came to Barcelona after an incident in a bar after a football match. Despite his Milanese roots he's an ardent Roma supporter, and this didn't go down well with some Inter Ultras one night after the Romans had come to Milan and stolen the points. A sensible man would have said 'OK, I'm going to leave now,' but not Luigi. He'd had a few drinks and wasn't about to take any shit. There were three of them and one of him. As he tells the story, the fight was just about to begin when he asked them to hold on while he took off his shoes. Which he duly did, leaving them rather confused as to why anyone would want to take off their shoes before a fight. Wouldn't your kicks be harder with your shoes on? Anyway, he put his shoes on a table, cracked his neck from left to right, then picked up a glass from the bar and smashed it right into the face of the first guy, who fell to the ground shrieking, and when his mates went to help him up and eventually persuaded him to take his hands away from his face, a jagged shard of glass was embedded in his left eye. Luigi calmly picked up his shoes, left the bar, and the very next day took a train to Barcelona.

He'd been there ever since. He spoke good English but sounded exactly like Super Mario. Well, at least, he did to me. And he had the most unusual line in insults I had ever heard. They generally involved calling you some kind of animal or household item or a combination of both. I hadn't seen him in years, obviously, and I got quite the shock when I caught sight of him behind the bar, his actress girlfriend making mojitos and other cocktails. His black hair was as long as a girl's, and he had it tied in a ponytail.

'Fucking hell,' I said, 'what the fuck has happened to you?'

'Nothing, Irish corn-holder bastard.'

'The hair? The beard?'

'I'm liking it so you can, you know, suck a big cock.'

'Charming as ever. Luigi, this is Jimmy,' I said, making the introductions, 'and this is Vicky,' I said, waving at the mojito-maker behind the bar. She waved and carried on her business.

'Hello Jimmy, sorry for you to have to spend time with this bitchface spoon-monkey.'

'Erm, yeah, he's a cunt all right.'

'So, why you come back to Barcelona?'

'Long story, hippy, but basically it involves that group

of lads sitting over there and a man in Dublin who's going to kill us unless we help him get his daughter's wedding called off.'

'You crazy half-baboon. How you get into these kind of problems?'

'You know me, I try to live the quiet life, but trouble just seems to find me.'

'So, what kind of ridiculous situation is this?'

I explained to Luigi what was going on and what we were planning on doing. He offered whatever help he could and went behind the bar to get us a couple of beers. 'This is going to be one hell of a chore,' said Jimmy.

'Hopefully we can set him up and get what we need early enough.'

'How long do we give it before we kill him?'

'You know we can't kill him.'

'If nobody finds the body he's just a missing person. Tony didn't say anything about not making him a missing person.'

'Well, if his beloved daughter is going to be too upset if he dies, imagine what she would be like if she never knew what happened to him? She'd probably turn into a miserable old spinster, living her life in her wedding dress like a modern-day Miss Havisham.'

'So, Tony's happy because no man ever has sex with his daughter. It's every father's dream!'

'It's a gift you have, you know?'

'What's that?'

'Being able to make murder sound so perfectly reasonable.'

'Each of us is talented in his own way.'

Luigi beckoned me from the bar.

'Here are your two large Perronis, you potato-peeler slutbag.'

'Thanks man. Listen, when I give you the nod can you bring us over a round of B52s? I'll pay you for them but announce they're on the house as a celebration for his wedding.'

'OK, I can do that.'

I brought the beers over to Jimmy, and we went over to the lads at the table.

'So, how was dinner then?' I asked.

'Great, yeah, really top-end stuff,' said a puffed-up Coleman, who gave me the eye to ask if I had a little something for him. I nodded and handed him over a wrap. And another each to Kyle and Breffni. Diarmuid looked on hopefully, but I made him aware he'd have to share with the other two. I had another one but I wanted to keep it spare just in case.

'So, what's the plan for tonight, like?' asked Coleman. 'There's a whole lot of this town that hasn't danced with Darcy-McNeill, and it would a shame to deny them the pleasure, har har!'

'A few cocktails here,' I said, 'then we can head to some of the other bars and clubs. I'm sure the lads here will want to make sure you have a good time.'

'I could have a good time on my own in an empty room.'

'Yeah, once you had a box of Kleenex,' said Jimmy.

'Why would he want to blow his nose to have a good time?' said Diarmuid.

'Christ, Diarmuid,' said Kyle, 'He, like, wouldn't be blowing his nose.'

'Yah,' said Breffni, 'more like his trumpet.'

'But the room was empty he said. And Coleman doesn't even have a trumpet. I know he had a Bontempi organ when we were kids but I don't ever remember a trumpet.'

I looked at Jimmy, who just shrugged. Well used to that kind of stupidity, you see. The bar was quite busy, some Italian disco-house music playing, so it took me a while to hear the phone ringing.

'Hello?' I said.

'He . . . twe . . . wher . . . com . . . for a bee . . . bit lat . . .'

'Hello? I can't really hear you. Hello?'

' . . . ear me now? Smee . . . bi . . . dinner . . .'

'Sorry man, you're breaking up,' and just then the phone went dead.

'Sounds like you got a bit of a Katy there,' said Coleman.

'A Katy?'

'Yeah, a bad line. Har har.'

'Indeed. Excuse me a moment,' I said as the phone started ringing again, 'I'd better go outside and take this.'

I left Jimmy sitting with them while I took the call. It was Big Ian checking in to say he was around later on for a few beers. I told him where we were and said he was more than welcome to join us. He said he had to meet a couple of people but he'd stay in touch and probably hook up with us later. I went back inside to hear them talking about a hilarious incident when, after a rugby-club disco, they'd all driven around in Coleman's Audi and had run over a guy, but it was OK because he didn't die – he was left a brain-damaged quadriplegic so he couldn't identify them.

'Can you believe how lucky that was?' said Coleman as he got up to go to the toilet. 'Back in a mo. Just need a little refresherino.'

'So, you all brought your stuff?' said Jimmy, in a way that made it very clear if they hadn't they'd be improvising right there and then.

'Yeah,' said Kyle, 'and, you know, the more I think about it, the more, like, totally hilarious this is.'

'Yah, it's going to be wicked funny,' said Breffni. 'Like *The Panel* on RTÉ 1, but even more funny, if you can imagine that.'

'Oh yeah, I can imagine that,' I said. 'Luigi, the guy who owns the bar, is going to come over in a while with a tray of B52s. We'll have to wait till Coleman goes to the jacks again, and then we can get things going.'

'Brilliant.'

'Totally, yah.'

'Cool, but I still don't know where the trumpet is.'

I said I was going up to the bar to tell Luigi to be ready to bring the drinks over on my signal, but Jimmy, obviously not wanting to be left alone with the threetards, jumped up and did it for me. It was make-or-break time.

24

Jizz, hmmm?

I was thinking it'd only be a matter of time before Coleman had to piss again or got the goo on him for another line, but I underestimated his ability to talk and the size of his bladder. It must have been like a manatee's stomach. I suppose when you give coke to an egotistical braggart, who already likes nothing better than to wax lyrical about how great he is, you have to expect him to be even more self-obsessed and motor-mouthed. We got to hear about how brilliant he was at rugby and about all the great tries he scored from his very first one in second class in Blackrock College to the last one against some fuckers I can't even remember. But every single try was almost entirely due to his individual brilliance and put Gareth Edwards' try for the Barbarians against the All Blacks to shame.

The other three simply sat around back-slapping and guffawing at the right moments. I'm pretty sure it was a routine they'd been through before and were probably destined to go through for the rest of their lives. Coleman made jokes about 'northsiders', slagged off people who didn't drive nice cars, or who didn't go to poxy nightclubs named after expensive Champagne and generally bored us to fucking tears.

I could feel Jimmy getting really twitchy – he has a very low threshold when it comes to people like this. He either leaves their company abruptly or makes them leave consciousness abruptly. So it was a relief when Coleman eventually got up and headed to the toilet again.

Luigi, being the clever bloke that he is, had already spotted this, and Coleman had barely gone through the toilet doors when the tray of drinks was on the table. 'Here you go, bearded ladle-hole. B52s just like you want.'

'Thanks man. Right, you three, you know what to do.'

I put the drinks around the seats so there was one in front of everyone. There were perfect B52s in the shot glasses, but Coleman's glass was ever so slightly empty. One by one the lads bent over, took out small plastic syringes and squirted a small measure of their own semen into the top of the glass until, like all the others, it was filled right to the top.

'This is gonna be so good,' I said to them. 'Just wait and see. Right, Jimmy?'

'Oh yeah. Seriously. I don't know how anyone could possibly not find this funny. I know if my mates did this to me I'd be almost overwhelmed by their creativity.'

'Tee-hee,' tittered Diarmuid. 'I put two wanks' worth in, and I was thinking about his chick for both of them!'

'Yah, I got a double dose too.'

'Jakers, like, I just did the one.'

'Then you only get one-fifth of the credit for this,' said Diarmuid. 'I'm a much bigger wanker than you.'

'Shhhh, here he is,' said Kyle as Coleman came back to the table. As he sat down again, Luigi made a toast. Holding a B52 of his own, he said, 'These cocktails are on the house. Your friends have told me it's a big wedding for you. Congratulations. As we say in Italy, Brindo a te, cazzo di finocchio irlandese!'

'Down the hatch,' said Kyle.

'Yah, make sure you swallow it all!' said Breffni.

We raised our glasses – there was no clinking though (I wasn't going to risk any kind of splashback) – and we all toasted the groom and drank the B52s.

'Man I love B52s,' said Coleman, smacking his sticky lips together a bit more than one might usually do.

'Yeah, me too,' said Kyle. 'I like their saltiness.'

'Saltiness?'

'Yah, for me though it's the sticky gloopy sensation as it slides down your throat.'

'I cum over all funny when I drink them,' giggled Diarmuid.

'Yah,' tittered Breffni, 'you need some amount of spunk to have more than one.'

'Haw haw haw,' laughed Kyle, 'but they're certainly much nicer than shandies . . . hand-shandies.'

At this point, the three of them were laughing, much

to Coleman's consternation. He didn't like not being in on the joke, whatever it was, and he wasn't so stupid that he didn't suspect that somehow the joke was on him.

'What's going on?' he said.

'Oh, nothing,' said Kyle, 'maybe we should have a look around the port for another bar. One with more seamen.'

'Har har har har. Yah, and we might meet some famous people, like the Three Spooges!'

At this point, they broke down into hysterics, tears streaming down their faces. Coleman was looking really freaked out. He looked at me, and I made a face which let him know I knew there was a joke being played on him but that I disapproved of it entirely. Jimmy also looked suitably unimpressed, shaking his head sadly.

'Right,' yelled Coleman as his mates hooted with glee, 'someone better tell me, like, what the fuck is totally going on here. Pronto.'

'Well,' said Kyle, trying to straighten himself out, 'that B52 you drank—'

'What about it?'

'It wasn't an ordinary B52.'

'What do you mean? You better not have spiked my drink with Special K or crystal meth or something, like.'

'Oh, it's nothing like that,' said Breffni, and they all started laughing again.

'OK, if you don't tell me what's going on I'm going to be totally super-unimpressed. Seriously.'

They were laughing too much to speak though so I thought I'd help out.

'Look, this is probably going to freak you out, but as a

kind of stag-party prank, they added something to your drink.'

'What? Drugs? Mud? Dust? Piss? Oh God! It's piss, isn't it?'

'Nearly.'

'Nearly? What's nearly piss? What are you . . . oh! . . . no! . . . they didn't!'

'They did.' The sheer look of disgust on his face was the highlight of the weekend to that point. 'We tried to stop them, didn't we, Jimmy?'

'Oh yeah,' said Jimmy. 'There's a line you shouldn't cross, and making your mate drink your own spunk is way over that line.'

They had stopped laughing at this stage and began to look at us funny.

'True,' said Luigi, 'I tell those cheese-grater bitches that this is too much but they don't listen.'

'Oh, hold on,' began Breffni, 'Wait just a minute here, it was you—'

'You made me drink your jizz?'

'No. Well, yes, but it wasn't our idea. It was—'

'You scummers. I'd expect that from someone who came from, like Inchicore or Artane or something, but not from you.'

'Coleman, really, it wasn't our idea. It was all their fault,' said Breffni, pointing at me and Jimmy.

'Yeah,' said Diarmuid, 'they made us do it.'

Kyle was staying quiet.

'Hang on,' I said, 'first, we hardly know you lot long enough to make you do anything you don't want to do.

Second, do we look like the kind of people who would make a man drink someone's sperm? If you were to accuse us of being reprobates, petty thieves, occasional administers of violence or mischief-makers then I wouldn't bother arguing for a second. But this? This is just the most disgusting thing I can think of.'

'Exactly,' said Jimmy. 'I mean, what if one of you has AIDS? Now Coleman has it too.'

'Oh, Jesus fucking Christ,' said Coleman.

'I hear them,' said Luigi, 'and I also say, "Don't do this. Is too dirty. Is your friend. This you would only do to your friend if you are toaster-head prick".'

'Fuck, you guys are supposed to be my friends. I invited you on this weekend to celebrate my wedding and have some laughs. Not so you could make me drink your man-custard. What were you thinking?'

'Yeah, what were you thinking?' I said.

'But—'

'Don't give me your buts, Breff. We've been friends since we were four, and now I have a stomach full of your spunk. Oh Christ, I'm not feeling well. How could you let them do this, Kyle?'

Kyle just shrugged.

'Jimmy, I'm gonna take Coleman to the toilet. He probably needs to be sick.'

'Good man, Twenty. You wouldn't desert someone in need, no matter how short a time you've known them. That's a real friend.'

So, as the other three sat there, open-mouthed, no doubt wondering about our complete about-face, I brought Coleman to the jacks.

'Right. If was you, I'd just stick my fingers down my throat and sick that all up.'

'Yeah, I think that's what I'll do.'

'Of course, it will mean that their spunk is in your mouth for a second time, but at least it won't be curdling away in your stomach on top of all that delicious fish from Don Pescado.'

'Bleeeeuuuurrrrgggghhhhh.' He spewed into the sink.

'That's it. Get it all up. Oh, look that squid ring is almost perfectly intact.'

'Bluuuuuuaaaaaaarrrrrghhhhhh.'

'Good man. Hopefully those bits stuck between your teeth are prawn and not lumps of, well, you know.'

'Aaaarrrrraaaaaaaaarrrraaaauuuuuurrrrruuuugggghhhhh.'

He stopped vomiting about five minutes later, but the dry-retching went on for a while. I got him a bottle of water from the bar, and he used that to swoosh around his mouth. And once he began to feel slightly better, the emotions kicked in, starting with amazement.

'I can't believe what they did. I told them I didn't want any jokes played. Jokes are stupid.'

'This was a bit more than a joke, wasn't it? I mean, drawing on your face in permanent marker is one thing, but taking the time to toss off, suck up the stuff into a syringe and then squirt it into someone's drink is another.'

'They're supposed to be my best mates.'

'And they've let you down in a big way. Imagine them

all the way through dinner planning to jizz up your drink. Laughing. Sniggering. Knowing you were going to have a mouthful of their filthy paste.'

'Those assholes . . .'

'They might as well have made you suck each of their cocks in turn. Who does that to a mate?'

'Damn, I'm going to kill them.'

'Would you do something like that to one of them? No way. You might be many things, but you're not a man who makes another man drink his wank wine. Especially not on his stag weekend.'

'Arrrrrgggh,' he roared. Excellent. The anger had kicked in. He went charging out of the toilets and back into the bar where the lads appeared to remonstrating with Jimmy, obviously unhappy that they, the tricksters, had been tricked themselves. They'd get no rise out of Jimmy though. Even when caught red-handed he would infuriatingly deny all knowledge of the incident. This time though, I suspected he was just sitting there letting them rant and not giving a shit, which was probably wrecking their heads.

'You total tossers!' said Coleman when he reached the table. 'You make me sick. In fact, you made me sick. Lots and lots of sick, and you know I hate getting sick.'

'Look, Coleman—,' began Breffni.

'SHUT UP,' he roared. 'I don't want to hear anything from any of you. You are dead to me.'

'It was all their fault!' said Diarmuid pointing at us. He looked close to tears.

'I just dunno,' said Jimmy, 'they're not even man

enough to admit what they did. Instead they try and blame it on somebody else. Tut-tut. Poor show. It really is.'

'He's telling the truth!' said Breffni. 'They came to us with this plan and said you'd like it.'

'Liars! Why would you go along with a stupid plan like that when you barely know these guys? You just got carried away with yourselves, but now you're going to be sorry. Remember who it is that plays rugby for Blackrock. Who has the profile? Who has got more than a thousand friends on Bebo and Facebook? Who can get you into the VIP areas? How would you score chicks if it wasn't for all the ones hanging around trying to score me? Let me tell you now you're going to find life much more difficult without me.'

'But Coleman,' said Diarmuid, 'it really was them! Tell them, Kyle. Tell them.'

'It was our idea, Coleman,' said Kyle, making sure that Coleman would ditch them and be left in our clutches. His commitment to the bigger plan was almost admirable. 'It was all our idea.'

'Well, you can get lost, Kyle. We used to be best buds but not anymore.'

'We still are.'

'No man, we're not. And I rode your mum.'

'What?'

'Yeah. When I was seventeen I rode your mum when I called around one day and you weren't there.'

'My . . . mum? Oh . . .'

'So, you think about that, and it serves you right for what you did to me.'

'But you did that first.'

'Yeah, well, now it doesn't matter. It was pre-emptive revenge. Enjoy the rest of your weekend, you saps. I'm outta here.' And with that he stormed out of the bar.

Diarmuid was openly weeping. Kyle and Breffni were shell-shocked – Kyle obviously having visions of his friend humping his mother. I gave Jimmy the nod, gave a Luigi a stealthy thumbs-up, and we followed Coleman out into the night.

25

Sandy crack

Leaving the bar, we looked left, saw nothing. Looked right, saw nothing. Bollocks. He must have taken off at a canter, and this lad was an athlete. My days of flying up and down a football pitch were long behind me, and the last time I had to run anywhere I ended up in intensive care. Well, I ended up at the end of Ron's bar gulping down some restorative pints, but the point is much the same. We had no choice but to split up and hope for the best. We made an arrangement to meet at a pre-defined bar should either of us find him, and off we went. Jimmy went left, back towards more bars and restaurants. I went right where the path led past a number of bars and up towards the Olympic towers. It being Saturday night, it was busy, and there were people milling about all over the place. I checked in the bars and their terraces as I went past but found no sign of Coleman. I went up the steps, straining to see if I could spot his deftly spiked head, but, again, I was out of luck. I hurried over towards the casino – maybe he'd gone in there. I wandered in, had a look around, but he wasn't. I checked every bar, restaurant, bench and disco, but he had gone – disappeared into the night like an invisible ghost burglar. Bollocks. He could have been anywhere. The night was young, so was he, and he probably had a goo on him for drinking like he'd never had before. Betrayed by his mates he could hop from bar to bar all night long and nobody would ever find him.

So that was it. We were fucked. Without Coleman, we had no way of getting the wedding called off. Without the wedding being called off, we were going to find ourselves on the wrong end of a Tony Furriskey solution. Fucking horse-buggering cunt blisters. I couldn't believe this had gone wrong. This was supposed to be the easy part. Making him fall out with his friends was the tricky bit. Following him and getting him pissed enough to do something stupid was something even Dirty Dave and Stinking Pete could have done. I sighed and wandered down to the beach. I took my flip-flops off and felt the cool sand on my feet as I wandered towards the shore. In the distance I could see various lights of boats drifting around the sea, and I wished I was on one of them. I could just live on a boat for the rest of my days, going from port to port. Then I remembered I don't much like boats since I was almost sexually abused by one as a child. Shit, that wasn't a boat, that was a religion teacher. But still, I couldn't live on a boat. Putting the cat out at night would prove rather too drowny.

I looked up and saw the full moon beaming down, its light refulgent on the water's surface. I sat down, thought about how nice it was, how warm, how beautiful, how I'd like to stay in that moment forever. I drew my knees to my chest, hugged them to me and breathed deeply. I don't mind telling you I was emotional. Wouldn't you be? I didn't cry though. Which is probably just as well, as, if I had, I wouldn't have become aware of the bloke sitting just to my right sobbing heartily.

Yeah, yeah, I thought, you've probably just been dumped or your parents have just been diagnosed with terminal SARS, or something. You're not facing the kind of terrifying and hideous death I am. Why don't you just shut up? He didn't, because I had only thought the words, and his blubbering continued. Frankly, it was getting in the way of my woe, and, as I'm not a man predisposed to melancholia, I felt rather put upon. Why couldn't I have a few minutes of self-indulgent woe without having to listen to someone else's increasingly hysterical weeping? I turned to tell him to shut up or move to a different part of the beach to do his keening and almost believed in God when I recognised the thick-necked, Fahrenheit-stinking presence of Coleman himself. 'Coleman?'

'A-boo-hoo-hoo-hoo,' he wailed.

'Coleman. It's me. Twenty.'

'What . . .' sniff '. . . are you . . .' sniff '. . . doing here?'

'Oh, I came looking for you.'

'How did you know I'd be here?'

'Where else would someone who has been cruelly betrayed by his best friends, living with the shame of drinking a shot glass full of their muck be? It's where everyone comes when they're upset.'

'I am upset. I'm . . . very upset.'

'I would be too.'

'I grew up with these guys. We've been friends forever, and I thought we'd never have this kind of thing happen to us. I mean, I thought they'd do something – it's a stag weekend for God's sake. You have to, but I thought if I kept saying I didn't want any jokes played they'd just take it a bit easy.'

'But they didn't, did they?'

'No,' he sobbed, 'and you know why I kept saying "no pranks"?'

'Why?'

'Because I was scared, man. I was scared they'd tie me to a pole and people would be able to see my peen or they would make me wear a sailor's outfit and I'd look stupid. But I'd rather have been scared than have that happen to me. Oh God, I feel like I've been violated. Our friendships are dead. Oh Kyle, oh Breff, oh Diarmuid. Why? Whyyyyy?'

He started to cry heavily again. I was almost feeling sorry for him. Almost. I couldn't let emotion get in the way though. There was a job to be done, and thankfully the job involved going out on a Saturday night in Barcelona. It certainly wasn't up there with my worst-ever job, cleaning the mallow machine at the Jacob's biscuit factory. In fact, I was quite looking forward to it now.

The realisation that I wasn't doomed to a slow and painful death was such a lift.

'Look,' I said, 'what happened was disgusting and, quite frankly, unforgivable. I can't imagine what it must be like, especially when I think about Dirty Dave.'

'Who's Dirty Dave?'

'He's one of my mates, and he's absolutely rancid. I bet his sperm has lumps of tartar and fingernail dirt in it. So, it could have been worse. Anyway, the point is that this is your stag weekend, and you can't sit on a beach crying, can you?'

'What else am I supposed to do?'

'You can pick yourself up, dust yourself off, dry those eyes, wipe the sand off your arse, and do what most lads do on their stag nights. Get as pissed as a cunt, go to as many bars as possible and end up in a strip club some-where.'

'But I don't want to go drinking on my own. I don't like being on my own.'

'I'm here. And Jimmy's around. We may not know you very well, but we'd be happy to be your stag mates.'

'Really?'

'Yeah, really.'

'OK then,' he sniffled as he stood up. 'You're on then.'

'Good man, and I know just the place to start.'

We walked up the beach for a bit, and almost directly underneath the towers was a place called CDLC. It was a restaurant/bar/nightclub place, and it was very, very trendy. It had those kind of seats like enormous beds, and they served you your food on giant silver platters.

The outside terrace was packed with people finishing their dinners – those crazy Spanish and their late dining. The bouncers on the entrance gave us the once-over, gave Coleman another look, probably due to his crying eyes being all red and swollen, and waved us through. We went down a couple of steps and inside, where there was a large bar to the right, on the left more of those bed-style seats, and in the middle a dance-floor area. There were some steps up to another bar which we headed towards.

'Hey, this place is cool.'

'Yeah, very "now", I believe. Quite the hangout for some of the Barcelona players, you know?'

'Not much of a soccer man, I have to say. I'm a practitioner of the oval arts, like.'

'Oh right. How about some drinks?'

'Yeah, like, good idea. Bacardi and coke, please.'

I sighed.

'Look Coleman, I know you're still a young man, but you should know better at this stage.'

'How do you mean?'

'Bacardi is like drinking the Devil's watered-down smegma, and I'm sure you've had enough of that kind of stuff for one night.'

'So, what should I drink?'

'If you're going to drink rum and coke, then you need to choose your rum from the Havana Club range. I recommend the 7, it's dark, sweet and delicious—'

'Like Halle Berry's fanny!'

'Erm, yeah, OK. Whatever floats your boat. Anyway, that's what you want. Havana 7, coke, slice of lime.'

'Cool.'

'I'll go get them.'

I left him sitting looking around the bar, his shoulders not as slumped as they had been. The many scantily clad young ladies bouncing around the place seemed to have caught his eye. His mouth hung open like a Down's syndrome fish. It was then that I realised I was now stuck with a young man with whom I had nothing in common. I liked football, he did not. He liked rugby, I did not. He was young, I was not. He liked to talk about how awesome he was, I did not like to listen to him talk about how awesome he was. This was worse than sitting beside somebody awful when you had to go to a wedding. Having to make small talk and laboured conversation simply because it was the done thing. And wasn't there always one absolute cock at the table? Except this was worse. At a wedding it's only for the duration of the meal. After that, you can get away from them and never speak to them again, but this was going to be an all-nighter. All night. With him. Having to talk. And listen. And pretend to laugh. All the time trying to engineer a situation which would give us what we need to get Tony off our backs.

There was only one thing to do. Get as fucked up as possible as quickly as possible. But then I had to try and stay somewhat sober in order to get the pictures. Right, slight change. I had to get Coleman as fucked up as possible as quickly as possible. That couldn't be too difficult, surely.

26

Cruising

I went to the loo to have a mind-clearing crap. I do some of my best thinking during the defecation process, you see. It took quite some time, and I was worried all of a sudden that I would go out and find Coleman gone, but, when I felt the burn subside to the point where I could walk without looking like John Wayne, and I made my way back inside, he was sitting on the same seat. I went to the bar, ordered a couple of drinks and brought them over. 'There you go,' I said, holding up my glass. 'Cheers.' We clinked glasses, and I thought about the situation. Two Dubliners in a bar in Barcelona, one of whom has no idea he's being set up completely so his wedding can be scuppered, the other having to do the setting up and scuppering to save his and his mate's life. It was a long way from Leo Burdock's, Moore Street, Christchurch and Chinese barmen we were.

I looked around me. The bar was really quite busy, and there were some famous faces there. I looked at Thierry Henry sitting on one of the bed seats, chatting away with a guy who was wearing a T-shirt advertising his own Arsenal blog. Pffft, what a ponce. Having a blog is one thing – but a range of merchandise? Talk about up your own arse. There were some vaguely familiar actors and actresses, a Spanish TV personality and Penelope Cruz, who was being chatted up by a bloke who looked suspiciously like Jimmy the Bollix. I had to do a double-take before I realised it actually was Jimmy. That old cad. We're supposed to be saving our own skins, and he was trying to get into bed with a famous film star. Sometimes I had to question his priorities. 'Hey,' said Coleman, 'isn't that your mate there chatting up Penelope Cruz?'

'Looks like it,' I said.

'Hah, cool. She's, like, a sick lash.'

'That's good, right?'

'Oh it's good. Diarmuid used to have a total obsesh with her.'

'Obsesh?'

'Yeah. Obsession, man. He was mad for her. If he knew she was in here he'd go mad. But not as mad as when I tell him.'

'Hmm, excuse me for a minute.'

I wandered over to where Jimmy was leaning casually up against a pillar, a glass of some kind of sparkling wine in his hand. He had his back to me while Penelope Cruz seemed enraptured with whatever he was telling her.

' . . . so when that happened,' I overheard him say as I

got closer, 'I just had to take matters into my own hands, you know? There are times in one's life when, as a gentleman, you have to say "Hey, you can't treat a lady like that," so I biffed him one right in the nose. I suspect he'll think twice about doing something like that again.'

'Oh my . . .,' tittered Penelope.

I tapped him on the shoulder. 'Oh, Twenty! How's it going? Did you find yer man?'

'Er, yes, no thanks to you.'

'Chill man, if you've got him now, everything's under control, right?'

'Well, I suppose so. Apart from the fact we're supposed to be engineering a situation so we can get the wedding called off, not chatting up Hollywood stars,' I hissed at him, smiling at the lovely Ms Cruz.

'Excuse me a moment,' said Jimmy to the actress. We moved away a few feet.

'Jesus, Twenty. Do you know how long it's been since I was in bed with a famous movie star? Too fucking long, let me tell you.'

'I'm sorry to spoil your fun here, but we have bigger fish to fry. And, anyway, I'm pretty sure you're wasting your time there.'

'Oh yeah? Don't think the old the Bollix charm is still working, is that it?'

'No man, but you know what they say about her.'

'What?'

'That she . . . you know . . .'

'I don't know.'

'Erm, if you were to give her a plate of sausage or a

cardboard container she'd prefer to eat the box.'

'Eh?'

'She would prefer the fish main course to the steak.'

'No!'

'Apparently.'

'But she's had high-profile relationships with men. In fact, didn't she go out with Tom Cruise for quite some . . . oh . . .'

'Exactly. Now, any chance you could give her the Jimmy nod and wink and help me get this cunt shit-faced so we can get ourselves out of this mess. There'll be plenty of time for you to root starlets once all this is over.'

'Right so. Gimme a couple of minutes. Gotta let her down gently – you know yourself.'

I wandered back over to where Coleman was sitting, and I stood there tapping my foot to the Italo-house music that had begun to pack the dance-floor. I realised my drink was empty, so I signalled to Coleman to go to the bar. It might have been his stag weekend but that didn't mean he couldn't get his round in. Jimmy came over then.

'Where's cockhead?'

'Gone to the bar. All good with Penelope Cruz?'

'Yeah, if we get this sorted quickly enough we're invited to a party in the Hotel Arse. Man, these Spanish have some strange names for places.'

'It's the Hotel Arts.'

'Ah, OK. I saw a bar yesterday though called "Can Quim".'

'I'll give you that one. So, what's the plan?'

'Well, you're the one who knows Barcelona. Where can we bring this twat so we can get him so fucked up he'll try and score some chick? Strikes me the ladies here are a bit out of his league.'

'Right, the obvious place is next door. It's the Baja Beach Club. It is to classy nightclubs what itinerants are to uncluttered gardens. It's packed full of tourists looking to get laid and locals looking to get laid by tourists and is populated by sluts, nymphomaniacs, male slatterns and gigolos of all shapes and sizes. The people who go there make Big Brother contestants seem well rounded and likeable. If we can't get him set upon by some young one in there then I'd be very surprised indeed,' I said.

'Nightclubs, eh? You know I fucking hate nightclubs. Have you got any of that stuff that Big Ian gave you?'

'Aye.'

'Right, well, if we're going to have to spend the night with idiot boy in a fucking nightclub then I want some of that.'

I handed over the wrap to Jimmy who went to the toilets to prepare himself for the sweaty carnage we were about to experience.

27

D.I.S.C.O.

I don't quite know how to describe the interior of the Baja Beach Club. To say it's horrendously gaudy and more tacky than one of those houses that gets lit up with flashing santas and snowmen at Christmas time would be downplaying it somewhat. It was similar to, but far worse, than anything you used to see on *The Hitman and Her*, the late night TV show which trawled the worst nightclubs in England every Saturday night. It was full of bright yellow late-eighties poles and tubular columns in blue. There was a car sticking out of the wall. The dance-floor was sunken and circular in shape. There were booths, podiums, strobe lights and occasional bursts of dry ice. On the dance-floor, people's teeth glowed white under the fluorescent purple strips that beamed down from above. The music was thumping, and, far from the sophisticated tunes in the last place, this was pure Euro-pap, relentless beats over cheesy but infuriatingly catchy choruses. The place itself was absolutely jammed, and the crowd was young – much closer to Coleman's age. I did feel slightly self-conscious, being that much older than them all, but another round of rums made me feel much more comfortable.

Coleman seemed impressed with the place. He said that his big brother had told him of this mythical Dublin nightclub when he was growing up, and he'd always wanted to find somewhere like it. Quite why he was so happy to have found Barcelona's answer to 'Hollywood Nights' in the Stillorgan Park Hotel was beyond me, but once he was happy I suppose we couldn't complain. I could see Jimmy looking around the place trying desperately to keep the look of disgust off his face. This was his idea of hell on Earth.

Jimmy's never been a man for nightclubs, not since that terrible incident in Tamango's back in the eighties. This was a Sunshine Radio party night to which Jimmy had brought his girlfriend. He was very smitten with this particular young lady and spoke openly of marrying her despite Dirty Dave and Stinking Pete slagging him off for being so gay he'd marry a girl.

The night was going well, and he had planned to pop the question when the moment was right. Now, this girl was a champion drinker, and, while Jimmy was taking it relatively easy, wanting to be in a good state of mind to ask that most important of all questions (well, second most important after 'Is it in yet?'), she was knocking back bottles of Satzenbrau and West Coast Cooler like there was no tomorrow. Realising he hadn't seen his sweetheart for quite some time, Jimmy went looking but found no sign of her anywhere. Not the toilets, not the dance-floor, not the nooks and crannies, not anywhere.

He decided, being the trendsetter that he is, that he'd go outside for a smoke, and, around the side of the building, he found his girlfriend sucking off another man. And the other man just happened to be his brother, Johnny the Bollix, who was looking at him with a 'har har' look on his face. Jimmy and Johnny were at loggerheads anyway after Johnny had swindled Jimmy out of his inheritance when their parents had died, and this was just another reason for him to hate him.

'Karen! What are you doing?' said Jimmy. She took Johnny's cock out of her mouth, looked at Jimmy, licked her lips a couple of times then got sick down her front, before going back to work on Johnny's manhood.

From that moment on, Jimmy never went to night-clubs, and he would wait years to extract revenge on his brother, which he did by poisoning him to death with his own bone marrow. Served him right.

As you might imagine, Jimmy's dislike of nightclubs has been somewhat intense. In fact, I think this might have been the first one he was in since that rather traumatic episode. I stood at the bar, having just ordered some rums, with Coleman on my left-hand side, Jimmy on my right. The music was thumping, and the roar of people trying to talk to each other over it made for a decibel surplus of epic proportions.

'Fuck me, this place is a right load of cunt,' yelled Jimmy.

'Oh man, this place is, like, totally cool!' bellowed Coleman.

'We need to get the fuck out of here as soon as we can.'

'Now, this is exactly what I had in mind when I pictured my stag night!'

'If I have to stay here much longer I'm going to slay somebody right in the face.'

'Kicking tunes, great people, this is the place to be. Thanks man, you really know this town. Without you, and this disco, my weekend would have been ruined. I'm gonna go dance, right after I get a bit more of this down me,' he said, tapping his nose. And off he went towards the toilets, holding his belt buckle and thrusting his hips forward as he boogied his way down.

'Seriously, Twenty. We can't stay here.'

'He likes it here, Jimmy.'

'Oh for fuck's sake. What exactly does he like about it?'

'As far as I can tell, everything. The decor, the music, the clientele. Everything.'

'Jesus Christ. What sort of a person could possibly like all this? How clueless and tasteless do you have to be to enjoy this thronging mass of cuntdom?'

'He plays rugby for Blackrock College, Jimmy.'

'Goddamn it. I know life is supposed to be a test at times, but this is too much. Look, here's what we'll do. Next time he goes to the jacks, I'll follow him in and strangle him, and we can just get the fuck out of here.'

'You know we can't do that. Tony doesn't want him dead.'

'It could be the Barcelona Nightclub Strangler. We read about it in the newspaper, right?'

'Hah, nice try.'

'Seriously though, you know I can't be in nightclubs. You know what happened. And I know, I know, you're going to say something about you coming back to Barcelona after all you went through, but Barcelona is big. You're not confined in a small space, surrounded by sweaty, muppetty twats.'

'OK, we'll try and keep it as brief a visit as possible. We need to find some girl and convince her to try it on with Coleman. I've got the camera here,' I said, patting my back pocket and finding it flat. 'Oh. Fuck.'

'What?'

'No camera.'

'Oh, you are kidding me. Where is it?'

'Back in the hotel. Sitting on the bedside table in my room.'

'Well, there's only one thing for it.'

'We find someone in here and buy their camera off them?'

'Nope. I'll go back to the hotel and get it. You can stay here and entertain our young friend. Gimme your key.'

'OK, but don't be long, you sneaky bastard. I know you'll take your time.'

'As if,' he grinned. I gave him the key, and Jimmy, promising to be back as soon as possible, made good his escape from the nightclub. I perched myself at the bar, just people-watching. I spotted Coleman on the dance-floor after a while, spinning round baby, right round, like some kind of record and, by the looks of it, thoroughly enjoying himself. With Jimmy sure to take the camera-gathering trip as slowly as possible so he wouldn't have to spend too much time in the club I had plenty of time to get Coleman rightly fucked up.

Now, I'd met rugby players before, and they did love their booze, but generally they were weaklings when it came down to it. Stick them in a pub at half seven and by eleven one of them is trying to lift up his kilt to show you his sporran or engaging in the kind of man-on-man high jinks that you wouldn't see in The George, but, because they were rugby players, it was far too straight for it to be in any way gay. I ordered myself a shot of Jameson, and, as I did, a pretty young girl beside me spoke.

'You can buy me one if you like.'

'Why would I like to do that?'

'Because you look like a gentleman.'

'Ha ha, that's the worst attempt at flattery I've ever heard. But go on then.' I ordered her a shot of Jameson.

'I meant you could buy me a drink, not necessarily what you were having.'

'You said I could buy you one, so I did. Now you're being fussy.'

'You elderly folk, so funny.'

'I'm Twenty,' I said.

'Lisa,' she said. 'I love your accent. What part of Scotland are you from?'

'Dublin.'

'Wow, I always thought Dublin was in Ireland.'

'And what part of Australia do you come from?'

'I'm not from Australia, I'm from New Zealand.'

'Ah, it's all the same, isn't it? Like Scotland and Ireland?'

'Aren't you a bit old for this place?'

'I'm young at heart.'

'On holidays?'

'You could say that. More of a mission of life and death importance.'

'Sounds interesting.'

'Oh, it is. Really. What about you? Just taking a year or two off and travelling around Europe, picking up work here and there, mostly as an au pair or a bartender?'

'Something like that, yeah. Are we really that typical?'

'Not at all, just a lucky guess on my part,' I smiled. She laughed and was still having a little titter to herself when Coleman, having had enough dancing for the time being, came over.

'Hey, those are some wicked sounds, man. I especially liked the Coldplay remix. Do you like Coldplay? I like Coldplay even though I think the singer is a bit of a fag. I know he's married to Gwyneth Paltrow or whatever, but he's still kind of faggy. Who's this?'

'Oh, this is Lisa. I met her at the bar.'

'Hi Lisa!' said Coleman, his jaws beginning to show the effects of the drugs.

'Hi Coleman,' she said, holding out her hand for him to shake. He kissed her on both cheeks, grinning slightly mischievously. Oh, here's a chance, I thought.

'Who's for a drink?' I said, draining my shot. Lisa did likewise.

'Yeah. Jägerbombs!' said Coleman.

'Jägerbombs?'

'You get a glass of Red Bull, right, and then you, like, drop a shot of Jägermeister in it and lash it back. Seriously, you've gotta try it man.'

'That sounds foul,' I said. 'Red Bull may give you wings but they're the kind of wings that you get on used tampons.'

'I'll have one,' said Lisa.

'Good woman, Lisa!' said Coleman. 'Come on Twenty. Get them in.'

Knowing that setting up Coleman and Lisa, or at least getting a picture making it look like they were being in any way intimate, would be the solution I was looking for, I had to play along. So I ordered a round of Jägermeisters and two glasses of Red Bull.

I had no problem with drinking a shot of the brown wine but there was no way I was going to drink that energy-drink muck. I read somewhere that its principal ingredient was bull semen. Imagine that. And imagine starting work as the harvester and going home to tell your family about your new job.

'I'm gonna work for Red Bull, Dad!'

'Good stuff, son. What are you going to be doing? Marketing? Advertising? Taste-testing?'

'No, I'm going to wank off a load of bulls, then add their semen to the vats we mix all the ingredients in.'

'I have no son.'

Coleman and Lisa dropped their shot glasses into the slim Jims half-filled with Red Bull and skulled them in one go. I looked at my shot of Jäger, thought 'fuck it' and knocked it back. I'm a bit wary of Jägermeister. My theory is that it's a drink invented by all the other drinks companies in the world because its main effect, besides getting you pissed enough to wet your pants in mid-afternoon, is to make you think that drinking more is simply the best idea you've ever had. Remembering I had to get Coleman pissed, I got in another round for the three of us.

'That's the greatest drink of all time. Imagine there was a time, right, when, like, people didn't have this to drink. I'd hate to have lived in those days. I heard as well, like, that they didn't have CDs and used big plastic things to play music on. How big must an iPod have been back then?'

'Jaysus. Look, I need a smoke. Why don't you two go dance or something? I'll be right back.'

I left them at the bar, hoping they'd start chatting and then click enough for Coleman to at least look like he was trying something on. I wandered outside to the terrace where I lit up a cool, refreshing Major and waited for Jimmy to come back.

28

Sexy beards

I sat outside smoking for a while, and I rang Big Ian to see if he fancied dropping down for a drink. When he discovered where I was, he just laughed and told me to give him a ring if we found ourselves somewhere decent. I sat and listened in to bits of conversations – guys trying to impress girls, girls acting all coy, pissed lads talking about scoring, girls comparing one guy to his friend and marking them out of ten . . . This whole place was like a giant pick-up joint. If we couldn't get Coleman set up here, then there was no hope for us. I smoked a final cigarette, went back inside and got myself another drink at the bar. I looked for Coleman on the dance-floor but didn't see him. This was promising. Perhaps he was in a dark corner snogging Lisa and trying to finger her without anyone seeing. Dammit if he was though – I had no camera to snap the evidence. The crappy camera on the shitty Alcatel mobile I bought wouldn't be good enough. I wandered around the club for a couple of minutes and didn't see them at all, then began to get worried that they'd taken off somewhere else. I needn't have worried though. When I got back to the bar, I ordered another drink because the Jägermeister was telling me to, and I saw Lisa, who waved.

'On your own?' I said. 'Where's Coleman?'

'Gone to the toilet. I think he's gone to snort coke to be honest.'

'Oh really?'

'He's sniffling away like crazy, and, unless he's caught one of those mythical summer colds, then I reckon it's got to be drugs.'

'To each their own, eh?'

'Drugs are for losers! My old boyfriend died from a coke overdose. He bled to death out his nose.'

'How terrible. Maybe he just has the summer cold.'

'Yeah, right.'

'He's a handsome lad, isn't he though? Talk about buff, what?'

'I suppose he does have a good body.'

'And he plays rugby for one of the biggest cunts . . . erm . . . I mean clubs in Ireland,' I said, desperately trying to talk him up.

'Rugby? I hate rugby. Another of my ex-boyfriends wanted to be an All Black more than anything else in the world. He trained every night, took steroids, lifted weights. I loved him, which is why I overlooked the terrible acne the steroids gave him. And not just on his face either. He had a back full of pus-filled blackheads. I put up with so much until the day he hit me when I just asked him to pass me the salt at the dinner table. "Roid rage", they call it. Complete arsehole, I called it. I swore I'd never go near another rugby player again, and, to this day, I hold every single one of them in contempt.'

Bollocks. This wasn't good. How was I supposed to get a picture of Coleman trying to finger some girl if the girl thought he and his ilk were utter twats. I mean, she was dead right and all, but this was no help to me.

'Actually,' she said, rubbing the back of my hand with her fingers, 'I prefer the older man.'

Double bollocks.

'Er, well, ha ha, erm . . . what can I say? Ha ha ha, not quite as old as me I'm sure.' I took a big gulp of my rum.

'I wouldn't be so sure about that.'

'Well, you know what they say . . . er . . . you know that thing, holiday romances give you . . . erm . . .'

'And beards. Mmmm, I find beards soooo sexy,' she said, looking at me coquettishly.

'Oh . . . erm . . . well, the thing is . . . ha ha. . . . uhm . . . I just have to go and find Coleman.'

'Hurry back,' she said, batting her eyelashes at me and licking her lips.

I went to have a wee and to think of a way out of it. Perhaps if I started sniffing all the time then she might think I was a drug user too and leave me alone. I certainly wasn't going to pass for a rugby player. I mean, it's not that I wasn't flattered. She was a very attractive young lady, but I didn't have time for amorous, lustful and nubile New Zealanders. I had to stay on topic, as it were, and what we needed to do was get someone to act that way with Coleman, not with me. I was no Lothario, my Casanova days long behind me, and this was a headache I just didn't need. Where the fuck was Jimmy as well? The night was getting on, and we still had work to do.

I ran into Coleman as I came out of the toilet, and he thrust a shot of Jägermeister into my hand. 'Here you go, Twinky!' he said.

'Thanks. Cheers.' I clinked his glass and threw it back.

'So that Lisa girl was asking me all about you at the bar, like.'

'Oh God.'

'I told her, like, that I didn't know you that long but from what I knew you were a totally decent guy.'

'You did?'

'Oh yeah, man. I mean, I had to tell her, like, about how you saved my stag weekend after what my so-called mates had done to me. How you showed me the kindness that not many strangers would have, like,' he said, his voice earnest with coke and booze. 'You know, seriously, I'll never forget what you've done for me.'

'Honestly, it's noth—'

'No man, no man. You might think it's nothing, but I know. I know in here,' he said, thumping his heart with his fist. 'In. Here. And it means the world to me. I don't know what I would have done without you. We should probably exchange numbers you know, do some stuff together in Dublin when we get back, like. We could hang out and stuff. Wouldn't that be awesome?'

'Forget it, reall—'

'Because, you know, sometimes you meet someone, and there's, like, a connection, and I can feel that connection. You might be sort of old and stuff but you're a gentleman, and that's something I'll remember forever. When I have my kids and I tell them stories about all the, like, totally awesome people I met in my life, you'll be right up there with the best of them, like Brian O'Driscoll and that black fella we met on tour in South Africa. You know the one, in jail for ages for nothing.'

'Nelson Mandela.'

'Yeah, Ernest Mandinka. You're my very own Ernest Mandinka.'

And with that he began to have a little cry again before wrapping me in a bear hug so tight I thought I was going to pass out. And people who take coke think it makes them interesting.

'There there,' I said, patting him on the back, trying to let him know that was enough. 'You're all right. Erm, let's get another drink.'

'Yeah, more drink. Oh, and what I was saying? I think that Lisa girl likes you.'

'Oh yeah. Ahh, she's not my type.'

'But she's gorgeous and I think she'd, like, let you get your hand under her jumper, if she was wearing a jumper instead of a skimpy little top.'

'I'm sure she'd prefer someone her own age, eh?' I said, quite literally giving him two nudges and two winks.

'Not me, man. In case you hadn't noticed, this is my

stag weekend, which means, you know, that I'm a bride to be. I'm about to give my life to the woman I love. I'm not going to do the dirt with someone.'

'But it's your stag weekend. Isn't that what every stag does? Isn't that why they go away these days? There was a time a stag night was just that, a stag night. You went to the pub, got pissed, went to some grotty club, maybe finished off with a thirty-pound bottle of some Italian vinegar down Leeson Street. Nowadays it's weekends away, and that's because of the code of honour among men. What happens on tour stays on tour. Am I right?'

'You do have a point, like, but—'

'And the reason they go to places where it's warm is because the girls won't be wearing many clothes, and the reason they go to places in Eastern Europe is because you can stay the weekend, engage in whatever manner of paid-for entertainment you so desire, eat, drink and generally be merry for half-nothing and still have money left over for a suit from Louis Copeland when you get back.'

'Yeah, but it'd be all wrong and stuff to do anything. Anyway, I don't want to. I love Cynthia with, like, all my heart. She's the best girl I ever met, and I met loads of girls in my time. I mean, look at me man. Look at me!'

'I'm looking.'

'If you were a girl, you'd be trying to shift me right now. In fact, I bet there's part of you that secretly wants to.'

'In your dreams, pal. Look, all I'm saying is that you're going to be married soon. You're going to spend the rest of your life with this girl, and, as wonderful as she is, this is your last chance to sample the à la carte before you get the set menu . . . forever. And ever. And, like, ever. See what I mean?'

'Yeah, but—'

'Code of honour. It's like Omertà.'

'Where the bomb went off that time?'

'That's Omagh. No, Omertà. The mafia code. The code of silence. I'm just saying that whatever you do nobody is ever going to find out. Look, your mates aren't around. How is anything you do going to get back to Dublin? And look at the chicks in here, man. Seriously, if I wasn't so old I'd be trying it on all over the place. Especially if I was going to be drinking from the same cup for the rest of my life.'

'I dunno . . . Anyway, let's get some more drink!'

And he took off towards the bar. I followed behind wondering how much fucking booze it was going to take to make him less coherent and far more suggestible. I wondered as well if I could keep up. His youthful stamina was proving more than a match for my resistance and experience. I wasn't going to be beaten though. Not yet, anyway.

29

Motormouth

We'd had another two rounds of drinks before Jimmy arrived back. I'd spent the time watching Coleman get more and more lively, dancing around the place like he was Boyzone on *The Late, Late Show*, just without the dungarees, and trying to fend off the advances of Lisa who had, with the drink, become ever more forward. Frankly, I was quite shocked. Girls didn't talk like that back in the days when I was courting. Lads these days had no idea how good they had it. 'Where the fuck have you been?' I said to Jimmy.

'Nowhere in particular. Just getting the camera. I figured there was no real hurry, you seem to have everything under control.'

'Oh yeah, it's all going swimmingly. Coleman has got the coke-plus-booze profundity going on, telling me all about how I'm a great person for saving his stag party. The poor fucker even wants us to be friends, and here we are trying to set him up. And not only that, he's got the constitution of a horse. And not one of those scabby piebalds you see knackers pulling carts with. No. He's like one of those enormous Budweiser horses. He's drinking Red Bull and Jägermeister mixed up, lashing the sniff down him, and he's like an unstoppable dancing machine.'

'There's the problem, you see.'

'What?'

'Red Bull and coke. It's got him so buzzed the booze is having no effect. It's just making him drink more. Give it some time. Eventually the drink will take over.'

'Oh, time. Great. It's already nearly 2 a.m. Anyway, not only that, I've got some young girl trying it on with me, telling me she loves sexy, bearded, older men.'

'You're certainly older and bearded.'

'Har har. She won't leave me alone, man. I think we're going to have to get out of here. I tried to set her up with Coleman, but it turns out she hates coke-snorting, and she especially hates rugby players.'

'A sensible girl then, leaving aside her bizarre attraction to you.'

'Yeah, well, I still think we need to go somewhere else.'

'What have you got in mind?'

'Strip club. It's the natural progression.'

'Right so, lead the way.'

I managed to get Coleman's attention without getting a slap in the face as he was thrashing around on the dance-floor like an epileptic in a room full of strobe lights. I told him we were moving on, and he said he had to go to the loo one more time before we left. I told him we'd see him outside. On the way up the stairs, I felt a tug on my shirt and looked behind to see Lisa there.

'Going without saying goodbye?'

'Ah . . . well . . . yes, basically.'

'Where are you going?'

'Not sure, somewhere else.'

'Can I come too?'

'Well, it's really only for lads, you know. Stag weekend and all that.'

'OK,' she looked disappointed. 'Can I at least have one kiss before you go?'

'Look, I'm not sure—'

'Just one kiss. What can it hurt?'

'Oh, all right then.'

She closed her eyes and puckered her lips, which was all I needed to turn around and get up the stairs as quickly as possible. I thought I heard her call my name but I ignored her. It wasn't as bad as the time when Jimmy had asked this girl out and they were having a drink or two in town when he realised he wasn't even slightly interested in her. So he waited for her to go to the bathroom, and, while she was in there, he took off, after leaving a note on the back of a beer mat saying 'Sorry, I died.' What a charmer.

Outside the club I expected it to be a little cooler, but it was a typically humid Barcelona summer's night, and there was little respite from the heat. I lit a cigarette and waited for Coleman to emerge. Thinking about where we were going, I gave Big Ian a ring, and a strip club seemed acceptable enough for him to agree to come along and meet us for a couple of drinks. Coleman came out from the club a couple of minutes later, full of vim and vigour, but, thankfully, out of drugs.

'I don't suppose you've, like, got any more of that,' he said.

'Sorry man, nothing left. I can see about getting some but it's probably going to be difficult.'

'OK, you can try though, right?'

'Oh yeah, I'll try,' I said, having no intention of doing so. The last thing we needed was him chemically awake for any longer. We needed him to start slumping, for the drink to start taking control.

'So Jimmy,' said Coleman, 'what's your story then? You know your pal Twenty here is a really cool guy? I'm sure you do. I mean, he's your friend, isn't he? You must know. I only know him for a few hours really, and I can tell what a cool person he is, and if you've known him for years and years you must be, like, hyper-aware of it. A good friend. Not like, like, my friends. What a pack of toads – and nobody's going to kiss them and turn them into bunnies, are they? In this life you get one chance with Coleman Darcy-McNeill, and if you blow that chance then there's no more chances. Forgiveness is for, like, priests and stuff. I'm a good friend but a terrible enemy. Wait. Does that mean I'm, like, terrible at being an enemy? Because that would be wrong, right? I'm brilliant at being someone's enemy, so I'm a brilliantly terrible enemy. It's not good to be on my bad side, you know what I mean? I remember this one time during a match this guy I used to go to school with, who then went on to play for some other lesser team, hit me one right in the balls during a ruck, and so that was it. Any old friendships were out the wardrobe, as they say. I got my revenge because his boss was a friend of my dad, and Dad had a word, and he got him fired, and then the bank repossessed his house and his car, and his girlfriend left him, and then he committed suicide by gassing himself in his dad's car somewhere up the mountains. But that's just the way it goes and . . .'

Coleman went on and on and on, obviously loving the sound of his coked-up voice, and, without the dancing to distract him and the loud music to make it hard to hear him, he was practically insufferable. I could see Jimmy's jaw clench as we took a taxi to the strip club, Coleman talking all the while. He even spoke to the taxi driver, who hadn't got a clue what he was saying and just stared back at him looking more than a bit confused. Jimmy ran his finger across his throat while making a pleading gesture. I'd like to say I was a bigger man than that, that I rose above, but I defy anyone to listen to that kind of incessant blabbering for long without wanting to cut it off at the source. Still, there was time, and surely we could get something incriminating in a strip club of all places.

Eventually the taxi pulled up outside El Strippertorium and let us out. The club was in a very respectable part of town and obviously not well liked by many of the neighbours. In typical Spanish style, they made their objections public by painting slogans on sheets and hanging them from their balconies. The apartments directly opposite and the ones above in the same building carried messages like 'No to Strip Clubs', 'Peace and Quiet in Our Neighbourhood' and, bizarrely, 'Too Much Strip, Not Enough Not Strip.' However, banners or no banners, there was a strip club in their midst, and there was little they could do about it.

'All right!' said Coleman, 'strippers are cool.'

'Yeah,' said Jimmy, 'it's tough these days to see women naked. This must be a rare treat for you.'

He didn't seem to hear though, so enthused was he with entering this mythical arena. He knew he could be out with the lads and someone would say, 'We went to Estonia for my stag weekend, right, and we went to this strip club, and, oh my God, you should have seen the women,' and he could bide his time then chime in with 'You think that's good? When I had my stag night in Barcelona, we, like, went to a place where if you think you should have seen the women in that place then you should really have seen the women in this place.' The one-upmanship would carry on for a while, both of them completely ignorant of the fact that you could simply exchange the women in both clubs and nobody would ever notice. We paid our twenty-five euro in at the door but it was good value because you got a ticket which entitled you to a drink at the bar. Well, it was good value when you discovered the price of the drinks. Anyway, we went in.

30

Flaming lips

It had been many years since I'd been in a strip club. Back then you went in, got treated to a flash of a lady's ankle, a glimpse of her petticoat or, if you were really lucky, a peep at her flowery bloomers. Well, times have changed, let me tell you. Everywhere you looked there were bosoms in push-up bras, skimpy tops, tiny skirts, cleavage, tanned skin (both natural and that lovely orangey hue of bottled tan) and girls made-up to within an inch of their lives. Essentially it was like any teenage disco in Dublin on a Friday night. As we walked in, there was a girl dancing on a podium with just her knickers on, her amazingly round breasts not moving as she gyrated in time to the music. They were like nipply, slightly less mottled cantaloupes.

There was a long bar to the right-hand side and a

raised area to the left. In front of the bar were some tables with low stools, positioned around a stage, which, at that moment, featured a lissom blonde who was spinning around on the pole that stretched to the roof, using only her legs to hold on. I have to say it was pretty impressive. I know if I'd tried a similar manoeuvre I'd have fallen flat on my face and most likely broken my back. She span around for a while before she began to take her clothes off, and it was only then I realised that the three of us were standing gaping, captivated by the performance, the athleticism, the boobs.

I shook my head, took the tickets off the other two and went to the bar. Knowing we had to get Coleman into a state of extreme drunkenness I thought for a few moments about what to order. Any kind of short with a mixer was going to be full of sugar, and the sugar on top of everything else would probably turn to speed in his body and keep the cunt awake until Tuesday afternoon.

There was only one thing for it. Straight whiskey. If there was any drink to help a man descend into the realms of 'Oh Jesus, what made me do that?' it was the golden firewater. All of my own worst moments have come with whiskey. Apart from the absinthe incident. Damn, why did I think of that? I pictured a keening, kidnapped Pete for a moment, but I had to put it out of my mind.

I concentrated on the whiskey again and the bad stuff it had made me do. Like the night I got up and went to the bathroom, which is at the far end of my house. But instead of continuing to the bathroom, I went out the back door and pissed into Bastardface's kennel thinking it was the toilet. The poor dog was pee-splattered. Or the time when I got so unspeakably drunk I actually laughed during an Adam Sandler film. Truly one of the most shameful moments of my life.

I went back over with the drinks and found Jimmy and Coleman still staring at the stage. 'Here you go,' I said. Neither of them said a word and continued looking at the girl who now appeared to be using her vaginal lips to cling to the pole, her arms and legs splayed out in a triumphant gesture, like a gymnast after a great dismount.

'OI! Drinks, you cunts,' I shouted, and this got their attention.

'Oh, didn't see you there,' said Jimmy.

'My . . . Who? . . . What? . . . How? . . . I mean . . . Jesus . . .,' muttered Coleman taking his glass.

'Quite the performer.'

'Remember that stag weekend we went to in Estonia that time, Twenty? Well, if you think the girls there—'

'Don't even start, Jimmy! So, Coleman. Can Cynthia do that?'

'I'm pretty sure she can't, although it's not like we have a pole she can practise on or anything.'

'And most houses these days don't have one, and I'd wager most wives don't do that kind of dancing for their husbands.'

'Yeah, but . . . yeah . . . Jesus.'

'How old are you, Coleman?' asked Jimmy.

'I'm twenty-four.'

'Pfft, twenty-four, eh?'

'What?'

'Nothing.'

'No, what?'

'It's just quite young to be getting married, isn't it?' said Jimmy.

'It is if you're marrying someone for the wrong reason, like for money or because you got them knocked up, and then, even though you paid for them to go and have an abortion in England, they don't get it, and then the father finds out, and he says he'll kill you if you don't marry his daughter. But I'm getting married because I love Cynthia. She's special.'

'Special needs.'

'What?'

'I said wives have special needs. More than girlfriends. Now just look around you. Look at all the beautiful women, yet you, at the tender age of twenty-four, are going to eschew the multiple-choice option for the rest of your days?'

'Chew what?'

'I just mean that you're restricting yourself at an age when you should be out enjoying yourself. A taste here, a taste there, you know? When I was your age I had girl-friends all over the place. One northside, one southside, one westside and so on. I was a right hoor when I think about it now. It's a good job they hadn't invented STDs back then. What you need is a roll in the hay here, a fumble there, a sordid tryst somewhere else when you're not rolling or fumbling. Look, what I'm saying is that you should take your time and make sure you've experienced all there is to experience before you decide to settle down.'

'So you're married now then?'

'Erm, well, no actually, but this isn't about me.'

'Yeah, but I love Cynthia. I knew it from, like, the first moment I met her. I know we come from different backgrounds and stuff, but that doesn't matter to me. She's my best friend. She's the first person I think of when I go to sleep at night and when I wake up in the morning. Sometimes if I, like, have a problem in my life, I just think of her face, and the problem seems meaningless because I have her. She gets me like nobody else gets me. She laughs at my jokes even though some of my jokes aren't really that good, but she laughs anyway. I know that no matter how terrible my day is, it's going to end well because I go to bed with her. Just thinking about living without her is making me want to cry. She means the entire, like, world to me.'

'Oh, fair enough then. If you know what you want then you know what you want. Oh, look at that girl there,' said Jimmy, pointing to another podium where a black girl was showing her pink bits. He took me aside.

'He's seriously smitten with Tony's young one. She must be a goer, and, unlike her mother, she probably doesn't have a quim like a wizard's sleeve. He said all kinds of mad stuff about her being his best friend. I mean, whose best friend is a girl?'

'Beats me, man.'

'So, unless we get him utterly shit-faced and he gets busy with some chick we're going to have to kill him.'

'Let's hope the whiskey does its work then.'

As I was up getting some more drinks at the bar, the girl on the stage finished her routine and left to a generous round of applause. A group of Japanese businessmen, some random holiday-makers, what looked like another stag weekend and some local pervs clapped enthusiastically. Then the music stopped, and there was a fanfare. The lights on the stage went out, and a spotlight shone towards the back of the room. Suspended from the ceiling was a small seat and, in the seat, a buxom redhead.

As the fanfare finished, a Tom Jones song kicked in, and the seat began to move towards the stage as the girl leant back, showing maximum cleavage. The seat went across the top of the bar, and all the men sitting there craned their necks skywards to get a good look. Her movements were slow and seductive, almost teasing, but eventually she got to the stage, let herself down and began her act. It was much the same as the other girls: she span around on a pole, did some dancing and ended up stark naked. Then when she'd finished, another girl did exactly the same, yet the men applauded wildly each time.

It was like they had goldfish memories. 'Hurrah, a chick stripping!' they thought. Then when she'd finished and another one took over, it was 'Hurrah, a chick stripping!' as if they'd never seen the likes of it before. I was bored with the place, and the booze was horrendously expensive. More expensive than going to one of those wanky pubs on Dawson Street where the 'beautiful people' hang out. I would have left, but this seemed like the best place to get what we needed from Coleman, so we stayed. A decision, as it turned out, that almost proved very painful and very costly.

31

Not quite Tina Turner

The whiskey didn't seem to do anything to Coleman but make him even more excitable, and he flitted around the club talking to anyone who'd listen. Oblivious to the fact that most of the girls there had ulterior motives for being nice to him, he'd chat for a while then go off and talk to another one, leaving a trail of frustrated faces behind him. He loved his dancing and almost got himself into ructions with one of the Japanese businessmen as he was strutting his stuff right in front of their table, blocking their view of the stage. Being so small, they couldn't see over him to where the chocolate-coloured girl was, shock horror, taking off her sexy underwear while twirling around to Grace Jones music. Fearing they might be secret ninjas, I went over and calmed the situation down and brought Coleman back over to where we were sitting.

His exuberance was exhausting. What was wrong with this fucker? Why couldn't he get hopelessly drunk and stupid? He was like a hyperactive toddler, and, far from looking a bit tired and suggestible, he was a Duracell bunny who could keep on keeping on for days yet. He got up and went wandering around the club, a huge goofy smile on his face, just as Big Ian arrived.

'Awright, Major. How the fack are you?'

'I'm fucking wrecked, man. This is proving more difficult than I thought.'

'Why?'

'This lad. He's a machine. He's so goofed up on coke and Red Bull that the booze is having no effect on him at all. We've been pouring whiskey down his throat for the last hour, and it's not making the slightest bit of difference.'

'He must have a hearty facking constitution. Get him a Benetton.'

'A what?'

'A Benetton. One of everything. Get him to drink it straight down. Guarantee you it'll work. It'll knock his facking head off.'

'You sure?'

'Yeah mate, not a facking doubt. One other thing, by the way.'

'What's that?'

'Mine's a Jack and coke.'

So off I went to the bar where I fended off the advances of an exceptionally tall lady who asked me if I was enjoying myself. I'm not quite sure she understood the sarcasm in my reply, but she most definitely understood my giving her two fingers and going to the far end of the bar where I ordered the drinks. Jack and coke for Big Ian, a couple of Jamesons for me and Jimmy and a Benetton for Coleman, which consisted of a shot each of whiskey, gin, vodka, rum, brandy, tequila, schnapps (regular and peach), grappa, Goldschläger and, rather digustingly, Bols Advocaat. I stirred it all together with a swizzler and brought the drinks back to the table.

I saw Coleman over at the far end of the bar talking to an Asian girl with pneumatic hooters on her tiny body. It looked like someone had stuck two footballs to her chest. I gestured him over, and he bounded across like an eager puppy.

'That girl is very pretty,' he said.

'Oh yeah? Tickle your fancy a bit, does she? A bit of the old yellow pearl, eh?' I said, thinking perhaps he was weakening.

'Not really, she's just pretty. Who's this, like?'

'This is my mate Big Ian. Big Ian, Coleman.'

'How the fack are ya?'

'I can see why they call you Big Ian, dude. You should do some more exercise. Then you wouldn't be as big.'

'You should shut your mouth, then you wouldn't be in danger of me kicking your teeth in.'

'Oooooh.'

'Leave it out, you two. Anyway, Coleman, as it's your stag, we've bought you a special drink.'

'There's no spunk in this one, is there?'

'Spunk?' said Big Ian. 'Where the fack were you cants earlier?'

'Long story,' I said. 'No, there's no spunk, jizz, snot, piss, bits of dried poo that are matted to your arse hair, ear wax or any other kind of bodily substance. I promise.'

'What's, like, in it then?'

'Everything.'

'Everything?'

'Yeah, there's a shot of every spirit from the bar, and this, my rugby-playing friend, is a proper test of your manhood. If you can drink this down in one go then you instantly achieve legendary status, right Jimmy?'

'Yeah, legendary cunt.'

'Ha ha, Jimmy,' I said shooting him dagger eyes, 'you're such a card.'

'He's right, Carlton, drink this and you become a hero,' said Jimmy.

'It's Coleman.'

'You've got to do it down in one though, that's the rule.' I said.

'Yep,' said Jimmy. 'You can only be a liquor luminary if it all goes down. I'm not sure you can do it anyway.'

'Oh really? Wanna make a, like, bet on that?'

'Sure.'

'If I do it, right, you've got to give me fifty euro.'

'OK, if you don't do it, you've got to call off your wedding and never see that girl again.'

'That's a little uneven, isn't it? I mean, like, fifty euro is nothing, but calling off my wedding and changing my whole life is a lot, like.'

'I knew you'd be too pussy.'

'I am not.'

'Well, if you're so confident, just drink it, Quentin.'

'It's COLEMAN.'

'Sorry . . . Coleman. Drink up. Come on.'

He looked at me. 'Twenty, you're a nice bloke, but your mate here is, like, a bit of a prick, I'm sorry to say.'

'They don't call him Jimmy the Bollix for nothing. Anyway, I'm sure you can drink that. It'd be no hassle to you.'

'Yeah, you're right!'

And with that, he picked up the glass and drained it in two seconds flat. A couple of seconds later I saw his eyes begin to water slightly, and then he shook his head as the burn kicked in. That must have been fiery going down.

'Right, that was excellent, thanks guys,' he said as he got up and continued his wanderings.

'Fucking hell. Surely that's got to make him pissed.'

'If it doesn't, Twenty, I'm going to lure him into an alley and strangle him with my bare hands.'

'Don't facking worry, Twenty. That's enough to knock an elephant on its arse. Remember Phil the Handyman?'

'Yeah.'

'We gave him one of those a couple of years back – a dare, don't you know. Anyway, he was fine for about five minutes then passed out flat on his back. We carried on drinking, sitting around in my flat actually, and then there was this gurgling noise and a fountain of puke erupted from his mouth and went straight back down his throat. He'd have choked to death if we hadn't turned him over after a couple of minutes.'

'Well, I don't want him to die. Not yet anyway.'

'What you need to do is get him a facking private dance, innit? See those booths over there?'

'Yeah.'

'Well, you pick a girl, ask her for a private dance, and in there anything goes.'

'Anything?'

'Anything.'

'If you wanted to be spanked and told you were a naughty boy?' asked Jimmy, one eyebrow raised.

'Anything, mate. So get him a private dance with that little Asian girl he was on about. Give it about five minutes, then nip in with your camera, snap snap, he's balls deep in one of her orifices, too drunk to know what's going on. Your problems are well and truly facking over. See?'

'Big Ian, not only are you big in stature you are big in brain power.'

I left Ian and Jimmy chatting. I could see Jimmy trying to explain how much he just wanted to kill Coleman, and Big Ian, being the kind of person who always goes on his first impression of someone, agreeing wholeheartedly.

As loathsome as he was, I didn't really want to have Coleman knocked off. And, anyway, it'd be much more enjoyable if he had to go home and face the music that our pictures would create. The pretty Asian girl that Coleman had been chatting to was standing in a group with some other girls, including the very tall one who I'd been so rude to a few minutes previously. I felt a little awkward I have to say.

I was never the smooth charmer, unlike Jimmy, who

could interrupt a group of girls with a smile and a witty comment. If I tried, I'd say something like 'So . . .' then wait for the tumbleweed to blow across the scene. I always just figured that girls had their stuff to talk about and that guys had their stuff. I tried to put myself in their position. How would I feel if I was having a good chat with the lads and some girl came over and started to try and put the moves on me? I figured I'd be mildly vexed, and, as I like to project my logical thought processes onto other people (foolish as I know it is), I then felt distinctly uncomfortable about going over and talking to the girl.

I tried catching her eye, but she managed to avoid my gaze. My rather gauche attempts at attracting her attention left me feeling even more self-conscious, when the tall one saw me, understood exactly what I was trying to do, smiled and stuck her own two fingers up at me before shifting around so she was standing in front of the Asian girl, right in my line of vision. I had no choice now. I had to go and introduce myself and all that other mortifying stuff. I brushed myself down, cricked my neck and went for it.

'Hello,' I said, talking in Spanish.

'Hello,' she smiled, as falsely as I've ever seen anyone smile. 'How are you?'

'I'm awful! Can we talk over here?' I said, pointing to a space by the counter. I could feel Tall One's eyes on my back as she took my arm, and we went to talk in a more private setting. Well, it wasn't private. The club was packed, but at least I didn't have to cope with a gaggle of girls.

'So, you like me?'

'Oh, I'm sure you're very nice but—'

'OK! Vodka and lime.'

'What?'

'You like me, buy me drink. Then we talk more.'
Christ, I was fed up getting drinks for people. On my way
to the bar, Jimmy gave me a nod and waved at his empty
glass. The look on my face didn't leave much room for
interpretation, and he waved me away, signalling he'd get
his own. I spent another small fortune on the drink and
brought it back over.

'Thanks,' she said, 'so you're a tourist?'

'Not exactly. Look, I need a dance, you know? In private?'

'Sure, come with me,' and she tried to drag me off to
the private booths behind the bar.

'No, not for me. For my friend.'

'You don't like me?'

'I do like you, you're truly lovely, but it's for my friend.
It's his wedding next week, understand?'

'Ahhh, wedding. We have many party in here for this.'

'So, I want you to do the private dance for him, OK?'

'OK!'

'And this private dance . . . you know . . . you . . . it's
. . . erm . . . special?'

'If you want special I do special.'

'Yeah, I want special. Really special, OK?'

'OK!'

'Excellent. How much?'

'Two-fifty.'

'Fifty? Compared to the drinks that's good value.'

'No. Two-fifty.'

'Two-fifty? Fucking hell.'

'It's special!'

'Jesus. OK, hang on.' I took out my wallet, which was now lighter than Karen Carpenter after a month on the Slim-Fast plan. I was down to my last two hundred, which meant I had to go over and borrow money from Jimmy.

When I came back, I gave her the cash and told her to hang on while I found Coleman. It took me a while – he was up in the elevated area to the left-hand side where he was chatting away to two guys who looked first like they couldn't understand a word he was saying and second like they wanted to be out of his company as quickly as possible.

'Hey,' I said, 'come on down here with me.'

'Cool, what's going on? Are there lesbians doing lesbionic things? I love lezzers.'

'No, just come on.' We wandered back down to where the Asian girl was waiting, the money I'd given her nowhere to be seen. Probably up her chuff, I thought.

'Oh, it's that girl again!'

'Yeah, and she's gonna give you a private dance.'

'But we can dance right here,' he said, beginning to jig.

'No. You're not listening. A private dance. Get me?'

'I think so. She's going to dance in, like, private.'

'Close. She's going to take you to one of those booths over there. Nobody can see you, nobody will disturb you. She will then do a dance which may involve her taking all her clothes off. And should your clothes come off as well then nobody will ever know. Now do you get me?'

'Ahhhh,' he said, the understanding spreading over his face like warm butter on toast. 'Oh, I don't know about this though.'

'It's your stag night, man. Everyone does it. And remember the code. What goes on tour stays on tour. And what happens in strip clubs stays in strip clubs.'

'Yeah, but—'

'Look at her, you said she was pretty. She is very pretty. And look at that body. This is your last chance for a breakfast roll before a lifetime of cheese sandwiches, Coleman.'

'Well, if you think so . . .'

'Would I do anything that wasn't a good idea? Did I make you drink a shot glass full of sperm?'

'I suppose not.'

'And, look, it's up to you what happens in there. Just go with the flow. Fair enough?'

'Yeah, fair enough. OK then Mary, let's go!' he said, taking her by the arm.

'Special,' she said to me.

'Special. Have fun, Coleman!'

And off they went together. I had to keep an eye from a discreet distance to see which particular booth they went into; it was the fourth one.

Behind the bar there was a bouncer there keeping an eye and making sure that nobody, well no man at least, came back there unaccompanied, so we were going to have to figure something out before I went to try and get the money shot. I went over and sat down with Jimmy and Big Ian.

'So, it's all set?' said Jimmy.

'Yeah, he went back there with her. I just have to get the pictures now. The only problem is there's a bouncer back there, and we're going to have to distract him somehow so I can sneak in and get snapping.'

'Leave it with me, Twenty,' said Big Ian. 'No better facking man than me, you know it.'

'Right enough. We'll give it about five minutes or so. That should be enough. In the meantime one of you cunts can get me a drink. I spent the last of my money getting that dance sorted for Pillock-Face, and I'm broke till we get to a machine.'

Jimmy went up to the bar to get me a drink.

'Guess what?' I said to Big Ian.

'What?'

'He found me.'

'Already?'

'Yep, and not only that, he's holding my mate Stinking Pete hostage to make sure I come and see him.'

'Oh, for fack's sake.'

'Aye.'

'Well, looks like you don't have any choice now, eh?'

'I guess not. I honestly thought that after all this time he'd have gotten over it. Not forgotten but at least moved on.'

'You know what he's like. When do you go to see him?'

'Tomorrow, I suppose. I can't even think about that now. Jesus. Change the subject, man.'

'Erm, this lad you're with, he's an ignorant facking cant, isn't he?'

'Ah, Jimmy just takes a while to get to know.'

'Not him, you twat. The other one.'

'Ahh, It's just his rugby-playing background. You know what they're like.'

'I do, they're all the same. Apart from Serge Blanco, who was a facking mad bastard, let me tell you.'

'I'll take your word for it.'

'So, you reckon you'll come back a bit more often now? Provided you get through the meeting with himself?'

'Pfft, if we can get through this without ending up as fish food then yeah, I reckon. It's not until you come back you realise how much you miss the place. I dunno, I love Dublin. It's home, but I feel very comfortable here. It's got something, this place. I know the change of seasons, the smells of different neighbourhoods, where's good, where's not, where to eat, where to avoid, and I haven't been back in so long. You still just know though. Sometimes you just make a connection with a place. It's a shame what happened, but I think it's time to put it well and truly in the past.'

'Probably for the best, mate.'

Jimmy came back then with a round of drinks. I have to be honest, I was feeling quite pissed, and I wasn't sure that I really wanted anything more to drink. But fuck it, if someone buys you a drink it's unspeakably rude not to drink it. We sat talking for another minute or two, then I figured it was time to go get the pictures we needed. Big Ian came with me to provide the distraction.

'You know what you're doing?'

'Oh yeah, don't facking worry. You just go in there and get the picture.

'We went around the far side of the bar. I hung back a little bit while Big Ian went down to where the private booths were. The bouncer, eagle-eyed and vigilant as he was, spotted him straight away and came over, making it quite clear he wasn't allowed in this part. Ian started gesticulating wildly, like an Italian being electrocuted, but this didn't do anything but make the bouncer look even more grumpy than he already did. He began to push Big Ian back towards the end of the bar, at which point my old mate froze on the spot, holding his left arm. The bouncer looked confused, then Ian's hands went to his chest, and he slumped to the ground. Brilliant, the classic 'I'm having a heart attack' move, and he was so overweight it was immediately credible. The bouncer knelt down to check him out while Ian convulsed on the ground, and, even above the pumping music, I could hear him groaning and moaning in pretend pain.

The bouncer now looked panicked – people dying on the premises was something to be avoided at all costs. He raced off to the front of the club to get someone out there to call an ambulance, at which point Ian gave me the thumbs-up. I moved quickly down to booth four, turned on the camera, made sure the flash was on, that it was set to 'auto' (no fancy exposures for me, definitely no pun intended) and went inside.

Like a marksman on a range I simply became one with the camera, pointing and clicking at the couple engaged in the frenetic and quite possibly illegal sex act they were performing. The problem was, it was one of the Japanese businessmen and the buxom redhead who had done that striptease earlier. I was a hundred per cent sure this was the booth Coleman had entered – I had seen it with my own eyes – but now there was no sign of him.

Absinthe Makes the Heart Grow Fonder

32

Fisticuffs

I left the booth to the sound of the Japanese businessman shouting at me (it seemed the flash photography had put him off his stroke) and found Big Ian standing just outside. 'Get it?'

'He's not in there.'

'Well, where the fack did he go then? You're sure that's the one he went into?'

'Positive.'

Just then, the bouncer who had witnessed Ian's heart attack came rushing back over with another two of his colleagues and a first-aid kit that you might find in the local supermarket. I wouldn't go so far as to say he looked like he'd seen a ghost when he saw Ian standing up healthy and chatting away to me instead of frothing at the mouth and on the brink of death, but he was certainly surprised. His surprise turned to sheer astonishment when the Japanese businessman burst out of the door of the booth, still doing up his trousers, and began to shout loudly in Japanese, gesticulating wildly and pointing in my direction.

Knowing there was no chance of the bouncer understanding Japanese I wasn't too worried. That was until the young lady who had been entertaining him followed him out, and, while looking at me, told him and his mates exactly what had happened. They took a moment to confer then moved towards us in almost perfect synchronicity. It was like they'd rehearsed it.

'Hey, did you take pictures?' said the lead guy in Spanish.

'No. Why would I want to take pictures?'

'You're a pervert. Or some kind of asshole.'

'Nope. I didn't take any pictures. Did I, Big Ian?'

'No, no pictures here.'

'And you, fat boy,' said the bouncer, 'feeling better?'

'Yeah, just a stitch, I think. Better now, thanks. We'll just be going.'

'Oh, I don't think you will,' said the second bouncer, who had a head like a Slavic Hellboy after he'd been worked over with a couple of baseball bats. 'There's a room at the back where we're going to have a chat, and we'll see if you took any pictures.'

'There's no need for any of that,' I said. 'We'll leave, you go about the rest of your evening, no problem.'

'I'm sorry, but there are things we don't allow in this club, and photographing our guests is one of them.

Imagine if word got out that people were taking cameras into a place like this. Who knows what they might do with those pictures? Websites, blackmail, you see? So we need to make it very clear to anyone else who might be thinking about doing that what happens if they do. We're going to make an example of you.'

'I don't think you are,' I said, picking up a glass off the bar. 'Come near me and this is going in your face.'

'Problem?' said Jimmy from behind me.

'You might say that,' I replied, over my shoulder. 'I went to get the picture of Coleman, and the little cunt wasn't in there. Instead I got a load of pictures of that Japanese guy. He's not happy, the bouncers aren't happy, they've got it sussed that Big Ian's distraction was exactly that, and now they want to make an example of us in some room out the back of the club.'

'Oh, that is a bit of a problem.'

'Twenty, I reckon we're ever so slightly facked here mate,' said Big Ian, picking up a bottle from the bar.

'You might be right there.'

'Jimmy, whaddya reckon?'

'I reckon we're going to have to take our chances. Where's Idiot Boy?'

'No idea.'

'Fuck. Big Ian, any idea how many other bouncers there might be in this place?'

'I know they have a control room upstairs, so at least another two or three there. There must be two more on the door and, behind the scenes, in the changing rooms and so on, I dunno, another couple.'

'Right, so we're fairly outnumbered. Are they armed in any way?'

'Possibly. Not armed in the traditional sense, but there are probably some batons or saps in the mix there.'

'Not so good. These blokes are big.'

And Jimmy was playing it down a bit there. These bouncers were a cut above the regular thick-necked, 'roid' monkeys you saw in Dublin. Guys who went to the gym and worked out religiously to ensure they had the kind of upper body that would be the envy of anyone. Yet when you saw them their massive pecs and biceps looked ridiculous against their skinny legs, which they singularly failed to do anything with. You didn't punch people in the back of the head with your legs, you see.

The ones we were faced with, though, were a mix of locals and some Eastern Europeans, who were monstrous. Their pale blue eyes were dead – you knew they'd kill you and bury you in a shallow grave as quick as look at you. Even under normal circumstances this would be a difficult task, even for a sly fighter like me, but being on the piss all day meant this was going to be trickier than getting George W. Bush to make any kind of sense for longer than ten seconds. The bouncers kept coming towards us; we moved backwards. I knew Jimmy would be handy in a fight, but this wasn't looking good.

'Whaddya reckon, Jimmy? Shall we go for them? Surprise attack? They might not be expecting it,' I said.

'Might be an idea all right.'

'Got any other ideas?'

'Not really.'

'Big Ian?'

'Fack this shit. Let's take 'em, facking cants.'

'All right. On three. Ready?'

'Yeah.'

'Aye.'

'OK, one . . . two . . . '

Just as I got to 'three', the fanfare blared out from the DJ booth up at the back end of the club. The last time that fanfare was heard, the buxom redhead made her way down towards the stage on the chair suspended from the ceiling. There was a gasp as the chair started its slow progress across the club, loud enough for the bouncers to hear it over the music and to stop their movement towards us.

I looked up expecting to see a truly exotic and beautiful woman – the astonished noises were surely evidence of that – but instead I saw Coleman, his T-shirt pulled up to just below his chest, suspended ten feet above us.

'Woooooooooooooooooo!' he yelled as the music kicked in and the whole bar turned to look at this six-foot-two Irishman looking more out of place than an Arab at a bar miztvah.

'Holy shit!' I said to Jimmy. 'Look at that.'

'Fucking hell.'

At this point the bouncers had kind of forgotten about us – this was far more important. The strip club prided itself on having hot females strip off, and this was all wrong. There must have been a girl waiting to use the chair. What had happened to her, and why was this hairy brute now getting ever closer to the stage? They followed

Coleman's progress, positioning themselves underneath him and jumping up to try and get him down. He remained out of reach, performing some rather acrobatic moves on the chair, teasing them and mocking them when they missed.

Every single person in the club was watching the scene unfold in front of them, and the gasps that met his first appearance were nothing compared to the ones when he, trying to hang on with his knees, lost his grip and fell right on top of the three bouncers, flattening them into the ground.

'Oh fuck,' I said. 'Here we go.'

The bouncers managed to right themselves, leaving Coleman laughing his head off on the floor at the sheer japery of it all. That didn't last too long when the three of them hopped on him and started laying into him with their fists. However, Coleman being a rugby player meant he was used to being pummelled by a load of guys and used his strength to kick one of them free, pull one of them over his shoulder and, from a position on his back, land the most incredible head butt right into the face of the remaining guy.

'Awww yeah! This is aaaaaaawwwesome!'

The bouncers didn't seem to share his sense of fun though. The one who got head butted crawled away behind the bar, his mouth and nose gushing blood, and began talking into a radio on his lapel. We went over to where Coleman was and formed a kind of circle – like wagons we were.

The bouncer who had been kicked off was getting

back to his feet, so I really had no choice but to try and stop him. I picked a bottle up from a table and cracked it over the back of his head, which made him cry out in pain but didn't put him down. What did put him down was Big Ian throwing a small chrome stool at him, the metal bits at the bottom catching right in the side of the head. The second one came at Jimmy, fists raised in the classic boxing style. He threw a punch, catching Jimmy in the ear. If there's anything Jimmy hates it's being hit in the ear. Face, nose, stomach, kidneys, anywhere else and it's all part of the game as far as he's concerned, but hitting Jimmy in the ear is like poking a stick into a hornet's nest. He just loses it, and when Jimmy loses it, you don't want to be in the way. He charged the bouncer, drove his shoulders into his stomach, lifted him up and carried him towards the railings of the raised area. He slammed the bouncer into the railings, knocking the wind out of him, then grabbed him by the hair and began to smash his head off the ground. When there was enough blood to suggest the bloke wasn't getting up any time soon, Jimmy stopped.

In the meantime, the bouncer who had gone behind the bar had obviously called for reinforcements, and another four bouncers came through the main doors and towards us. These ones were carrying things in their hands, and were just as big and much less defenceless than the others.

'Fuck, these cunts mean business.'

'I know what to do!' said Coleman.

'What?' I said.

'The haka.'

'The what?'

'You know the mad dance the All Blacks do before a game of rugby?'

'Yeah, why the fuck would we want to do that?'

'It's intimidating.'

'Look, this is no time for gay South Pacific dancing. Join a musical society if that's your bag. We should—,' but he had started.

He started beating his chest and slapping his thighs and chanting what I assume was the haka, but it sounded more like gobbledygook crossed with mumbo-jumbo with a healthy dose of hogwash on top. I have to say, I stepped back. It wasn't that I was trying to get out of the fighting thing, but I just really didn't want to be associated with that kind of carry-on. It was fine when you were a sixteen-stone Pacific Islander who has mysteriously become a New Zealander, but this wasn't something for Irish people. It didn't stop Coleman though as he continued his bizarre ritual until he was almost right in front of the incredulous-looking bouncers. They were used to perverts and overly touchy middle-aged men who were easy to intimidate and throw out. This wasn't something they'd ever encountered before, and, I have to say, they did look a bit nervous.

By now, most of the girls knew something was going on, and they had stopped trying to chat up the men and were transfixed on what was about to unfold. I looked at Jimmy and shrugged while Big Ian, the most unflappable person I have ever met, was looking on with his mouth open, unable to quite understand what was happening. The four bouncers stood shoulder to shoulder, like a macho Il Divo, with Coleman now in front of them, wailing and grunting and beating his head between his hands like a mad person. Eventually, he stopped the haka, stood with his hands on his hips and began shouting at them in English.

'How about that then? What about that, eh? You shitting it? You should be!' he bellowed. He turned around to me and said, 'I told you that would intimidate them,' which was exactly when one of the bouncers decided that would be the perfect time to grab him while one of the others smacked him over the head with some kind of baton.

'Owwww, you fuckers, like, hit me,' said Coleman, turning back around. The one thing I had to give him credit for was his ability to break out of situations where he was being held. Perhaps there was an upside to rugby after all. Forget fitness or the enjoyment of playing a tough, physical sport, winning trophies and such, the only good thing about it was the fact that it was handy when someone was trying to pummel you.

He shook off the first bouncer and drove his elbow into the face of the second one. Despite the fact the music was still on I could hear the noise of his cheekbone breaking. He then turned his attention back to the one he'd shaken off, getting him in a kind of choke hold. Actually, it was exactly a choke hold because the fella went red, then blue, then his tongue flopped out of his head, his eyes bulged, and he began to foam at the mouth a bit.

Coleman let go then went after the guy with the broken cheek who was trying to get to the front door but was so dizzy with pain he was careering from one side of the club to the other.

'Here we go then,' said Jimmy, who went straight over to one of the other gigantic bouncers and hit him with a right hook. The guy didn't even flinch. Jimmy hit him again. Same thing. A sly, smug smile appeared on the bouncer's face, almost daring Jimmy to hit him again, which Jimmy did. Again the guy didn't even move a muscle, despite the fact that his nose had started to bleed. By now his smile was most sinister indeed and made it clear that it was his turn to start throwing punches.

Jimmy held up one finger in a 'just one more go' gesture to which the bloke agreed, safe in his own head that Jimmy's punches weren't going to bother him or his big, thick skull. Jimmy cracked his knuckles, drew his arm back, threw the punch but, at the last second, ducked down and landed a powerful uppercut straight into the bouncer's groin.

No matter how well you can take a punch, being clobbered right in the bollocks is enough to send any man down, no matter how strong. Only the truly insane can withstand their testicles being slugged like an Illinois prize fighter, and this bloke certainly wasn't from Illinois. Or insane. Whichever.

With Jimmy now laying the boot in good and hard, it left just one bouncer for me and Big Ian to deal with. I suppose between us Big Ian and I were the perfect fighting machine: I was nimble and dextrous; he was big and powerful. However, we hadn't quite thought about how we were going to team up together to fight this guy, and, before I knew it, I'd been sent flying back across the room with a kick which caught me right in the solar plexus. As I was struggling to get my breath back, I saw him try a similar kick on Big Ian, but he might as well have been trying to kick an oak tree out of a field. He then took a sap out his pocket and started trying to beat Ian around the head with it.

'Oi, you facking cant, stop that. Fight like a facking man,' Ian shouted but the bloke wasn't interested in fighting like a man. And who could blame him? If I was fighting someone I'd be much happier if I had a weapon of some kind. Ian was trying to protect his head from the battering, and I knew I had to go over and help him. I struggled to my feet, took a few deep breaths and was just about to launch myself into the fray when the Japanese businessman, now practically insane with anger and fear that the pictures I had might end up on some voyeur's website, leapt on my back.

'Camela!' he screamed. 'Camela!'

'Get the fuck off me you little ninja bastard,' I said, but he clung to me, his arms around my neck, and his hands scraping at my face. In the meantime, I could see Coleman doing the kind of moves on the bouncer that Randy 'Macho Man' Savage himself would have been proud of. Big Ian was toe to toe with the bouncer with the sap while Jimmy was still trying to make sure his opponent didn't get up.

'Camela!'

'Fuck off, I need the fucking camela,' I said, spinning around trying to get him off me. I backed up and tried to smash his back into the corner of the bar but he was a clever little fucker and, at the last minute, let go so my own weight carried me into the bar. It got me right in the kidney which made me want to puke and piss myself at the same time, but I couldn't let myself as the Japanese businessman was standing in front of me yelling at me about the camera again. He was fucking relentless.

The bouncer Big Ian was fighting was getting the upper hand, and he needed my help. I didn't want to hurt the little Japanese fella, he was really an innocent party in all this, but I didn't have any choice. I stood up straight and gave him one of my patented karate chops to the neck. Perhaps it was being Oriental and brought up with martial arts, but he appeared to have some kind of immunity to my powerful blow. It did seem to make him more irate though, and he came at me again. I ducked out of his way and shimmied left, but he still came after me. I needed something to hit him with, so I leapt over the bar but slipped and ended up lying on my back.

I figured he'd come after me so I picked up a couple of margarita glasses from the shelf beside me. I held them by the base right up in the air, and, just as I had extended my arms fully, he came over the bar shrieking like a demon. This was nothing compared to the shrieking he did as both glasses broke on his face, one of them embedding itself in his cheek up to the stem. I felt sorry for him, but fuck it.

I got up, took a bottle of Champagne from the fridge

and jumped across the bar again.

Big Ian was now taking a bit of a beating from his bouncer who was so busy trying to hit him with the sap he didn't notice me come up behind him. This made it quite easy to crack the back of his skull with the heavy bottom part of the bottle. He fell forward on his face, so I hit him a couple more times. I know they say you shouldn't hit people when their back is turned, but, you know, that always struck me as the best time to hit someone. Less chance of you being hit back.

Jimmy's bouncer was unconscious on the floor, so I hit him in the head with the bottle too. The one Coleman had choked looked half-dead so I hit him as well, while the one with the broken cheekbone was still being toyed with like he were a mouse and Coleman a tomcat. 'Coleman!' I yelled, 'leave him alone.' Coleman stopped, which is when I hit the bouncer in the head with the bottle. Just to make it all even. 'Right you cunts, we need to get the fuck out of here,' I said.

'That's a good idea,' said Big Ian, bleeding slightly from the top of his head, 'they'll get cops down quick enough, and we do not want to be here when that happens.'

We all made our way out into the entrance hall, past the one bouncer who was still standing there, looking incredibly shocked at the state of us going out of the club, particularly as Coleman let out a guttural roar as we went past. We left, turned right and ran down as far as Passeig de Sant Joan as we could before ducking into a doorway to get our breath. We stood there for a bit licking our wounds.

'Fucking hell,' I said, exhausted.

'Jesus, that was a bit much,' said Big Ian.

'A bit too close for comfort there,' said Jimmy.

'That was awesome!' said Coleman. 'Now where are we going?!'

33

Never-ending story

I couldn't believe after all that booze, the supposedly foolproof Benetton in the strip club and everything else, that Coleman didn't appear to be slowing down at all. It was now 3 a.m., and most of the bars would be closing. The only option was another nightclub, so we jumped in a cab and headed to a place called Le Terrazza. This was up in Poble Espanyol in Montjuïc, and the place itself was originally built in the late twenties as part of an exposition. It was like a Spanish village but featured all the various architectural styles of the time from all over the country. Le Terrazza was a trendy nightclub that took advantage of the great climate by having a large part of it outdoors, so you could mix with the trendies and dance under the stars. On the way there, we drank the bottle of Champagne – even the taxi driver had a bit. The Spanish really don't give a fuck about drink-driving. He told us some crazy story about picking up a Barcelona player from an apartment in Gracia where he kept his secret family – secret because his mistress had a child who was a mutant and if he ever was viewed in public people would think less of the footballer. He wouldn't tell us who it was though, teasing fucker.

We paid into the nightclub, Jimmy went to the bar, Big Ian went to the bathroom to clean himself up a bit, and I was left with Coleman.

'So, what happened with your private dance?'

'Oh, thanks and all that, but I could see from that girl's face that she wanted to suck my cock. After all these years of being so attractive to women because of who I am I can just tell when they want to suck my cock. And I'm getting married so it wouldn't be right for her to do that. I just said thanks and went up to the toilet.'

'Right. I see. Well, how the fuck did you manage to end up on the chair?'

'Ahh, see, I went into what I thought was the toilet, and it turned out it was, like, a kind of dressing room. There was a girl in there and all, but she was just sitting in the corner crying.'

'Why was she crying?'

'Who cares? She's just a stripper – they're not real people. Anyway, I sat in the chair, and next thing I knew I was heading towards the stage. So I thought I'd better play up a bit, give them a flash of the old Coleman six-pack, you know?'

'Yeah, you're always thinking of others.'

'I have to say, this has been, like, the most fun I've ever had. For an old bastard you really are all right, Twenty. Coming dancing?'

'I'd rather suck your cock.'

'I know you would!'

And with that he took himself off to the dance-floor.

I sat down at a table, and, when Jimmy came over, I explained what had happened with the private dancer, the dancer for money.

'Fuck this, Twenty. I'm wrecked. I really can't take any more. Let's just kill him.'

'Did you see him in that club? He creamed those two bouncers without breaking a sweat. If we're going to kill him, we need to get him somewhere quiet then shoot him in the back of the head. And, anyway, we can't kill him. Tony might not kill us if he ends up dead, but he'd get us somehow. We'd end up vegetables or cripples or more fingerless than we'd like. We've got to try and do something here.'

'Yeah, like what? If we can't get him to do something in a strip club when it's laid on a plate for him then he's unlikely to do anything here, is he?'

'I suppose not.'

'And why is the cunt not that pissed yet? I can drink. I've been drinking my whole life. I pride myself on being able to drink lots and lots without becoming a slurring monster, but he's ridiculous. He must have hollow legs or something.'

'I have no idea. I'm like you but I've had so much to drink tonight I feel like Homer in that episode of *The Simpsons* where he has the steak-eating contest, and each time he puts a bit more meat in his mouth it just plops back out,' I said, taking a sip from the beer Jimmy had brought over, which just spilled out of my mouth and down my front. 'See?'

'What the fuck are we going to do?'

'You know what? I don't have a fucking clue. At this point, we just need to wait and see if something happens that we can take advantage of. Trying to manufacture a situation hasn't worked.'

'And what if nothing happens?'

'Then I guess we might as well just enjoy the rest of the night.'

So, while Coleman danced, and we kept feeding him with drink in the vain hope that he might get drunk enough for us to set something up, the night passed.

I sat in the outside area smoking a big joint that Big Ian had brought with him. I thought back to the time when we asked Tony Furriskey for help, and I wished I could, like Cher, turn back time and look elsewhere for help. In fact, it might even have been better to just let those guys deal with us. They weren't cruel and vindictive, just mean and nasty (there is a subtle difference in the world I inhabit) and would probably have gotten it over and done with quickly.

As the joint fogged my brain, I watched the people – the young, healthy, energetic people – dancing to the uplifting house tunes the DJ was playing. They were here because they wanted to be, because they wanted to have fun, dance, meet people, socialise – and at the end of it they could go home, or go to a party or another early morning club without worrying. Here I was, once one of those young people, now utterly jealous at their freedom, how liberated they were, how they weren't worrying about being tortured to death by a notorious criminal.

I thought about just staying in Barcelona and not going back, but Tony would find me, and he'd make it his business to find me. And if I put him to that much trouble, he'd be sure to make the end even worse. Then I thought about my home, and my trusty hound Bastardface. I wished he was here with me, sitting beside me. I'd give his massive big head a rub, and he, knowing I was feeling a bit maudlin and sentimental, would rest that head on my lap, and we could both sit there smoking the joint. He loved White Widow. I had to go back. I couldn't abandon him.

Then I had a brilliant idea. Did I not have a friend who was an assassin? I took out my phone and rang Lucky's house. It rang for ages and ages until a voice said 'Che cazzo vuoi?'

'Lucky, it's me, Twenty.'

'OK, I say again, but a this time in English: What a the fuck do you want?'

'I need you to kill somebody for me.'

'You know a what time is?'

'Sure. But this is very important.'

'I'm a tell you what is important, that a my pregnant wife not wake up because then she get a more tired, and my life become even more difficult.'

'Lucky, seriously. This guy is going to kill me and Jimmy.'

'Why?'

So I explained to him the whole situation and the predicament we found ourselves in. I asked him, as my friend, to do this for me and told him I would pay his normal rate. I wasn't looking for a freebie.

'No. I'm a not kill him.'

'What? Why the fuck not?'

'You a know I am compassionate assassin, only kill a the people I think deserve to die. Now, this man he a save your life and when he ask for you to a repay him you fail a worse than Mary Harney with a health service. Why he a deserve to die and not you?'

'You poxy assassins and your moral code. Thanks for nothing.' I was just about to hang up when he spoke again.

'Twenty, wait.'

'Yeah?'

'If you ever a ring here again so early I will a kill you like a the dog you are.'

I didn't even get to call him a cunt before the phone clicked off. It's during difficult times that you find out who you can count on, and I now knew that I couldn't count on Italian assassins when you ring them at some ungodly time of the morning. I sat there for a while hoping his wife would have mutant children, then I realised that was a bit harsh – a lifetime of caring for them and their peculiarities would be just too much – so I wished they were all stillborn.

I sat outside for another bit before going back inside to drink the rest of the night away with Jimmy and Big Ian. I discovered that I could stomach the mojitos so I ordered them two at a time. It seemed like an age since we'd been in Else's bar drinking the best mojitos in the whole world. Now I wasn't sure if I'd ever drink a mojito again. In the end, I just stopped worrying and tried to get as drunk as possible.

We left the club about 6 a.m., and wandering down the road, so high up above the city, the view was just magnificent. The whole of Barcelona spread about below us, parts of it sheathed in a golden light as the sun came up. It really was beautiful, and, despite being tired, drunk and more than a bit emotional I felt a sense of calm and well-being.

'Now what?!' said an eager Coleman.

The sense of well-being evaporated. Here I was, banjaxed with the tiredness, Jimmy's eyes were hanging out of his head, Big Ian looked fit to drop, and this cunt was like the Duracell bunny. I hated him. Hated him with every fibre of my being. More than I hated terrible folk music or cloves, and let me tell you something, I hate cloves really a lot. Why would anyone want to eat something that tastes like licking the top of a battery?

'What say you we go back to my place?' said Big Ian. 'I've got some beers in the fridge, a great big bag of grass and a terrace to sit out on.'

'That sounds like a plan,' I said.

'Cool,' said Coleman, 'we can drink some more and tell jokes about northsiders and immigrants.'

'I don't suppose you have an axe, do you?' asked Jimmy.

Coleman told northsider jokes all the way back in the taxi. It was like hell on Earth, but in a car.

34

Beaten

We got back to Big Ian's, and, sure enough, he had beers in the fridge. The sun was well and truly up now, and I had to borrow a pair of sunglasses to protect my eyes from the burn. There is no sun brighter than the one you're faced with after being up all night. I sat out at the table, a condensation-covered bottle of Estrella in front of me, and I got busy rolling a joint. 'You shouldn't smoke, man. It's bad for you,' said Coleman, his beer almost finished. 'Oh aye? That's a bit rich coming from you, isn't it?'

'Why?'

'Well, drinking is bad for you, isn't it? And snorting coke is bad for you too. Especially if you're a finely tuned athlete.'

'Everyone drinks man, and everyone snorts coke. It's just what people do these days. You're just too old to understand.'

'I'm people too, and I'll smoke, and I'll smoke without any fucking lectures from you, right?'

'Oooooh!' said Coleman, tweaking his nipples, 'listen to her!'

I figured if I said anything it wouldn't be good so I just kept my mouth shut, finished the joint and lit it up. Big Ian and Jimmy were talking about football, debating it like reasoned adults even though they supported teams who were direct rivals. Coleman wasn't having it though.

'Football is rubbish.'

'So's your face,' said Jimmy.

'What's so facking rubbish about football? You probably don't like it because you can't get a handful of some guy's balls like you can in rugby.'

'They're just so, like, wimpy, you know? I mean, look at that Cristiano Ronaldo guy. The moment anyone touches him he falls to the ground, rolling like a, like, girl. In rugby, at least the players can take a bit of physical contact.'

'Yeah, I suppose you have a point there. Still, at least if he grabs a handful of someone's balls it's in his own time and not in a stadium full of people.'

The rugby-versus-football debate went on for quite some time with Coleman getting quite excitable and saying our reasons for saying football was better were rubbish. My contention was that if rugby were better than football then more people would play rugby than football instead of the other way around. Also, instead of Sky paying millions and millions for the rights to show football, we'd have Super Sunday Rugby – if it was truly better than football. Rugby players would be much better paid than their round-ball counterparts if it were a better game. Where was the David Beckham of rugby?

Coleman said I was mixing up better with popular, but he missed the point: the better something is, the more popular it is. Like Westlife and X-Factor.

As we sat there on his terrace, we drank the beer from Big Ian's fridge, smoked joints and generally got more and more tired. Coleman went to the toilet at one stage, allowing me to talk to Jimmy.

'I'm done, man.'

'Me too. I can't drink any more, I can't smoke any more, and all I want to do is crawl into bed, pull the curtains and sleep for eighteen hours.'

'Doesn't that mean you're completely facked with that bloke back in Dublin?'

'Yeah,' I said, 'it does, but this lad is like the Terminator. He just doesn't seem to be getting drunk at all. There isn't a drink we haven't tried to get him pissed, and he's immune to it all. I bet he could keep going all week without any sleep. I know when I'm beaten. And I'm as beaten as a ginger stepchild.'

'Oh,' said Jimmy, 'I've got an idea.'

'What's that?'

'Lucky!'

'Nope. Already tried.'

'You what?'

'Yeah, I rang him when we were in the nightclub up in Montjuïc. He said he wouldn't kill Tony for us and said I was the one who deserved to die for ringing him at that time of night.'

'Oh, he's got a point, although that is a bit cunty. Well, then, we're well and truly fucked. Gimme that joint.'

We passed the joint around until I realised the beers were all gone. I went into the kitchen to get some more but opened the fridge to find it empty – empty of beer anyway.

'Oi, Big Ian. No beer left.'

'That's a facking pain. You fancy going to get some more?'

'No, fuck that, man. If I go out the front door I'm getting straight into a taxi and heading for the hotel. You got anything else?'

'Don't think so. Had a party in the week, and everything's been guzzled. There might be a half bottle of peach schnapps.'

'Fuck that. That stuff is poison.'

Well, that was it. Time to call it a night. An incredibly long, difficult, trying, wearisome and problematic night.

We'd have to go back to Dublin and throw ourselves on the mercy of Tony, knowing full well he had about as much mercy as a woman with breast cancer has chance of getting a correct diagnosis in an Irish hospital. Well, we all had our time, didn't we? This was going to be ours. It would have been nice to just have one more drink on top of all the other drinks but with nothing there we couldn't do anything.

But then I spotted something on the ground between the sofa and the wall. A familiar-looking plastic bag. I went over. There were the two bottles of absinthe that Jimmy had bought the previous day on the way down here. We hadn't taken them with us, and now here was more booze.

And the type of booze which reminded me that even when we called it quits here I couldn't go and crash. I had to face my past and rescue Stinking Pete. That absinthe that fucked up my life in Barcelona. I had avoided it ever since, but desperate times and all that.

'Look what I found,' I said, carrying the bottles out onto the terrace.

'Oh facking hell, here's where it all starts going wrong!'

'Fuck it,' said Jimmy, 'at this point it can't get any worse.'

I went back into the kitchen and started rummaging around for glasses and small spoons. I brought out glasses and teaspoons, and, although Big Ian didn't have sugar cubes, we were far too fucked to be worried about the niceties of absinthe-drinking. Normal sugar would do. I balanced a sugar-filled teaspoon over each glass then poured a large shot of absinthe over the sugar and into the glass. I then used the lighter to light the sugar, which burned and melted into the alcohol.

'What's this?' said Coleman, just back from his trip to the bog.

'Absinthe.'

'Oh cool. I heard some people talking about this before. It's supposed to get you proper mashed. I've never had it before though.'

'There's always a first time, eh?'

After the sugar had burned off the spoons it created a

cloudy mixture in each glass. Cloudy like my future. Cloudy like an old man's urine. Just cloudy.

'OK then, before we drink these, I'd like to propose a toast. To the groom, I hope your life is miserable and you regret marrying that girl every day of your life—'

'Har, I get it. That's, like, ironic!'

'Jimmy, it's been a pleasure. To the good times. And Big Ian, thanks for having us. It was good to see you again before the end.'

'Facking right, Twenty.'

'Cheers everyone,' I said. We clinked glasses, and we all downed our shots. I could feel the burn start in my mouth, drip down my throat and into my belly. Eighty-proof booze will do that to you.

'Jesus, that's strong.'

'Blubalubalubalub,' said Big Ian, shaking his head like a wet dog. 'Fack me.'

'Oh,' said Coleman, still holding his glass. 'That's . . .'

'That's what?' I said.

'That's . . .'

'What? Come on, spit it out.'

'That's . . .' he said again, before toppling backwards off the chair. There was a sickening thunk as his head hit the terrace and the glass fell from his hand and shattered. I went over to have a look, and he was out cold. I slapped his face a couple of times, not a movement or acknowledgement. I pinched the bit of skin on the back of his upper arm, the most painful bit of skin there is to pinch, but he didn't move a muscle. Alarmed, I checked to see if he was still breathing, and, thankfully, he was.

'He's out cold.'

'Thank fuck for that,' said Jimmy. 'Now we don't have to listen to any more of his fucking shite. Shame it didn't happen earlier in the night.'

'What are you going to do with him?' said Big Ian. 'Leave him there, and he's going to burn to death in the sun.'

'Can we use your spare room?'

'Sure. You just gonna let him sleep it off?'

'Eventually.'

'Eventually?'

'Yeah. Jimmy, I've just had a fucking great idea.'

I took out my phone and dialled, almost praying for an answer.

'Hello,' said a voice eventually.

'Dave. Twenty. I need your help.'

'You need my help?'

'Yeah. It's quite literally a matter of life and death. I need you and Gloria to come and meet me.'

'Gloria too?'

'Oh yeah. Definitely Gloria,' I said and gave him Ian's address. I told him to get here as quickly as he could, no messing, no typical Dirty Dave stupidity. I hung up and waited. Perhaps there was a way out of this after all.

35

Stripped ease

I have to say that despite my instructions I was expecting something to go wrong so it was a pleasant surprise when about half an hour later the buzzer went. Even then I expected it to be the police or somebody looking for some of Big Ian's stuff, but it was Dave and an immaculately made-up Gloria. 'I came right over. What's going on?'

'Well, you know the way we came over here to try and stop that guy marrying the girl back in Dublin?'

'Did we?'

'Yeah. Remember me telling you on the plane on the way over and how important everything was and that if you didn't help that me and Jimmy would be killed in a most awful and painful way?'

'No.'

'I told you all about that time Tony went after Stinking

Pete's cousin and flayed him alive, rolled him in salt, dipped him in vinegar then set him on fire in that warehouse out in Cabinteely. You did the reading at the bloke's funeral and everything.'

'Are you sure it was me?'

'Jesus Christ. Look, forget it—'

'Forget what?'

'Dave, shut up now. Anyway, the point is we have to get some evidence so Tony can show it to his daughter and so that she'll then call off the wedding with this bloke.'

'Where is he?'

'In the spare room, absolutely out for the count.'

'Right, well, what do you want from me?'

'Nothing from you exactly, but . . .'

'But?'

'We need to catch Coleman "in flagrante delicto", so to speak.'

'You need to catch him with ice cream? I'm confused.'

'Let me try and spell this out for you, if I can. Coleman is unconscious. I have a camera. We need to get some pictures of Coleman involved in "sexy time" with some sexy dame. Now, are you a sexy dame?'

'I am not.'

'Would you say that Jimmy or Big Ian or I were sexy dames?'

'I would not.'

'Right then. Who does that leave?'

'That just leaves Gloria. She's certainly a sexy dame and . . . oh . . . no! NO!'

'Look, she doesn't actually have to do anything. We

just need to get some pictures to make it look like she is.'

'But Twenty, this could upset the delicate balance of our relationship. We've had the most wonderful weekend together. You know how I have despaired of ever finding true love, but I think this is it. We connect on so many levels.'

'Probably one less level than you might like.'

'What's that supposed to mean?'

'Nothing.'

'We can talk and talk and never get bored or tired. If we were on the phone we'd definitely do that "You hang up. No, you hang up" thing. I've never had that with anyone before, and I don't want anything to mess it up.'

'Look, I promise you nothing I do will have an effect on your new relationship.'

'Promise? And not one of your promises that you make with your fingers crossed which ends up with me bleeding from somewhere or locked down a basement for days or anything else.'

'I promise. Look, doing this will save our lives, mine and Jimmy's. And we won't forget that, will we Jimmy?'

'Absolutely not. And Twenty's right, nothing he does or asks you to get Gloria to do will have any bearing on your future.'

'OK, if you're sure. I mean, I'm asking her to do something with some passed-out guy, and I've never even seen her naked. She might be shy.'

'She might be quite reluctant, all right, but you're going to have to convince her this is the right thing to do. For your mates, Dave, and you don't turn your back on your mates like some kind of shitbag Italian.'

'Right, well, let me go talk to her,' he said, and he went out to the terrace where Gloria, perhaps sensing something was up, was sucking away on one of the joints that was lying in the ashtray. I saw Dave talking to her, using a lot of hand gestures as his non-existent Spanish and her pidgin English still provided many barriers to effective communication.

'You reckon he'll get her to do it?' said Jimmy.

'I'm sure he will.'

'Your mate, he does know that girl isn't a girl, right?' said Big Ian.

'Nope. He hasn't got a clue. He's a good bloke, but he's as thick as jellied vomit.'

'Well, this is going to be a big facking surprise then, isn't it?'

'You could say that all right.'

'Poor fucker,' said Jimmy. 'I feel a bit sorry for him in a way. It seems wrong to spoil his happiness, but we need to do it. Plus, we're saving him a bit.'

'How's that?'

'We're going home tonight, so chances are they weren't going to consummate the relationship. This would result in a long-distance correspondence, expensive phone calls and the like, and, eventually, he'd come back here to satisfy his most base of urges. He gets her into bed, goes for a lick of the bearded clam and gets a mouthful of cock instead. We've saved him money, time and emotional investment.'

'A good point. He might not thank us now, but, in the long run, it's for the best.'

Just then, Dave came back in with Gloria holding his hand, her mascara running a bit where she had obviously been crying.

'She doesn't want to do it, but I told her it was important and it would help my friends so she said she'd do it . . . for me.' He looked at her and smiled sadly at her.

Perhaps it was all the booze and smoke and how tired I was, but I felt my heart sink a bit for poor old Dave. So long looking for true love, and, God help him, the one time he found it, it was like this. I smiled back at him.

'Thanks, Dave.'

'No problem, Twenty. Anything for a friend.'

We made our way into the spare room where Coleman was flat on his back, his tongue lolling out of his mouth and snoring like a pig with sinus problems. 'We're going to have to get his clothes off,' I said. I gathered from the silence that nobody was too interested in helping me with this part, so, bit by bit, I stripped him. As I was pulling off his T-shirt, his arm shot out and grabbed me, scaring the shit out of me. It was just an involuntary reaction though, he wasn't waking back up. I got his T-shirt off, and he was left there in his boxers which had the Silver Surfer on them.

'Nobody?' I tried. Nobody was right. I grabbed them and pulled them down his legs, lifting his feet to try and get them off without having to get a good view of his chocolate starfish. I stood back.

'We may have a problem here,' said Jimmy. 'Look at that!'

'What?'

'His lad. It's shrivelled up because of all the booze and coke. If these pics are going to be realistic, it's going to have to be a bit more standy-to-attention than that.'

'Well, what the fuck do you want me to do about it?'

'You're gonna have to do something.'

'Why me?'

'Because I'm not going to.'

I looked around the room. There was no eye contact. Oh Jesus. Over on the counter I spotted a feather duster which I picked up and used to tickle his mickey to try and make it look vaguely active, but that didn't work.

'I heard that even if someone's unconscious,' said Big Ian, 'if you stimulate their prostate it'll give them a stiffy.'

'Oh fuck. I can't do that.'

'Look, Twenty,' said Jimmy, 'if someone gave you the choice between stimulating someone's prostate and being killed in a barbaric manner, which would you choose?'

'Fuck. Shit. The prostate.'

'Well, there you go then!'

'You have the same choice.'

'I know, but there's no way I'm going anywhere near his arsehole.'

'Fucking hell, what kind of friends do I have?'

I went into the kitchen and had another look around. Eventually I found a knife with a round yellow plastic handle which I took back in. I sat down on the bed and tried to lift Coleman's legs but trying to hold them up and use the knife was too much. 'Dave, c'mere and hold his legs up in the air.'

And Dave, being a good friend, did exactly that.

Holding the knife by the blade I rammed the handle up Coleman's hole and started wiggling it around. I figured I'd whack off the prostate every so often. After a couple of minutes, I had a look over the top, and, unbelievably, it had worked. 'Right, I'm going to keep this going. Dave, can you tell Gloria to get herself ready?'

'OK, Twenty,' he said sadly. 'If that's what you really want.'

'It is.'

'OK.' He let Coleman's legs down while I jiggled the knife handle a bit more. By now Coleman had something approaching a respectable boner which I had to ensure was maintained until it was time to get the pictures.

I jiggled while Gloria stripped. She took off her top and stood there in her bra. She sighed before taking it off.

'Hmm,' I heard Dave say to Jimmy, 'she's a bit flatter than I would have liked.'

'Oh yeah?' said Jimmy.

She kicked off her shoes, let her skirt fall to the floor and moved over to the bed in her knickers. 'All of it,' I said to Gloria. She looked at me, almost pleading, but I returned her gaze, not giving an inch. Slowly she took off her knickers from which a mighty pair of balls and a large mickey emerged, having been taped in place and kept there by the underwear.

'Oh . . . my . . . God,' said Dave. 'She's not a she at all.'

'I'm sorry you had to find out this way,' I said.

'She's a transceratops!'

Gloria looked at Dave, her big brown eyes glistening. Jimmy and Big Ian were speechless while Dave stood staring at what he had thought was the love of his life, a single tear rolling down his face. 'Let's just get this over with, Twenty,' he said.

So without any further time-wasting I got a series of shots of Coleman naked with Gloria, penises being put in mouths, Gloria teabagging Coleman, Coleman with a yellow plastic-handled knife sticking out of his arse and as many other incriminating shots as I could muster.

This all took place to the soundtrack of Gloria weeping and Dave's occasional sobs wracking through the room. It was more uncomfortable than when you call someone a cunt and the faces on the people you're talking to make it clear that person is standing right behind you.

Eventually I had enough pictures, and Gloria grabbed her clothes, ran back into the sitting room and got dressed again. She and Dave went out onto the terrace, where a rather intense discussion took place. It looked like two deaf people beating flies away from their faces.

'I'm going back to the pension, Twenty, ' said Dave, when he came back in.

'Flight's at 9 p.m.,' I said. 'See you there.'

'OK.'

'And, Dave?'

'What?'

'Thanks, man.'

He didn't say anything and left the apartment. 'Is it OK to leave that lump sleep it off in your spare room?' I asked Big Ian.

'Yeah. He's not going to remember anything.'

'Have you got a pen and piece of paper?'

'Sure,' he said and went off. When he came back, I took the piece of A4 and the marker that Big Ian gave me. I wrote, 'It was all Kyle's idea, seriously' on it, folded it up and put it on the pile of clothes that belonged to Coleman. 'Look,' I said to Big Ian. 'We're fucking bollixed. I've got to go. Thanks for everything, man.'

'No facking problem, good to see you again, Twenty. Don't leave it so long next time.'

'I won't.'

'And good luck with you-know-who.'

We gave each other a hug – a very manly hug – and Jimmy and I headed back towards the hotel.

The day was well and truly up and running. People were out and about in the streets. I looked at them with pure jealousy. They'd been asleep all night, they didn't feel like bags of shit. That tinny, hollow feeling where you don't quite feel part of the world.

'That was fun, eh?' said Jimmy.

'There are about five hundred words I can think of to describe that, and I'm pretty sure "fun" isn't one of them.'

'Aye. We got what we needed though.'

'That we did. Now I have to go find Stinking Pete.'

'Want me to go with you?'

'No, this is something I need to do on my own. I'll see you back at the hotel.'

Jimmy nodded. He hailed a cab and went on his way. I called Stinking Pete, found out where he was, and took a cab of my own.

36

Showdown

I suppose there comes a time in every man's life when he has to face up to something he doesn't want to. I had gone a long time without having to do that. Mostly because I didn't have much to face up to. Apart from this one thing, everything else in my life had been dealt with as and when it happened. I wasn't a fan of loose ends. I didn't like things hanging over me, but what had happened in Barcelona all those years ago had been so terrible, so utterly shameful, I just couldn't deal with it. When I woke up the next morning and found out what I'd done, I knew I had to leave straight away. This wasn't something that could be mended quickly. I figured I'd leave it a while, then when things had died down I'd come back, face the music, and everything would go back to normal again. But you know yourself, the longer you leave something the more difficult it is to sort it out. It became more and more awkward, and soon it got to the stage where I had decided it would be easier to never go back to Barcelona again, much as that would pain me, than to try and make things right. In time I forgot all about it, although every so often it would flash back into my head out of nowhere and I'd cringe, mortified at what I'd done and how I'd dealt with it. Or failed to deal with it.

I sat in the cab heading towards Sarrià, the upmarket area of town. My head was swimming, the sunlight and the heat of the morning were almost too much. I was exhausted. With so much booze and no sleep, it was like being inside a weird kind of dream sequence. I felt hollow, things that moved in front of me left traces as they went and I really wanted to brush my teeth. It was like there was a party in my mouth and everyone had stepped in shit before wiping their feet on my tongue. I considered just going back to the hotel, but that would have meant abandoning Stinking Pete. It was tempting, but I just couldn't do it.

Eventually we arrived, I paid the driver and stepped out of the car. The heat made me queasy and dizzy. I steadied myself against the side of the building. I slapped my face a couple of times to try and right myself enough for the confrontation. Fuck it, I thought, just do it. I walked up the steps and rang the buzzer for the apartment.

'Yes?' said a voice, slowly, smugly.

'It's me.'

'At last,' he said. 'Well, let's not hang around. Come on up.' The door buzzed, I pushed with all my might but it wouldn't shift. Then I pulled. That worked. The lift interior was all frosted glass and dimmed lights. It seemed to take about fifteen minutes to get to the penthouse apartment. I stepped out. This was my last chance to turn around but at that stage it would have taken more motor skills than I could call upon. I breathed deeply, rubbed my face with both hands and knocked on the door.

I heard the footsteps approaching, felt my heart quicken, hoped briefly it was some kind of coronary so I could avoid seeing him again, but no such luck – it was just nerves. The door opened.

'Come in,' he said.

I stepped inside. The room was spacious with dark wooden floors reflecting the light and light curtains shifting slightly in the breeze that came in through the open windows.

'Where's Pete?' I said.

'He's in one of the bedrooms. Don't worry, he's fine. I wouldn't hurt him. I wouldn't hurt anyone. Unlike you.'

'Look, it was an accident. You must know that.'

'Of course you would say that.'

'It was just one of those things that could have happened to anyone. A completely chance event. Wrong place, wrong time and all that.'

'Oh, it was certainly the wrong place and undoubtedly the wrong time.'

'So really you should have gotten over it by now. I know what happened was terrible, and if I could take back what I did I would, but I can't. Life goes on.'

'Yes, it goes on, but it's not the same, is it? Had you not

done what you did then life would be different. Better. I wouldn't have had to carry that burden around with me for so many years.'

'Burden? You know how things change so quickly. People forget,' I said.

'How can they forget this?' he said, and I couldn't help but remember that fateful day.

It was a Saturday evening in late April. I'd been out with Big Ian since the previous night. Back then we had proper stamina, you see. We spent the day flitting from bar to bar, eating some tapas here, making friends and talking loudly in every place we went.

We'd managed to score tickets for the big match, FC Barcelona versus Real Madrid. One of Big Ian's pupils had season tickets, and, due to a death in the family he couldn't go, so he gave them to us. We drank steadily right up until the game, then followed the crowd up Travesera de les Corts, joining in with some of the songs although making up our own words. We shared a couple of joints with some other fans and bought some food outside the ground.

Eventually we were inside, and the atmosphere was incredible. It was Johann Cruyff's first season as manager and the expectations were high. The noisy Catalans were hating the Madrid team and fans with every fibre of their being. There had been so much political history, and, on a sporting level, this was up there with the great footballing rivalries like Celtic versus Rangers, United versus Liverpool or Bohemians versus Shamrock Rovers. We found ourselves in the standing area and the place was buzzing. It wasn't that warm, despite the imminent arrival of summer, so having something to keep you warm on the terraces was an absolute must.

To this day I'm sure that had we brought a bottle of whiskey the events that unfolded and led to my hasty departure from Barcelona would not have happened. But Big Ian brought out of a bottle of absinthe from his jacket, and we swigged as the match went on. Already well oiled from being out since the night before, and more than a little stoned from the joints, I found myself becoming more and more distant from myself. It was like I wasn't me, I was part of this huge throng of people. Jumping, shouting, cheering, roaring. It was primal. The more of the fiery green liquid I drank the more it was like I was watching myself in a film.

The game began. Barcelona scored first – I have no clue who got the goal – only for Madrid to equalise. The home side scored again, and, at half-time, they led 2–1. The race for the title was well and truly on and this game would be vital in deciding its outcome. Early in the second half Real Madrid equalised, and, from then on, the game was deadlocked.

We continued drinking, and, looking back, I probably drank a bit more than I should have. I was just caught up in the excitement of it all. With about fifteen minutes to go I realised I was absolutely bursting for a piss and made my way through the crowd and into the toilets to relieve myself. Well, that's what I thought anyway. So blindly drunk from the absinthe was I that I had somehow made my way onto the pitch, and, instead of urinating in the foul-smelling trough underneath the stand, I was pissing right down the leg of Barcelona goalkeeper Andoni Zubizarreta. The noise in the stadium stopped – Big Ian told me afterwards you could hear a pin drop – and I was jumped on by stewards and police and taken away from the ground.

Late in the game, Real Madrid were awarded a free kick outside the area. The effort was tame, but Zubizarreta, his mind elsewhere, flapped at the ball and could only watch helplessly as it trickled over the line to give the hated whites the result that would see them take the points and eventually go on and win the title.

The incident was replayed over and over, the horrified look on the keeper's face clear to everyone as I, eyes closed and oblivious to it all, aimed my stream of urine at his knee thinking it was the toilet. He claimed afterwards that his normally unflappable concentration had been shattered by being pissed on in front of the 100,000-plus crowd in the stadium and the millions more watching on live television.

I spent the night in a cell and was released the next morning. Walking down Passeig de Gràcia I stopped at a kiosk to buy a copy of *El Mundo Deportivo*, one of the daily sports newspapers, and was horrified to see myself on the front cover in mid-slash, Zubizaretta's expression of disgust captured perfectly. I could feel people looking at me, pointing. I was utterly ashamed. The headlines about 'Madrid Taking the Piss Out of Barcelona and Zubizarreta' made my skin crawl.

I telephoned Big Ian to tell him I was leaving, going

back to Ireland for a bit until it all blew over. I wasn't
back in Dublin long when I rang him again to check in
and he told me the goalkeeper, still smarting from what
had happened, had called into the school, having been
given my details by the Catalan police, to see if I was
there. 'Tell him if he ever comes back to Barcelona I will
find him,' he told Big Ian. 'And revenge will be mine.'

And now here we were. Face to face after all these
years.

'Do you know the pain you caused me?' Zubizarreta
said, standing in his full 1988 Barcelona kit, gloves and
all.

'I'm sure it must have been embarrassing for you—'

'Embarrassing?'

'—but you just got weed on, it was me who had his
mickey in all the papers. How do you think I felt?'

'How you felt? Nobody cared about you. You were just
a drunk Irishman. The only surprise was you weren't
fighting someone. But me? We lost the title that year
because of my mistake and they began to call me "Piss
Legs" at every ground we went to.'

'But you went on to win so many titles. Four in a row
from 1991 to 1994, the European Cup, so many caps for
Spain . . . surely that made things better?'

'They were good things, but, to this day, I remain the
only goalkeeper in the history of football who has been
urinated on in the middle of a match. That's something I
can never live down. "There is Zubizarreta," they say.
"Remember the time that crazy Irish bastard did a slash
on his leg?" They don't remember the saves, the medals,

the great performances – only the piss.'

'So what do you want?'

'Isn't it obvious?'

'You want me to untie Pete and go for a game of three-and-in?'

'I simply want to do the same to you as you did to me!'

'I think the chances of me playing in goal for Barcelona during El Derbi are rather slim.'

'I'm no fool. I don't want to replicate the circumstances, merely the act itself. And you shall then feel the shame that I felt.'

'You want to piss on my leg?' I said.

'Precisely.'

'Well, it could be worse, I suppose.'

So Zubizarreta took me to the terrace of the apartment where he had set up a video camera. There were professional style marks on the floor to ensure everything was captured properly. I stood on mine, he stood on his and he went to the toilet on my leg. With the booze, the tiredness and everything else it was as surreal a moment as I can ever remember in my life.

'Now, I can rest easy. When the world discovers the YouTube video "Zubizarreta pisses on Twenty Major" they shall laugh and point at you and call you "Piss Legs".'

'Is that it? Can I go now?'

'You may leave,' he said, pouring himself a celebratory glass of Cava.

I found Stinking Pete in one of the bedrooms and untied him.

'Twenty! You came to rescue me. I was settling in here for the long haul, you know.'

'I told you I would. I'm a man of my word, Pete. Apart from when I lie to carry out elaborate practical jokes.'

'You're a pal, Twenty. And . . . ewww . . . you smell.'

'I know.'

'You smell of . . . well . . . you smell like Dirty Dave. Why do you smell like wee?'

'It's a long story.'

'You wet yourself? Hah! I knew it happened to everyone.'

'I did not wet myself, Pete.'

'Wait till I tell the others about this.'

'I didn't wet myself,' I said, then thought that it was probably better if people thought that than know the truth. That I had stood idly by and let Andoni Zubizarreta relieve himself down my leg. 'Oh, tell them what you want, man. I'm too tired to care.'

We made our way to the front door. There was no sign of Zubizarreta. I assumed he was uploading the footage to YouTube already.

'So did you feel all warm at first and think it was quite pleasant then realise that when it gets cold it's altogether a most unpleasant experience?'

'Yes, yes I did,' I said, eager to just get back to the hotel as quickly as possible. The sunlight was blinding, I was as tired as I could ever remember being, and Stinking Pete was going to tell everyone I pissed my own pants, but despite all that I felt pretty good. We had what we needed to get Tony off our backs, and I'd finally laid to rest the ghosts of the Camp Nou that had haunted me for so long. All I needed now was a bit of sleep . . . and to clean the goal keeper's piss off my legs. The simple things in life.

37

Return journey

I dropped Pete off at his pension and got back to the hotel some time around 11.30 a.m. Check-out was supposed to be 12 noon. That wouldn't do, so I had a quick word with the manager. The promise of a few bob into his hand meant he was happy enough to leave us until around six.

I have to say it was the most wonderful sleep of all time. I had this brilliant dream where Coleman was sitting having dinner with Tony Furriskey in some kind of Japanese restaurant but when Coleman told Tony about all the sex he was having with his daughter Tony lost it and cut his head off. The head then went round and round on the conveyor belt while Tony ate sushi and miso soup. When I woke up, I wasn't feeling half as bad as I thought I was going to, but I was upside down on the bed, naked apart from my flip-flops and clutching the pillow to my chest. I jumped in the shower, and, afterwards, gave Jimmy's room a ring.

'What?' he said.

'It's me. Flight's in three hours. We need to get out of here.'

'Christ. My head hurts. Last night seems like a terrible nightmare. When I think about it . . . that really was poxy.'

'Aye, still we got what we came for, that's the main thing.'

'Have you spoken to Dave?'

'No, I'll ring him now.

I arranged to meet Jimmy in the lobby in half an hour then rang Dave.

'Yes?' said the saddest voice I'd ever heard.

'It's me.'

'Oh, hi Twenty.'

'You all right, Dave?'

'I . . . don't . . . think so. I'm not sure I want to talk about it now, if that's OK?'

'Sure. No problem, man. Look, get Pete, then come meet us in the lobby of our hotel and we'll drive out to the airport, drop off the car, and have some pre-flight gins.'

'OK,' he said and hung up. That poor bastard. All his life he just wanted somebody to love and when he finally found her she turned out to be a transvestite. Admittedly quite a convincing transvestite, but a transvestite nonetheless. Some people were just born unlucky, I supposed.

I packed my bag and went up to the roof of the hotel and ordered an Estrella. I finished the weekend as I had started, looking out over the city, the rooftops shimmering in the summer heat, drinking a beer. There are simple pleasures in life, and this was one of the best of them. I vowed I wouldn't leave it so long to come back the next time. What had happened all those years ago was now just history, and you can't change history. Not without a time machine anyway, and I didn't have one of those. I smoked a cigarette, finished my beer and took one last look at Barcelona before we made our way to the airport.

The flight back was uneventful. I drank my G and Ts, Jimmy was surly from tiredness and quiet, Dave was heartbroken and quiet, Pete looked smug as if he couldn't wait to tell his story. It suited me fine.

I bought a book and read that the whole way – not even the little pockets of turbulence bothered me. Compared to what we'd gone through all weekend, a bit of bumping was just a bit of bumping no matter how high up in the sky you were. We landed in Dublin, grabbed a cab back towards the South Circular Road where we dropped off first Dave, then Pete, then Jimmy and finally I got out at my place.

I opened the door, smelled the familiar smell of my house and left my bag in the hall. I flicked on some lights, which alerted Bastardface to the fact I was home. His enthusiastic woofs continued until I opened the back door, and he greeted me like he hadn't seen me in a hundred years, not just a couple of days. I rubbed his big head, and he leapt about the place like a demented lamb.

It was good to see him too, and I thought about how it would have been to come home and find him Furriskeyed. It didn't bear thinking about. I gave him a snack of a side of beef which he settled down just outside the back step to devour.

I opened up the French doors from my office, put on some music and sat in my chair, as glad as I have ever been to be back home. I was almost dozing off when I heard a strange yowling getting closer and closer. Imagine someone yodelling and being tortured to death at the same time, that's what it was like. There was a thud as something landed in the garden and made its way over the stones. Two eyes flashed in the light and then, as black as the ace of spades, Throatripper the cat appeared. He'd obviously been locked in somebody's coal scuttle and had only just managed to claw his way through the metal. That, or someone opened it and got a good slashing for their trouble, just to teach them for locking him in there in the first place.

'Where have you been?' I said.

'Myaroarororoaaawww,' he said.

'I see. Hungry are you?'

'Rowowowowwwwww,' he said. I opened a large tin of tuna and put it in a bowl for him. He scoffed it up in no time, purring away to himself. I figured I'd better get in touch with Tony who would no doubt be waiting for an update. I made the phone call.

'Ahh, howya Twenty,' he said. 'Good news for me?'

'Wouldn't have it any other way.'

'Good man. I was hoping yeh'd come through. Not

just because it'd mean the wedding's off but also so I wouldn't have to . . . well . . . yeh know.'

'I know. What time is good for you tomorrow?'

'Come round about eleven. Bring the other fella with yeh too.'

'Will do.'

I sat there for a while but couldn't get comfortable. It was like I'd forgotten something. Maybe it was just the routine of having a few late pints in Ron's. That's probably what I needed. So I left the animals with their food and wandered around to take my place at the end of the bar.

'Evening, Twenty,' said Ron. 'Pint?'

'Do you even need to ask?'

'How was the trip then?'

'Oh, it was something all right.'

'Get what you needed?'

'Yep, thankfully.'

'That's good. Did you see my cousin?'

'We did. He sends his regards. Says he'd come visit but Dublin's a shithole where it's always raining and too cold.'

'He's not wrong there. What about the rest of the lads?'

So I told him about Jimmy wanting to kill Coleman for the whole weekend and Dave's lost love and how badly it had affected him.

'Only he could go have a holiday romance with a tranny,' said Ron. 'Still, it'll be a great slag once he gets over himself a bit.'

Ron put the pint down in front of me, and I took a

deep breath before taking a great swig of its creamy goodness.

'You know what, Ron?'

'What's that?'

'It's good to be home.'

Jimmy and I went to see Tony Furriskey the next morning. We showed him the pictures we had of Coleman and Gloria, and he was more than a little enthused with them. He kept saying we'd well and truly paid him back and that if we ever needed anything from him again we just had to ask. All the while I was thinking to myself that I would rather ask a gummy old man to bite off my cock than ask Tony for a favour ever again. Dirty Dave descended into the doldrums of despair, so crushed was he by what had happened. We did our best to try and cheer him up by not playing any terrible pranks on him, by Stinking Pete repeating the 'Twenty Wet Himself' story over and over and even by bringing him to his favourite restaurant, but not even a night out at Captain America's cheered him up. I figured his heart was just going to have to mend itself in time. From time to time he'd say something like, 'But she, I mean he, had the soft lips of a lady, Twenty. Those weren't a man's lips,' and all I could do was nod and pretend to be interested.

Things were a bit tense with Lucky. I eyed him suspiciously when he came into Ron's, but we put it all behind us when his beautiful wife gave birth to triplets, three girls, all alive. Naturally I taunted him about how his sperm could not produce a boy because he was a fannyarsed Italian, but he didn't rise to it. Even when I tried to paint graphic pictures of what boys were going to do to his girls when they were old enough he just shrugged and said that anyone who touched his daughters deserved to die and who better than him to kill them? The fucker was just unflappable. That didn't stop me blowing a snot rocket into his pint one night when he was in the toilet. I figured that made us even.

So life got back to normal, and I like normal. It's quiet, reliable, perhaps a touch predictable, but that's no bad thing. Between the weekend in Barcelona and Folkapalooza I'd had enough of adventures for a good long time.

Epilogue

A week after we'd given Tony the pictures, I woke up, head swimming from the night before in Ron's, and reached out to get the water beside my bed.

'Here yeh go!' said a voice.

'Aaarrrggh,' I said, sitting up quickly and lifting the eye mask from my face. 'Fucking hell, Tony. Would you stop doing that?'

'Hah, didn't mean to startle yeh.'

'How are you getting in here? I just had a new system put in since your last unannounced visit. It's supposed to go off at the slightest movement.'

'Alarm systems are easy to override when the bloke who owns the company that installed it owes yeh a significant favour.'

'What do you want, Tony? We're all square. We did a good job for you.'

'Yes, Twenty. Yeh certainly did. It was a good job. Perhaps too good.'

'What do you mean "too good"?'

'The young one. She's at home distraught. Cryin' all day. All night. Won't go out. Won't eat. Heartbroken.'

'What did you expect? She got pictures of her fiancé with a cock in his mouth, a set of balls on his chin and a yellow knife handle up his arse.'

'I blame yerself, Twenty.'

'You what?'

'This is all yer fault.'

'But you told us to get those pictures. This was all your idea.'

'Ideas aren't real, Twenty. Pictures are real. Yeh provided the fuckin' pictures, therefore it's yer fault.'

'So what do you want me to do about it now? It's a bit late to make things better, isn't it?'

'Get them back together.'

'What?'

'Reconcile them. If yeh can break them up, yeh can make them get back together.'

'I can on my shite. Who do you think I am, Cilla Fucking Black?'

'Listen, Twenty. I'm not askin yeh here. I'm tellin yeh.'

'I don't owe you anything, Tony. We're fucking even.'

'We're even when I say we're fuckin' even.'

'Fuck that.'

'Fair enough, Twenty. Of course I don't have to remind yeh about Scally Walsh, Eddie Drinkwater, The Boot Molloy, Micky Fitz . . . do I need to go on?'

'Fuck you, Tony. That's not right. It's just not right.'

'Sometimes the world just works that way.'

'I can't deal with that cunt again. Seriously. He's the biggest prick I've ever met in my life. And what's to stop you, if I do get them back together, coming after me for making a twat like that your son-in-law and ruining every family occasion you have?'

'Nothin', I suppose. It's just a chance yeh'll have to take.'

'Fuck. I need a smoke.'

'I'll join yeh.'

'Come on then, you cunt.'

'I can understand you're a bit pissed off, but watch who you're fuckin' calling a cunt, Twenty.'

I got out of bed, went into the kitchen and grabbed my delicious Major from the counter. In my shorts and vest I opened the back door and stepped outside. I lit one, handed one to Tony and lit his. Bastardface poked his head out from the kennel and came wandering over.

'Ahh, there's that mad dog!' said Tony. 'What a beast.'

'Yeah, he's a beast all right.'

'Howya there,' said Tony, getting down on his hunkers to rub Bastardface under the chin. I took another drag of my cigarette, exhaled, and said 'knacker', Bastardface's code word for attack. He tore at Tony Furriskey's throat, and, in moments, the notorious Dublin gangster was dead, bleeding all over my backyard. I'd probably opened up a massive can of worms, but fuck it, at least I didn't have to deal with Coleman again.

I finished my cigarette and went inside to call Jimmy. This was going to take some cleaning up.

Absinthe Makes the Heart Grow Fonder

Acknowledgements

When you write your first book you end up thanking nearly everyone you know. Second time around it's not quite as in-depth but there's still some appreciation to be dished out like pints in Ron's on a Friday night.

To the Running Lady, a true font of ideas, wisdom and inspiration, my eternal gratitude.

To 19 and the man with the white beard, cheers for the beers and everything else.

Monkey, you still smell but you're all right really. Hope you enjoy this one as much as the last one.

My editor Ciara Doorley for her help and direction which is always fantastic, and for her continued enthusiasm. Thanks as well to everyone at Hachette for all the behind the scenes stuff and support.

And finally to all the readers of the blog (Retired? What? You must have been dreaming . . .) and to everyone who bought the first book your support is greatly appreciated. Remember, in this world of techno-failure you should really buy two copies. Always keep back-ups, everyone knows that.

Until next time.